FISHING

for
BIRDS

We gratefully acknowledge the support of the Canada Council for the Arts and
the Ontario Arts Council for our publishing program. We also acknowledge the
financial support of the Government of Canada.

Fishing for Birds is a work of fiction. All the characters and situations portrayed
in this book are fictitious and any resemblance to persons living or dead is purely
coincidental.

Cover design: Val Fullard

Library and Archives Canada Cataloguing in Publication

Title: Fishing for birds : a novel / Linda Quennec.
Names: Quennec, Linda, 1969- author.
Series: Inanna poetry & fiction series.
Description: Series statement: Inanna poetry & fiction series
Identifiers: Canadiana (print) 20190094389 | Canadiana (ebook)
20190094443 | ISBN 9781771336130 (softcover) | ISBN 9781771336147
(epub) | ISBN 9781771336154 (Kindle) | ISBN9781771336161 (pdf)
Classification: LCC PS8633.U45 F57 2019 | DDC C813/.6—dc23

Printed and bound in Canada

MIX
Paper from
responsible sources
FSC® C004071

Inanna Publications and Education Inc.
210 Founders College, York University
4700 Keele Street, Toronto, Ontario, Canada M3J 1P3
Telephone: (416) 736-5356 Fax: (416) 736-5765
Email: inanna.publications@inanna.ca   Website: www.inanna.ca

FISHING

for

BIRDS

A NOVEL

LINDA QUENNEC

inanna poetry & fiction series

INANNA PUBLICATIONS AND EDUCATION INC.
TORONTO, CANADA

To Oma—for the stories

"Never make yours the subject of islands," she cautioned the young woman.

"But what else?" the young woman asked, knowing nothing of other places.

"You can't know the story of an island. It's unfathomable, disconnected."

"You would understand," the young woman said.

"No, I never did. And I still don't."

And so she stayed, until the islands told their own stories.

The older one was right though, they were never hers. Even after the telling

KATE: BRITANNIA ISLAND, 2005

EVERYONE ALWAYS CALLED HER accident prone. "That's Kate," her father would say, palms-up. "I get it." To herself, she was just clumsy, hovering somewhere outside her own body, the product of a childhood devoid of ballet classes and figure skating lessons—pursuits that produced muscle memory and a rigid spine. Testaments to confidence. As for Kate, she wasn't certain she was actually occupying her body, and in more existential moments she wondered whether she'd been born at all, or if in fact, she was still making up her mind.

But Kate's birth was very civilized, as far as births go. The doctor said she was *transverse*, lying sideways in her mother's womb, as though sunning herself in a lounge chair. *She can't decide which end will come out first.* A C-section was scheduled, as was usually done in such cases.

Seemingly, Kate's ambivalence was contagious—at thirty-seven weeks, her mother Nora's blood pressure rose slightly, but not enough that the doctor knew for certain it was time to intervene. So another week passed and at thirty-eight weeks' gestation and much insistence from the bloated mother-to-be, a decision was made.

Nora was not a fan of tardiness, and when the doctor was a half hour late shouted to her husband to "go and find that woman." At 2:10 p.m. on a Friday, Kate was born in the presence of a highly drugged mother and a father in tears.

When she was two, Kate pulled her mother's electric frying

pan full of spattering pork chops off the counter; when she was four she swallowed a quarter and turned blue. At five she fell off a thirty-foot dock. In all instances she traipsed away without scratch or scar. This was telling, but her mother was still afraid of borrowed time.

KATE SHIFTS IN THE LOW ARC OF THE KAYAK. At the end of the inlet she dips the right blade of her paddle, then the left. The small craft wiggles, slaps ocean at her hips. She pauses to search a break in the wall of forest up the bank. She notices a shaking bush, but can't strain far enough to see whatever small animal is there without tipping. You can see so much more from a kayak, smaller things you'd miss from a speedboat or ferry. Morning is the most illuminating time, when it's as calm as this—the ocean a heady, viscous ink. Other folks have yet to rise and fill the air with competing intentions.

Paddling makes her forget, causes her to sing in an operatic style that might be embarrassing if she had an audience composed of more than birds, otters, and other undiscriminating creatures. As her torso swivels, her mind skims over water-gloss, and tension releases itself through her voice. Normally, this brings a sense of calm, a thinning of the membrane between her body and what surrounds it, but today she notices something else in the muted air as she approaches the tiny bay, something inscrutable, like a shifting tide. Autumn is losing patience. Soon winds will begin to lift the ocean and tease it into tiny, whipped peaks. Summers aren't very long on the west coast.

At the mere suggestion of Autumn's presence—its exposure—her voice weakens. She feels a familiar pull, as though something like a fisherman's net has replaced the fascia throughout her body, encasing her organs. This net has an opening somewhere near her chest area, one that she can cinch closed quickly whenever she needs to. The cinching pulls her fetal, wraps hard bone around the tender places. Someone else put the net there. Not her.

She watches a gull pick and pull at the gummy contents of a mussel. Maybe this is the sign—creatures everywhere taking their fill of abundance, storing up. Their movements have accelerated in the last few days. And how will she prepare for a season she's never seen on this island?

At sea a mind drifts, and hers almost always goes back to the time when she wasn't alone. Not ever. Jeff's hand, possessive on her back, at a party. She doesn't remember the occasion, but the words are still there. His words ... replacing her own. She, disappearing, shoulders hunched, guts churning. Sick life inside of her. Hers, a half-life.

"Kate's pretty much a zero on wine," he'd said. "But of course she remembers to buy the one that makes me sick." Laughter, including hers, condemning her own self. From the outside this must have looked fairly innocuous; maybe only she could feel the dagger penetrate. This was both good and bad. Others always found him funny.

She slides in alongside the silvery dock. It looks ancient, but Kate figures it's got a few years left. At least that's one thing she won't have to fix—yet. She ties up the kayak with a deft anchor hitch, creaks along the dock and up the steep ramp, entering the beginnings of forest and the tiny home hidden there. She nudges open the door to the front room, once so familiar. For the last nine months following Jeff and his parents' deaths, however, the room has felt as though it's holding its breath. The photos, mementos, paintings, and books all look disoriented, fearful of becoming irrelevant.

But she has no plans for change; she doesn't yet feel she has permission. She still half-expects to see Jeff or one of his parents round a corner into the open, bright living room and start shuffling books around or lighting a fire in the wood-stove. For now she can pretend that they are all still asleep. She's become used to getting up and going out for a paddle while everyone is still in bed. After that her routine has been to tiptoe in to sit and read alone. Silence. Up until this time of day she can fool herself into believing everything is normal. When she first made plans to come to the island at the beginning of the summer, people were edgy. Everyone told her to stay busy, to take another week or so before getting back to some sort of routine. None of this made sense to her. She supposed her friends weren't to blame, though. Of course they can't know what it is to be widowed at thirty-two. Someday they'll become familiar with divorce maybe, or abandonment of another sort. Kate is the first to encounter death. Although her husband was the one who had died, after so many years of making herself smaller in an attempt to escape his scrutiny, Kate finds that she has become little more than an apparition herself. The years had driven silence so deeply into her body. Her thoughts, what she wanted, were at the least irrelevant, at the most disdained. She doesn't remember happiness.

She stands on one leg, lifting the other behind her to stretch her quadricep as she pulls an open canister to her nose, inhaling the bright musk of coffee beans, and moving hypnotically into the ritual of the grinder and then the French press. When her toast is ready she grabs mug and plate and curls into the plump sofa. She reads a few paragraphs of her novel, then puts it down, restless, and grabs a travel magazine about Rome. She glances at her mother-in-law's meticulous underlining and commentary within the margins of almost every article. Ann and Mike were big travellers, but always in groups with itineraries planned by someone else. Still, Ann never failed to enhance these excursions with her own unflagging research. She would think it unwise to extend complete trust to strangers.

They'd raised Jeff with the same attention to detail. When Dr. Spock was *de rigeur* it was his technique that predominated, when Whole Language was the way to teach reading, so it went as well. Kate's husband was the product of "one right way" for everything. Grey areas were for those without the confidence to commit, and ambiguity was simply a sign of weakness of character. Unsurprisingly this translated into rules at the cabin, not to mention places for everything, and as far as Ann was concerned, that was the way everyone ought to be doing it. If you weren't aligned with Ann, you became the unfortunate subject of her afternoon tea conversations, or worse, a topic at the monthly "Stitch and Bitch." Remembering this, Kate can't help but smile, knowing she's been the source of entertainment at more than one of those gatherings. Now that Ann is gone though, she follows the rules with a numbed sort of reverence. She can probably admit to missing the comfort of her mother-in-law's attentiveness. Habitual things.

She picks up yesterday's letter from the table next to her. Nicole. In Kate's world, when you're in the throes of your twenties, you lay certain claims upon friends' lives. Intimate details are consistently shared and to an equal degree. Some people have trouble moving beyond this in spite of age, jobs, or spouses. This is Nicole. Kate lifts the envelope's flap, pulls out a card she recognizes is from a boxed "for all occasions" collection, embossed with the words *Thinking of you…*

K—

> *I can't explain how sad I am to know you're alone in that place. Why do you need to lock yourself away? Hiding doesn't work. I miss you and I'm worried you're depressed. What do you do all day long? At least let me come visit. I'm an excellent distraction. There, now you're laughing. It's the least I can do.*
> *Love, Nicole.*

Kate counts the "me's" and "I's" for a total of seven. She wonders what colours Nicole's showing up would paint on the canvas of her emotional landscape. Whatever common ground they'd previously known had shaken loose nine months ago, in the rapid severing from everything that Jeff's death had created. Now Kate can no longer place a sense of normalcy around the things she and Nicole did together:

the gym, shopping, pub nights with perky friends who had always been more Nicole's than her own. This letter is a remnant, she thinks. An artifact. And never mind who she is now or what she is doing. Who the hell *was* she then? Past and present weave unfamiliar strands around each other, but none can connect her from there to here.

I need to eat, she realizes. The Saturday market, with its stacks of fresh fruit and vegetables, beckons. She folds the letter back into its envelope and under *Fall on Your Knees.*

THE MARKET, ON THE MORE HEAVILY TRAVELLED, touristy side of the island, never fails to be an eclectic treat. Farmers and gardeners bring fresh offerings of course, but there are also a number of contributions from local creatives. Photography, knitwear, wooden toys, imported Asian clothing and knick-knacks, whittled creations, pottery, and hand-hewn furniture. It all looks quaint to the weekend warrior, but this is serious business, particularly in the "sell or starve" months. Some of the locals are friendly to Kate, others suspicious—you are an islander full-time or not at all.

Kate walks into the throngs spilling out over the grassy field that the market takes over once a week. Her feet, exposed in flip-flops, brush cool blades of grass. The air is moving now, disturbing tents and hairstyles. She'd stopped noticing how still it had lain, for so long. A few leaves begin to give way to the decay edging in, the consumption of fall. Her skirt swings, tickles her ankles.

"Come, come, I have new stuff." A petite woman with dread-locks, her tongue thick with Montreal, emerges from the crowd, luring Kate to a table covered in an array of colourful clutter.

Kate embraces her, inhaling patchouli. "Claire. Glad you're here."

"What do you think, eh? It's for the Bodum. You know, for the coffee." She points to a hunk of fleece with a zipper up the side.

Kate tilts her head. "A cozy?"

"Yes, exactly. For keeping it warm. I don't know the size though. Do you have one? Can you check for me?"

"Of course. Great idea. Perfect for camping."

"Completely. You are reading my mind. How much, do you think?"

About islanders: many of them come from somewhere else, but no matter the duration of their stay, they all lay fervent claims to the place. The more elusive types—the writers, potters, and glass blowers, for example—live year-round in hidden homes you'd never see while driving the curving roads. They skitter like tentative cats when approached by outsiders, or the breed of part-timer who treats their home as a playground. Island politics. "The smaller the island, the weirder the people," her mother used to say. Jeff's dad was less tolerant and would threaten to "stop buying their crap" at the market. "Half of them are house-sitters," he'd rant. "If we all lived here full-time, they'd be out of work." Kate disagrees, however. Since her arrival, this island has stretched out its arms to her, holding her pain along the span of its quiet, empty beaches, within its wise, intimate forests, and in the slow-moving attentiveness of the few who have welcomed her. Kate thinks of the solidity of the local farmers, everything about them rooted in clear intention, their connection to land and purpose essential. Some part of her has perhaps always understood the value of sitting close to the earth, asking it questions. Kate's father-in-law Mike had different intentions, though. He had bought land on Brittania a few years into his marriage, and he and Ann spent several summers camping on it before building their cabin in 1982, shortly before Jeff was born.

"A woman was asking for you," Claire says almost nonchalantly, but Kate's neck hairs rise at these words.

"Who?"

"Tall. Suit. I don't know her." Claire runs her hands smoothly down the sides of her body to indicate the form-fitting nature of the woman's clothing.

"Did she say what she wanted?"

"Nothing."

Claire shrugs and returns to shuffling her wares. In her head, Kate goes over the people she knows on the island, but there aren't many who wear suits, even the business people. She must be from the city. A lawyer? A relative of Jeff's? She decides to drop it for now.

Included among the rednecks and the drinkers, the blue-collar folks and the artists, are people like Claire, the blithe ones who make a home here, befriend most of the community, and move on in a year or so. As much as Kate hates stereotypes, Claire is the sort of islander who ironically loans the island its romanticized reputation as earthy and esoteric, despite roots elsewhere and a relatively brief sojourn. *There is something more real than this, though,* Kate thinks. She still hasn't figured out what this place really is, and for the moment, that's fine.

She continues to roam, her fingers worrying the fleece in her skirt pocket. She reaches the tomato guy with his tremulous girlfriend who sits vigil each week, knitting an anaconda of a scarf.

"I have five varieties today," he points out. "The heirlooms are fantastic." He says *fantastic* with both a's elongated, like a stoner, Kate notes. Or someone who attends a lot of festivals ending in *-palooza*. He also has loads of cherries, he tells her: orange, red, and green. She fills her bag—tiny bursts of a concluding summer.

On the way out, she picks up a coffee from the Wellspring, the local bookstore/coffee shop, and hurries into crystalline air. The sky is a lighter shade of blue now, but the ocean has turned to indigo. Against this backdrop, the whites of boats in the still-busy harbour pop like so many astonished eyes. Winds are still warm, but a little more intentional. Kate sits on the usual bench and stares toward the ocean and the neighbouring islands. She feels a slap of grief. Without Jeff, the scene takes on a different quality. *Not for you now*, it seems to say. She sips her third coffee of the day, breathes. What is she doing here?

She feels a tap on her left shoulder. The guy with the "therapeutic digeridoo" twirls his instrument in a manner meant to be enticing. A market regular, he never speaks. He hands Kate a pamphlet outlining services he can render, from the curing of headaches to the taming of pesky cowlicks.

She shakes her head, and with the lever of her raised hand, waves him away. Unless he can make women in suits disappear, she isn't interested.

NORA: VANCOUVER ISLAND, 2005

ON THE EVE OF THE FUNERAL, Kate's mother Nora is bustling. She made all the pigs in blankets from scratch and two hundred cupcakes as well. She picked up the rest of the food at Costco, and as she shopped she wondered why she'd made anything at all. No one ever appreciates the work.

Ada Jackson from up the road did the flowers. Thank God Nora managed to convince her friend Loni that Ada and poor Mr. Clark were related. If she hadn't, they'd have ended up with a whole crap load of Loni's artificial arrangements and that just seemed, well, tacky. Nora would pound on the lid of the box if there were fake flowers at her funeral. And they'd open it to find her rigid middle finger poking up to tell them all what she really thought.

This will be a big one. Lots of people want to pay their respects to Charlie Clark, she thought. He'd run the local grocery for forty years, and for a big chunk of that time it had been the only market in town. Kids went there to get candy with their allowance; moms bought milk, bread and eggs; teenagers got their first jobs there and snuck into the bushes to make out during break time. It had been the centre of the world in this town before the big box stores rose up in forests made bald for their arrival.

Mr. Clark didn't have much in the way of family: a brother in Winnipeg and a sister in Toronto. They're coming, too, but the rest of the guests will be local. Everyone liked Charlie, and it definitely isn't every day that someone gets struck by lightning. Nora shakes her head. Mr. Clark didn't even have a chance to let the cancer get him. He didn't have to go through a hip replacement or move into a home. Nope, he had been just as healthy as he ever was, still managing the store at the age of seventy something. He got to go out with a bang—literally.

She fusses with her apron and puts the pigs in blankets in neat little rows on her real silver platter. The kids had given it to her and Ed for their twenty-fifth wedding anniversary. Ugliest damned thing she's ever seen, but it's the best she has for the occasion. A couple sprigs of parsley for garnish, and her preparations are done. She hopes that Molly did a decent job decorating the hall, but doubts it. Girl's a space cadet when it comes to anything practical, too busy thinking up ways to catch a third husband. Nora covers everything in plastic wrap twice lengthwise, twice width-wise, and sets the platter down on her counter. The phone rings.

"Nora here."

"Hello ma'am. How are you this evening?"

"Who's this?"

"I'm calling on behalf of Island Cable to see how you're enjoying our services."

"Well, you want to talk to my husband. He's the only one in this house who watches that damn thing from morning to night. I'd get him for you, but he's too busy watching the game."

She puts the phone down. That was a waste of fifteen seconds.

A floatplane flies over the house. Goddamn. When did it get so busy here? She's gone on living the quietest life she can, but somehow it's gotten harder and harder to even find a parking spot at the grocery store, even though there are more shops to choose from now. People whizz by all frantic nowadays, talking on cellphones and looking as though they're on their way to put out a fire. *And who are these folks anyway?* There was a time when Nora knew almost everyone in town.

Shit. Almost two and she hasn't gone out yet. She obliges the doctor by taking a walk every day except Sunday. No way is she going to piss off God. The walk takes her downhill on the way out and uphill on the way back. She dreads the return, but she's sometimes lucky enough to run into someone who'll bring her back by car if she's too tired. She'd enjoy those hills a lot more if they all pointed down. She considers the blood test results again. *Best get it done.*

The city—it was a city now—had begun what they called a "revitalization project." It involved kicking out all the bums and pouring a mess of concrete over the shoreline. Now there's a curving path along the downtown harbour for walking and riding bikes, and the mayor's office is boasting that tourist numbers are up. Nora doesn't really see them as tourists though, just people from Vancouver, and some of the bums seem to have found their way back. Uphill from the "seawall," as they call it, is the funeral home. Nora watches it up there as she walks, just as she's glanced at it for years driving by on the other side. It perches like a white raptor on the side of the bluff, ready to swoop down, claws exposed. With every recent death she'd become more wary. Even as a kid she had known it was inevitable that she'd wind up in that spooky old house someday.

Nora dodges what seems like hundreds of crotch-sniffing dogs on the path—she refuses to call it a seawall. Stupid animals can't figure out if they want to go left or right, and those god-forsaken retracting leashes that are almost invisible—dog way over on one side of the path and the owner on the other. She has to be more aware than she wants to be so she doesn't trip over one and go flying into the salt chuck. It's already the beginning of September, but lots of people from the city are still around, whining about there not being a bridge from Vancouver. Nora figures she'll turn herself in to the funeral home if that day ever comes.

Why does she have to share the best time of the year with a

million other folks who don't like where they live? She waits all year long for sunshine, and just this past summer she was hard pressed to find a space to put her chair down at the beach. The worst part is that these folks are starting to hang around after summer. The mountainside is beginning to itch with houses creeping flea-like up its side. Her friend Barbara, enamoured with the newness of these homes, and with their sizes, often drags Nora along on her walks at dusk, so she can peek in the windows and marvel at the new cul-de-sacs, but Nora can't think of any good that can come from all the crowds. She isn't political, so she deals with it by minding her own business and pretending things are as they've always been.

She decides to cut her walk short. No time for wandering around when there is a funeral to get ready for and she's fresh out of funeral clothes. She walks up to Horton Street and jumps into a cab. She doesn't usually like going to the mall, but today she'll make an exception—she needs to check more than one store.

Soon she finds a long black skirt, a black blouse, and a cream-coloured hat. The hat is less understated than what she'd usually choose, but since she's on the executive for the Moose Hall she needs to dress a little more "up." She's got a cream shawl at home that will go nicely with the whole thing and offset some of the black. Mr. Clark will be properly honoured.

She checks her lottery tickets carefully before leaving the mall—each number representing a family birthday: hers, Ed's, the girls', her brother's, her sister's. Nothing. She's been choosing these same numbers for years and can't stop now. What if she chose differently and her numbers came up? On second thought, considering some of her sorry bunch, maybe this wasn't the luckiest way to go.

One more stop to pick up the photo collage at Marian's. Marian doesn't drive—too scared to ever learn, so she can't carry such a bulky thing to the hall. She's ready for Nora with tea.

"Can't today. Way too much to do."

"Nonsense, Nor. There's always time for tea. What if it's us next time? Gotta make the most of it." She giggles and the rolls of fat on her stomach bounce on top of one another in her tight T-shirt. Nora's girls used to ask, "Why does Aunty Marian have a front bum?" Nora can't laugh too hard, though. She's working on one of her own. She follows Marian inside.

"That looks fantastic, Mar. You must have been up all night."

"Well, I did some this morning, too. Glad you like it."

"It's him all right. Look at that, in his old grocer's visor. And this one must have been taken at the river."

"Mmm-hmm. He loved to swim at the dam. She points to another photo. "I'm not sure about this one. I can take it off if you like."

Mr. Clark stands on his front lawn wearing nothing but a red string bikini. Nora has a hard time looking away from the photo. No doubt about it, Charlie was colourful. Anything for attention.

"I don't know, Marian. Maybe we should stick to the serious stuff for the occasion."

"But on the other hand"—Marian offers her palm in illustration—"don't you think it'll be nice to show everything? I mean, the other ones are so proper."

"Another time. There're things you do and don't do at a funeral."

Marian shuffles back to the kitchen to get the tea. Nora looks again at the collage. Another photo shows Mr. Clark at his "Holiday of My Own Invention." Every summer he'd close his store for a whole day, for no reason other than to have fun. He'd then turn the parking lot into a carnival with games for kids, three-legged races, a carousel, a wishing well, and tons of food. It's a great photo, an action shot that freezes the familiar faces in happiness. Nora has a sudden vision of the lightning bolt that struck Mr. Clark. It seems to have immobilized everything familiar in this town into one photographic still. Aged and antiqued.

Marian needs to know who's doing what tomorrow. Nora fills her in on all the roles and tells her to get some rest. She calls Ed to pick her up and puts the collage in the back seat. Ed grumbles about missing the game most of the way home. *When did he turn into such an old fart?*

As always, Nora finishes everything. After dropping Ed off back at home she slides over to the driver's seat and heads to the Moose Hall to check on the decorations. She takes down the balloons. *What was Molly thinking?* The hall is musty and the blue pleather bar seats haven't been reupholstered since 1975, but you don't go jazzing a place up with balloons on a funeral day.

KATE

BECAUSE IT'S SATURDAY, she has to look in on Ivy. Kate had offered to relieve Nancy, one of the locals, twice a week from her job as a live-in care aid. On Saturdays and Wednesdays she cooks, cleans, reads, and converses for a few hours at Ivy Lanwick's ancient home. Ivy's family farm predates almost everything else on the island. At one time she was an English professor, and she still runs a book club at the coffee shop. Many of her contemporaries have, in their dotage, left the island for care homes in Vancouver. Others no longer have complete use of their faculties, but, at ninety-two, Ivy is fully present in her stooped and failing body, spending most of her time with people much younger than herself. And Kate thinks that perhaps this is one reason why.

Ivy sits in her wheelchair in the doorway of the house as Kate approaches. Her face brightens as Kate's bicycle winds down the gravel pathway toward the house. "You've brought gladiolas. How elegant."

"Glad you like them."

"There's nothing like fresh flowers. I only wish it hadn't taken me fifty years to realize it's essential to have them around at all times."

Kate touches her hand. Thin skin clings to protruding knuckles. She brings the flowers close, and Ivy moves her fingers delicately over the blooms in a gesture that seems to recognize fragility.

Inside the house Ivy's entire being seems composed of questions. "Tell me who was at the market today."

"You'd be surprised." Kate roots in a cabinet for a long enough vase. "Warren Matthews wasn't there."

"And why not?" Warren's too proud of his squash to miss a September market.

"Apparently his daughter from San Francisco is here and he's been busy showing off the island. Nancy said she talked him into a trip to the city to see the fair."

"Well, that's news enough to make the local papers, isn't it? Bloody hell. I can just see his cranky face, dragged all over that ridiculous fair."

"Hopefully the mini donuts are a consolation."

Time spent with Ivy is easy. She doesn't force Kate to talk about the "dead husband." "Hell, I've got a couple of those myself," she'd said, laughing.

"Would you join us for dinner, Kate? Nancy's picked up a pork roast. Recipe's on the counter. She'll be back by then, and I thought that a ladies' night would be nice."

"That sounds great. Have we got time for Steinbeck today?"

"Finished two days ago. I'm on to Kingsolver now. Early years." She wrestles a stack of papers and *Pigs in Heaven* shoots out, landing on the linoleum.

"I can do that." Kate races to pick it up, troubled by Ivy's ineffectual reaches from her wheelchair.

"I wasn't always a feeble old woman." Ivy laughs off the embarrassment.

Kate looks at her giant blue eyes, fire and water in the same space. "Course not."

Ivy sizes her up. "Come here a moment."

She glides over to a wall of photos and removes a black-and-white portrait of a woman and two teenaged girls. The woman in the foreground sits in a chair wearing a black dress with a wide collar and black satin tie. She holds her left hand in her right, and her ankles are crossed in lace-up boots that protrude from her dress. She slouches a little, and her eyes are drawn together by two sharp vertical lines between her brows. Glowering, eternal worry.

"My mother," Ivy says, pointing.

"Is this you?" Kate asks, recognizing thinness, and the wide eyes of one of the girls.

"Yes, and my sister Eve. This was taken before I left home."

"For school?"

"No. I was fortunate enough to visit my grandparents first," she raises her eyebrows, "on a Cuban island shaped like a teardrop."

"Your sister—"

"Younger than me, but she died in her forties."

Kate shakes her head slowly.

"She still turns up sometimes. You know how you think you see someone's face in a crowd?"

"Mm-hmm."

"Some faces you never stop seeing. For me it's always her. She saved my life, in a way. In that place."

IVY: ISLA DE PIÑOS, 1926

IT'S BEEN TWO WEEKS since the steamer wound its way past a gateway of mangrove swamp and into the Rio las Casas. Two weeks since she'd first seen the mountains, verdant haystacks plopped on an otherwise flat, semi-jungled landscape, bizarrely punctuated by pine trees. Two weeks, but it has taken Ivy less time than that to recognize that Isla de Piños is speaking to her.

At first it told her that she was unsuitably dressed, that her stockings would become an implement of torture, that her jewellery, cheap beads swung round her neck, would slacken with sweat. As though to illustrate the point, trade winds had in no time dismantled her pin-tucked curls and set them free and fuzzy into the atmosphere, creating a cloud-like halo around her exhausted-yet-intoxicated head.

While the things she had first noticed about Cuba—oxen, almost every man in a Panama hat, women in long skirts, the impossible height of a royal palm, the stick of humidity and the omnipresent, churned percussion of *son* music—were beginning to fade into normalcy, there was usually at least one surprise enfolded within the confines of a day on La Isla.

"Come look at this, Rubia."

Opa bends over in baggy, grey pants held up by red suspenders. His white beard catches a delicate yellow blossom as it floats by on warm, invisible currents. Ivy watches it move up and down as he talks. He picks up a piece of fallen fruit.

"Is it an orange?" She moves toward him with caution.

"Try it," he tells her.

She turns it over, running her fingers over the nubbled skin. Too large to be a lemon. She peels it and removes a segment, bites into it, and spits immediately.

Opa bends over, laughing. He's been doing this this repeatedly since Ivy's arrival on Isla de Piños. Almost everything he introduces her to here happens within the context of one practical joke or another. Something in her enjoys humouring him, playing along.

"What *is* that?"

"Grapefruit. A little sugar and you'll learn to love it."

Her lips purse. "I doubt it."

They walk the red, dusty roads into Santa Barbara, stopping every few minutes to talk to another of the expats Opa knows. Ivy can't speak German, so her mind wanders away, spreading itself out and around the village, watching butterflies and birds rest on the spiny limbs of the pine trees that named the island.

When they reach the store, Opa goes inside to order flour and Ivy notices a group of teenagers speaking English on the steps outside.

"You're the Rubia he's been waiting for," says a boy with pebbly freckles.

"He couldn't wait to see you," adds the curly-haired, equally freckled blonde standing next to him. The humidity has added to the circumference of her head, and her face is dwarfed by yellow fuzz, her tiny blue eyes incongruous to the rest of her.

Ivy introduces herself.

"Come to the river sometime. We're always there in the afternoons. It's too hot to do anything else."

"I'll ask my grandparents."

"Sure. They know us. I'm Maureen, and this is Mark. From Virginia."

Ivy extends her hand in awkward formality. "Pleasure."

"I see you make friends quickly, not like your Oma." Opa chuckles and unwraps a sweet on his way out the door. He hands it to Ivy. "Eat quickly. It melts."

They walk back home very slowly, Opa's eyes in the trees, his thoughts seeming to travel well beyond the distance of the copper-coloured road. "You like to hike?"

"I don't know."

"Your mother was a hiker. She would often do two summits a day when she was a teenager. Did she ever tell you about that?"

"She doesn't talk about Germany very often, except to tell me how easy I've got it in Canada."

Opa looks at the ground. "She's right in a way. When we get home I'll tell Oma to pack a lunch. I'll show you the beach."

THE SAND IS BLACK. Impossibly tall, skinny palms pepper the beach and stagger themselves forward into the open space, where the more exposed ones bend generously in the wind. Ivy looks at the ocean, gazing into the distance toward the long, half-dead mangrove gate that had welcomed her here, like some sort of eerie portal.

"Bibijagua," Opa explains. "The only black sand beach on this island."

"Why black?"

Opa nods at the mountains. "There is marble everywhere. It erodes and eventually we find it here. Later I will show you the hills. This is a rich island, although many here are poor."

"My father told me that the U.S. held Isla de Piños for a long time."

"He is right. They only relinquished sovereignty last year." Opa scratches his beard. "I am happy to be in a Cuban place."

"Me too," she tells him.

"I will show you the Sierra de las Casas and you can become a hiker, like your mother.

"Today?" she asks, astonished.

Opa laughs, peeling off his shirt. "Today is for swimming." And he sprints like an Olympian into the cresting waves, Ivy not far behind him.

KATE

IT TURNS OUT TO BE one of those rare evenings that, although it arises organically, is better than if you'd spent months planning it. The energy of transitional air, everything in motion. And very good company.

Nancy returns with samplings of sweet summer whites: Reislings and Gewurstraminers courtesy of a friend in the industry. The chemistry of the sullied grape finds its way into their bloodstreams, bubbling up in uninhibited conversation, mostly on the topic of island people, but also about other places, farther away. And Ivy's photos.

"Here I am topless on Santorini." She's on to Greece now, having produced an album on Western Europe. Kate surprises herself with a pang of prudishness. It's as though some curmudgeonly part of her feels that when one enters the realm of "old," one is obliged to take vows of conservatism. She didn't realize she thought this way.

Sometime around two a.m., Kate finds her way back down the dark paths to her cabin door. Nights are chillier now and the noisy summer critters are already gone. She walks in, hangs her coat, and feels a sudden, swift surge of blood to her temples. Something is different.

"Is someone here?" She pulls her sweater more tightly around her torso. What is it? A smell? She edges along the wall to the fish bonker that hangs from a nail in the kitchen and grips its smooth wooden base. She rarely locks the door. *This is the island, for chrissake.* She glances outside at the huge moon, low in the sky, melting an orange puddle out over the water. She forces deep inhalations and wills herself to relax. It's silly, no one would make the effort to come here for the little this cabin has to offer. Still, she remembers Mike's stories about squatters in the off-season. Harmless for the most part, but disconcerting still. She moves room to room—there isn't a lot of space to check, and eventually washes up, grabs her book, and sinks into bed. A fitful night.

NORA

MORNING DAWNS GREY. An abrupt shift in weather. If only Charlie had gone a week earlier they would have dodged the monsoons. Now the clouds will have their way. Once rain and fog settle in on the coast they make themselves at home for a good nine months. How to describe it? Words like gloomy, dismal, and bleak come close. In some parts of the world sunshine is the default, what's expected after the storm, but here the default is cloudy and grey. Nevertheless, Nora is wearing her heels today—no gumboots for this occasion. She's thought everything through, but the weather is always unpredictable this time of year. At least it's still warm. Wouldn't seem right to have sunshine at a funeral anyway.

Ed sits with his coffee and paper, every now and then looking up to rant about something the government is doing.

"I can't believe they're going to let those bloodsuckers stay." He's referring to eighty migrant stowaways found recently aboard a cargo shipment into Vancouver. "Another drain on our medical. Goddamn bleeding hearts gonna bleed us dry."

"Mmm-hmmm." Nora stops herself from wondering aloud whether or not the country might need a few more hardworking souls. She busies herself by packing things into yellow plastic crates to bring to the Moose Hall. Best just to hear Ed out, there's never much sense in engaging. The funeral is four hours off, but she still has to drive to the ferry and pick up her youngest. It's good of Rachel to come home. She worked for Mr. Clark four years in a row, coming back summers to help pay for university. Nora and Ed did all they could, but that school was expensive, and the scholarships didn't cover it all. Nora doesn't know what drives her youngest daughter, but she's proud of her. Some of those kids that never left the island didn't seem to fare so well. Things aren't the same here as when she grew up. Unless you left for the city, opportunities at the time were limited to the pulp mill, waitressing, or other service jobs. University means leaving, except in Kate's case—she'd gone to the local college. She pauses a moment to consider her older child, lost and sad on an even smaller island, surrounded by hippies.

The waiting area for foot passengers has been renovated. Fancy and new, with lots more space. She remembers the days of being crammed in with everyone, bumping into peoples' rear ends as they bent over to hug their grandchildren. The greeters are now all staggered throughout a sterile, heavily windowed room. There might be a good friend of forty years waiting with you right there and you'd never know it.

The first passengers off the ferry are speedy teens racing to cram onto the bus, then clumps of adults, and university kids. Rachel turns the corner before families with small children and the wheelchair-bound emerge. With her red trench coat and smooth black hair she looks, well, shiny.

"My girl! Look at you, all sophisticated."

"Hi Mom."

Nora runs her fingers through Rachel's short, choppy hair. "You cut it all off. You look too grown-up now. I don't like it."

Rachel laughs, rolling her eyes.

In the car, Rachel chatters about how crazy her class is this year and what a big difference two extra students make. Nora keeps trying to picture her at a teacher's desk, but images of an eleven-year-old with braces keep coming to mind. She doesn't think it will ever be possible to see her baby girl as a grown-up with a proper job—a career really. It still feels like she's playing make believe. "…And I was lucky enough to get Ryan this year," Rachel says, squaring her bottom lip and gently pushing a chunk of bang aside. "He's a great kid, really, but I can handle about one of him in the class, with no other students."

"Just make sure you take care of yourself. Do you still go to that beauty parlour for massages?

Rachel giggles and Nora bristles, knowing she sounds like a bumpkin.

"I haven't been to the spa in ages. Thanks for reminding me, Mom. Hey, maybe we can go to one together while I'm here."

"No way am I letting some stranger push my fat around. I like it where it is."

"You'd love it. Kate's not coming, I guess."

Nora shakes her head. "Still on Brittania. She wasn't really close to Mr. Clark anyway."

Rachel looks out the window. "I guess she's had enough of funerals." Then she switches back, pushing thoughts of her sister out of her mind. "Mr. Clark was such a great person. I really am sad he's gone. This place won't be the same."

"Honey, it hasn't been the same in a long time."

NORA, RACHEL, ADA, MARIAN, LONI, and Barbara buzz like angry hornets in the Moose Hall. Molly, upset that her balloons were taken down, broods in the corner. The conversation was brief:

"What's the problem with balloons? It's a 'celebration of life' isn't it?"

"It's not proper for a funeral," Nora said.

"But I put some black ones in there!"

"Enough." Nora's usual closing words. She then got busy delegating tasks:

"Marian, you can put your collage over on that table. It needs a tablecloth put on it first, and a wipe before that. Ada, the flowers should go at the front and on the collage table, too.

Rachel and Loni, come help me straighten out these chairs. Barbara, you can put out the sandwiches and finger food."

Two hours to go. Nora sweats. Doesn't seem like enough time. It never does. She knows every corner of the Moose Hall and every item in it, but even still, time is always tight during events.

Around quarter to two, everything has more or less come together. The bartender is there and all the food's laid out. Nothing to do but wait for people. Nora whisks around, straightening. She always likes a bit of buffer time to make it just right, but she never enjoys the fruits of her labours. By the time the food is prepared, the decorations put up, and the million trips to the shops for forgotten things have been completed, she's usually too exhausted to eat. Not that she's supposed to enjoy anything today anyway.

Reverend Morris arrives and starts testing the clip-on microphone. His head resembles a friar's, with a sharp ring of hair encircling a shiny scalp that beams back a reflection of the overhead lights. Tiny dewdrops of sweat are visible in the glare. Nora feels a wash of nerves, realizing that Edgar Watkins isn't here yet. He's done a lot of eulogies in the last couple years, and Nora feels lucky to count him as a friend. He can put things into words that she can feel in the pit of her stomach. She hopes he'll still be around to talk about her when the day comes.

People start to spill in. Everyone dresses in the best thing they could dig up. They are a simple bunch, except for Edgar's wife Marjorie, who is always going to Vancouver for new clothes and wearing way too much makeup. As for the men, some have a suit in the back of the closet kept just for these occasions, but very few work a job that calls for one. The problem is that as the years go by the suits don't fit so well anymore, so most men walk around tugging and pulling the material to cover parts the suits are no longer able to. Women who never wear skirts or dresses also bring them out for today.

There is an assortment of eras: while the odd person sports a fairly current style, others hearken back as far as 1985, Nora guesses, glancing at a set of shoulder pads. There are also a few people she recognizes only slightly, professionals of varying kinds who knew Mr. Clark too. There is a lot of fussing over Marian's collage. She'd been thoughtful and tried to fit most of the old-timers into the display. Some people dab at the corners of their eyes. *Where is Edgar?*

Nora budges through the crowd whispering to folks, asking if they've seen him. No one has, and start time is five minutes away. She wonders who might be able to take his place. No one comes to mind and no way in hell is she going to do it. She knows where her talents lie, and it sure isn't in talking to a room full of strangers. Her heart begins a rapid *tocking. What's happened to him?* She racks her brain for possible solutions. She's solved a lot of last-minute problems at the Moose Hall, but she's never had to find someone to do a last-minute eulogy. Her chest sits beneath an anvil, her stomach churning.

Fortunately, the Watkins' son Evan is here to act as Master of Ceremonies. He clips on a microphone and starts blowing at it.

"Ladies and gentlemen, we're about to begin. If you could take your seats, please."

Nora waves her arms, trying to gesture to Evan that they need him to stall, but he won't look her way. *Goddamn it Edgar, please get here fast.* Nora mutters her own variety of prayer. Everyone settles into a seat.

"We are here to honour an unforgettable person today," Evan begins. "Our friend, neighbour, our surrogate parent in many cases…. We all loved Charlie Clark in our own respective ways, but one thing is certain, it wasn't possible to know Charlie without loving him. I know there's a lot to say, but we'll start first with some guests."

What in the hell is Evan talking about? This is not the plan. What guests? The hall is hot and muggy with cigarette breath and old, wet leather. In her head Nora composes a tongue-lashing for Edgar. He'd better be dead, too.

Then all eyes on the door.

The group that struts in seems to do so in slow motion. Like a large, splattered blob of India Ink on a bland, off-white canvas, six figures in black enter the hall. They glide to the front of the room and sit in six empty chairs. Nora had been so busy losing her mind she didn't even notice the chairs.

"Holy shit."

Words from Mr. Clark's cousin Steve, spoken for everyone sitting agog in the silent room.

People then start to turn and whisper to each other. Nora grabs a support beam. More silence as one member of the group takes the microphone from Evan and clips it to her tight-fitting, black satin shift. Nora doesn't even hear her words at first; some man is droning on in the background as she takes in the exposed garters and fishnet tights, the impossibly high-heeled shoes made of white leopard print, and the feathers sticking out the top of her head. Nora has never seen anyone dressed like this, except in the movies. She is trying to figure out how much makeup is on the woman's face when she realizes the droning sound *is* in fact the woman's voice, and that she's not actually a woman at all, despite the hourglass figure and cascading blonde hair. Who the hell are these people? Did they know Mr. Clark? She's never seen eyes as huge as the ones in that room. Not a single sound but that woman's (man's?) voice.

"I loved Charlie." She pauses. "He made things great. It's that simple. I think that today we are all asking the question, 'What am I going to do without him?'" Her voice catches a little and a helpless sort of look comes over her face as she starts to cry. Immediately two of her friends get up. Each takes an arm, one of them handing her a tissue, as they bring her back to her seat.

Another one goes up to the mic. She wears a long white gown covered in sheer black organza. Her hat is black and massive.

A silver piece of mesh hangs from the brim, covering her face, but Nora knows as soon as she speaks that she is a he, too.

What should she do? She's supposed to be in charge and now it's all gone to shit. Edgar still isn't there. Who planned all of this? Obviously Evan was in on it. Why didn't they tell her? Does anyone else here know these people? Nora had planned almost every noteworthy event at the Moose Hall in the last fifteen years. She'd worked her way up by showing she was capable, in control. How could Evan disrespect her like this? She seethes.

She can't catch the eye of a single board member. The whole room is riveted. She thinks of wielding her power, how good it would feel to go up to the front and say, "Excuse me, but this is a private event...." But Nora can't move. She doesn't like scenes anyway. The man (woman?) in the hat speaks.

"I remember the night Charlie did 'dueling Joni Mitchells' with Camille." She shakes her head. "...so creative. I can't tell you how much I learned from him. I'm sure you all remember."

Some muffled laughter and then, "No doubt our community is going to suffer without him. We have a lot of wonderful people, but Charlie was so incredibly special. He was brave enough to be in two places."

Nora listens. Although she doesn't want to believe it, Charlie Clark clearly had another life. And he didn't want to share it with any of them. Or did he? *Why are these people here today? Who are they?* She can't find a logical place for the millions of thoughts swimming like dumb, confused sperm in her head. To her, Charlie was a community man. Someone wholesome, someone who'd talk to her when she was alone raising two little girls and the rest of the world had gone back to work. He *related* to her, which now makes absolutely no sense. How could a person be one thing to her and something completely different to these strangers? No wonder he waited until he was dead to share it with the folks who felt they knew him best.

One by one each of the six gets up to speak, and each story paints an unfamiliar portrait. Each person shares a particular memory: the time they dressed as the Point Grey Housewives and walked all over the west side of Vancouver, the time they shocked a busload of Japanese tourists by pole dancing on the cluster of flagpoles in English Bay. The many, many nights out. And then, a slideshow.

There he is. Nora has to admit he made a great-looking woman, despite the Adam's apple. Some people giggle or snicker at the photos. Some of the men outright guffaw. Several people get up and leave the room. A few pictures are pretty racy. They aren't all of Charlie dressed as a woman, though. There are a few of him with his arm around another man. In one photo, taken from behind at sunset, they look out across the ocean, heads touching. While something about it is incongruous to Nora, she can't help admitting, at least to herself, that it is a beautiful picture. *Snap out of it.* She shakes her head. Soon it's obvious that one person won't be speaking. He sinks against the one sitting next to him, shoulders rising and falling with rhythmic, invisible tears.

And Edgar. He finally appears at the microphone, looking sheepish until the buzz of conversation in the room gives way to his presence.

"Respected members of our community, we are here to bid our own farewell to a gracious man, a loyal citizen, and a loving friend. Edgar continues as though nothing is amiss. The funeral then morphs into something familiar, and Nora half-relaxes into the lull of his soft voice. The memories Edgar speaks of are ones she is a part of, and his words provoke tentative laughter and tears of recognition from the people in the room. She looks at Rachel a few seats over, nose bright and cheeks stained red. Ed sits hunched over, looking at the floor, knuckles entwined. *Look at me,* she thinks. Doesn't anyone care about what just happened?

A handful of people get up to speak at the open mic. The

lawyer who helped Mr. Clark set up shop a long time ago, a couple kids who worked for him, a neighbour, and an old lady who said she'd never forget the personal service she got from Mr. Clark every Thursday when she bought her weekly staples. And Rachel.

"...What we need to remember is our shared love for Charlie. And that love needs to refrain from judgment, recognizing only how we can all connect, if we want to."

Nora listens to her daughter, surprised and sad. When she left their town, the little girl Nora knew had gone with her. This is a poised and articulate woman who has travelled beyond her mother's experience to a place where Nora doesn't even know how to walk. She feels faint, no longer knowing who sits in the room. Why do people who go away change so much? How has she missed what was between then and now?

The six strangers stay for the reception, sticking close together while occasionally someone from the community goes up and offers them a piece of cake or a sandwich. Before long, there is a big group of mostly younger folks in their circle, laughing and crying at the same time. They're drinking too, and getting louder. Most older folks take a couple bites of food and high-tail it out of there as politely as possible, trying not to look like they are fleeing. But instead of winding down, the afternoon starts to take on the feel of a beginning. Nora's bones ache. She wants to leave too but takes refuge in the usual tasks—refilling trays of food and making sure there's always a fresh pot of coffee. People stop by and tell her what a good job she's done, as always. She gives her usual *humph*, and talks about everything she's screwed up. Edgar and Evan slip out long before Nora can get anywhere near them. The music gets louder and people start moving around. Nora corners Marian, hands on her hips.

"What is this?" She waves a hand toward the room and places it immediately back on her hip.

"Dancing?"

"At a goddamned funeral?"

"What do you want me to say, Nora? It's not exactly the most surprising thing that's happened today."

"Jesus Christ." Nora storms back into the kitchen.

Hours later, apart from the social committee, there are only a few people of Nora's generation left in the hall. Someone's dimmed the lights and the bartender is getting busy. More young folks arrive. Rachel comes out of the crowd to see Nora.

"Can you believe this?"

She feels a moment of choice in the air between them, but decides to go with disapproval.

"Not at all."

"Come meet these people. They've known Mr. Clark forever."

Nora mumbles, keeps wiping the counters. "I have work."

"C'mon, Mom."

"You go."

Rachel pinches her face into judgment. The face she's pulled out since she was nine on occasions when she thinks her mother is an idiot. The face that separates them. Nora never feels more alone than when her daughter looks at her like this, and tonight it stabs more keenly than ever. Isolated, diminished, and adrift, she spins and leaves the room just as the show begins.

THE TELEPHONE RINGS FOR THE SIXTH TIME that morning. Nora, propped in bed with her magazine, tries to focus on a recipe for Yorkshire puddings. On the seventh ring, she picks up.

"You okay?" Barbara's voice is plaintive; in it, Nora reads an attempt at sympathy.

"What do you think?"

A pause. "You know you'd probably feel better if you hadn't said those things to that woman."

"That was no woman."

"You're missing my point."

For a moment, Nora's confused, but then her memory of the night returns. Had she really almost gotten into a fistfight with a drag queen? Her head starts to throb with the combined remnants of red wine and MSG, but in the lifting fog she hears herself:

"How much longer do you plan on staying?" She'd asked the broad back of one of the group of six, emboldened by drink and fed-upedness.

There was a beat, and then the woman made a slow turn. Nora took in her impossible eyelashes and bulbous, burgundy lips. "As long as we need to."

She was an imposing figure, dwarfing Nora in her black, lacy shadow. She cast her eyes deliberately up and down Nora's body, arms crossed.

"You know, this is a private party," Nora managed weakly.

"Indeed. A place for Charlie's friends to say goodbye."

Nora's rage bubbled up before she could help herself. "Exactly. So you might want to just let us get back to that."

The woman's neck strained forward until her face was so close to Nora's that she thought she might spit in it. "We *are* us."

By then, Rachel had shown up again and whisked her back into the kitchen. "Mom, can we talk?"

"NORA?" BARB WAS STILL ON THE LINE. Nora let the receiver tumble off her shoulder. She picked it up, turned it off, and placed it back on her bedside table. She rolled over, willing herself back to sleep.

KATE

THE MORNING JERKS ITSELF around like a feral, bewildered animal. Kate flits unfulfilled between normally simple tasks that today for some reason have become exceedingly complex. Taking out the compost is interrupted by an urge to fill the hummingbird feeder; lighting the wood stove fire requires more than five matches and a trip to the washroom. Along with this, things aren't where she thinks she left them. Nicole's letter is no longer on the table where she'd stuffed it under her novel. She makes excuses—wind, her constant shuffling of things—but under this sits a kernel of unease. She decides to walk.

It's a half-hour walk down to the shore. In the picnic area, the tables and benches are all dedicated, most in typical ways: *Sit here and ponder awhile. We miss you, Janice*, and *In loving memory of Mitchell Harrison. 1935-1999*. Others attempt originality: *To the left of the unnamed boats is where I now sail*, and the overtly poetic: *I am you, in tree, sky, and soft ocean*. Kate reads all of these and wonders not only about the people who died, but also about the loved ones who wrote the dedications. Can a bench provide solace? A table?

She can't help but wonder what sort of inscription she'd display in memory of her young husband. Nothing comes to mind. What would their sadness look like, if extracted, distilled? The most withered parts of her—depicted, rendered, cooked away like fat from a bone. It would look nothing like this.

She snaps a few photos of the small plaques, sits awhile, and then plods the shoreline, edged in sun-baked wrack and smelling of the inhabitants of low tide: sea stars, fish, tiny crabs, and the things that burrow into soft, hidden niches, perforating mud. She snaps more photos: a small Inukshuk made out of stacked rocks, an assortment of smooth, multi-coloured pebbles in macro. As she walks on, images present themselves one by one—an old rowboat beached next to a cabin, its peeling paint revealing a palimpsest of changed names; the legs of a raised dock forming a gateway to the ocean; black, mussel-clumped appendages hiding worlds within their crevices. *Snap, snap.* She doesn't see the woman watching at first.

"You look productive this morning," she calls out from her tabletop perch, paper coffee cup in hand.

Kate jolts, feels her camera swing.

"You ever sell your work at the market?"

"God, no."

"Have you seen some of the stuff at the market?"

Kate grins. Some of it's good, but conservative—scenes of boats, ferries passing by. What the tourists want.

"Maybe you can put something in the shop. Have a gallery showing, see how people react. No harm in that, right? Kris owns the coffee shop portion of the Wellspring.

For one suspended moment, Kate floats the idea. With this, something lighter begins to poke playfully at her thoughts, but just as quickly, a different sensation creeps in to smother it: Another attempt at rescue? Pity?

"I'll think about it," she says. "I'd better keep going."

"Mind if I join you?"

She wants to say no. Kris seems decent, but Kate knows her as the chatty sort who spends most of her time in the village. She would fix you with her small brown eyes, asking intrusive questions before she even opened her mouth. Kate hasn't been to any of her events at the coffee shop, but hears they can go late, with lots of noise and the odd table dance. Kris makes her anxious. She thinks that if she spends too much time around her she'll say more than she wants to.

"How long you been here now?" Although Kris is walking alongside her, she somehow manages to turn her torso to face her, offering fixed attention. "Couple months?"

"About two and a half."

"You thinking of staying over winter?"

"I think so."

"Good. We need more interesting people here in the off-season. Gets boring sometimes."

"Look at this." Kate turns sharply to the craggy oak perched impossibly from a rocky outcropping. She starts snapping again, twisting herself down into a squat, facing her lens up through branches. She looks for an angle where she can get only tree and sky, excluding the foundation of rock, but on the slippery leaves her leg scoots out from beneath her. Falling, she shoots the sky. "Shit."

"You artists. So distracted all the time."

Kate raises an eyebrow. "I'm hardly an artist."

They walk on, a chain of questions forming link by link: What does she do? How many summers has she spent here? Finally, Kris makes her final suggestion.

"Let me put your stuff up. You don't even have to come in."

"I don't know. Maybe."

By the time Kris lets up, Kate has grudgingly agreed to letting her display her photographs in the coffee shop. *Fuck,* she thinks to herself.

At the next juncture, Kate says a goodbye of sorts and breaks off onto a different trail before another link can be added to the conversational chain forming between them, a piece of her life she would not yet be willing to share, without coercion.

Back at home, her phone is ringing. Nora's voice.

"How are you?"

"Good. You?"

"I don't know. Mr. Clark's funeral was last week. Did you talk to your sister?"

"No. I completely forgot about the funeral."

"We had some crashers."

"Funeral crashers? Really?"

Nora goes on to describe the day: The preparations, all the work of the community. And then these people show up unannounced," she continues, "taking complete control of everything, ruining the service for everyone."

"Were they friends of his?"

"Guess so. But nobody here knew them."

"Mr. Clark. Wow. It sort of makes sense, though."

"Your sister and I can't find common ground on this one." A pause. "What would you say to me coming over?"

"Sure?"

"How does tomorrow look?"

"Soon."

"I'm bringing soup."

Kate spends a couple more hours shifting dust motes around the cabin, then sits down to look at the novel Ivy loaned her. She pulls out her bookmark, but instead of following the story she thinks of Ivy and her carefully curated circle of friends and caregivers. She can't help but think that Ivy would be more decisive than she is about the people she'd let into her home, more forceful with her privacy. And now Kate's pictures—something so nascent, so embryonic in her—would be stuck up on a wall for a bunch of strangers to look at. You have something to learn from this old woman, she tells herself.

IVY

DEAR FATHER AND MOTHER,
The days are passing quickly here on Isla de Piños. It's such a treat to see sunshine during the time of year when we're usually bundled up and barely going outside. I am helping Oma and Opa in the bakery and sometimes on the farm, when I'm not worrying about snakes and other insects. Did I mention before how huge they are here?

I know that you aren't pleased about my decision to delay university, but I hope you'll understand how much I'm learning here. Everything is different. My whole life already feels as though it's expanding.

Opa has loaned me his horse, Bonita. She's beautiful, and she's been a sort of a guide to this place.

Please give my love to Eve. I miss you all, and thank you for allowing me to come here.
Love, Ivy

THE AFTERNOON HEAT INVITES LAZINESS. Ivy waves to her grandmother in the kitchen window and instantaneous pools of sweat form in her armpits. She walks toward the barn and releases the white mare. Opa, now napping, had pointed out a trailhead past the fields and orchard and told her to follow it until she came to the river. Then, if she turned to the right she would eventually come to a spot where the waters widened and formed a sort of swimming pool.

It's not long before she and Bonita reach the river's edge. They continue on until she sees it: a sparkling little mini-lake that promises a heavenly reprieve from the punishing humidity. She tethers Bonita to a tree up the grassy bank from the water and peels off her dress, having worn her swimsuit underneath. She'd thought maybe the Americans would be here, but maybe they came later in the day. Testing the water with her foot, she discovers that it's almost the same temperature as the surrounding air. Still, she walks in.

Ivy's never been a fabulous swimmer, but that doesn't bother her. She's content just to float around, enjoying weightlessness and a moment of slight refreshment. Would she ever get used to this heat? She spends a few minutes in the river, then dries herself off and sits down on her towel.

A few minutes later she notices a flash of blonde out of the corner of her eye. Maureen, Mark, and Peter Freisen, the son of her grandparents' German neighbours, emerge from the trail.

"You came!" Maureen shouts.

"Thank goodness," Mark adds. "She's been looking for you every day."

Maureen strips down to her swimsuit, flicks a towel at her brother and taunts, "Last one in!"

"Not everything is a race, little sister."

Maureen runs and dives into the river. Mark follows behind. Peter seems uncomfortable to be left with Ivy. He spreads out his blanket and sits quietly on it. Ivy knows his English isn't very strong. Most of the time he blushes when he sees her, or simply walks away. His older sister Sonia lives with the family, along with her husband and three-year-old son. The Freisens are always back and forth from their house to Ivy's grandparents', and her grandparents tread the same route in reverse, borrowing, lending, lifting, speaking German.

"Ivy, come in!" Maureen calls.

"Coming!"

She marvels to herself that it feels so easy to find her way into the group of collected strangers on Isla de Piños. Easier, strangely, than making friends back home. At eighteen, distance and youth embolden her.

AS THE WEEKS PASS, LIFE FALLS INTO a new sort of routine. Each day after helping her grandparents, she goes to the swimming hole. Oma and Opa own a bakery and also grow vegetables—including eggplant, peppers, and cucumber—on their farm. There are also a couple of cows and some hens scratching about. No single source of income is sufficient for Oma and Opa. A rare frost in Florida means they can export fruit and vegetables to the United States. If there is no frost, there's nothing but a large freight bill. There are always hints at new opportunities, but very little stability. *Nothing we can be sure about*, Oma is fond of repeating. They are always working.

There are several regulars at the swimming hole. Apart from the predominating Americans, there are other Europeans: a few Italians, some Spanish, and even some folks from the Cayman Islands who speak English very well. Sometimes there are Cubans, and when they come, Ivy always listens closely to the dance of their language, which interests her more than German, much to Oma's displeasure.

"You are making friends?" She asks.

"Yes."

"It's good, but I think you need to work too."

"I'm working in the bakery, and the farm a little."

"Not enough. I had a job when I was your age, made some money to help the family."

"But I want to explore, too."

She'd swatted the air as if Ivy's idea was an offending mosquito. "Exploring is the work of a lazy mind. It will bring trouble. I put the paper on your bed. There's work at the phones."

She doesn't want to give Oma any reason to send her back to Canada before she's ready. It had been hard enough convincing her parents that she needed time off before college, so she agrees to look for a job. Soon, she finds herself working as a telephone operator on various evenings and weekends. On Sundays, everyone goes to church. Ivy's grandparents are Lutheran, as are her parents, and there is a fairly large gathering of Germans there each week. Things are removed, but somewhat predictable. Ivy has never been good with that sort of thing; where many people find comfort in routine, Ivy typically finds only restlessness. Her biggest flaw.

KATE

KATE SITS IN THE BOOKSTORE pretending not to watch the movements of an unfamiliar man. He is craggy-bearded, with clothes from the Mountain Co-op, R.E.I., or possibly the Free Store. He looks like he stepped out of a kayak just moments before, and is still walking on sea legs. He knocks over the magazine rack.

"Crap."

The customers look up at him subtly, brows first. All mundane things become interesting here in the cooler, quieter months. The bearded man re-erects the rack, picks up fallen magazines, and approaches the front desk.

"I'm looking for marine charts."

"Right against the back wall."

"And can I have a latté?"

A sigh. "You have to order on the other side. Just books here."

It's a rainy night, but still warm. Steam fogs the windows of the shop and the local poets are mid-reading. Claire, at the microphone, ruffles her papers and glares at the barista when the espresso machine begins its hollow, sucking noise, as though attempting to inhale everything in the room.

It's been a few weeks since Kate last saw her mom, or any family for that matter. She talks herself into wanting to see Nora, and it's true that she could use some time away from her spinning head. Nora will fuss and make food. She'll brood and nag, but she hopefully won't force Kate to talk too much.

Having her here without Ed, Kate convinces herself, will be a welcome break from the otherwise inevitable family dynamic. Her parents have always been more palatable in individual doses.

The man heads toward Kate's table—all others in the coffee shop are full. Hers is half in the bookstore, half in the café, on the periphery where she likes it. Up close, she sees he's younger than she first thought.

"Mind if I join you?"

She looks up at him and shrugs. "No, that's fine. I'm leaving soon anyway."

"Don't let me chase you away."

"It's okay."

"You live here?"

"More or less."

"What does that mean?" He smiles, looking curious.

She's glaring now. Nosy idiot.

He holds out a hand. "Luke. I just washed up on shore today. Still getting my bearings." He laughs.

"I figured."

"Everyone as friendly as you around here?" He's still smiling.

Kate lowers her shoulders and forces herself to soften a bit. He is—if nothing else—trying.

"Sorry, I was just focused on something else."

He smiles. "So, is this the place to be?"

"Of course it is." Kris swoops by, collecting Kate's mug. "You done?"

Irritation and claustrophobia blossom in Kate and extend out to both Kris and the stranger.

"I have to get going," she tells them.

"What do you mean? Where?" Kris says, sensing nothing.

"I need to make a phone call," Kate answers, getting up quickly. Disoriented, her breathing shallow, she swings her bag over the table, knocking Luke's full coffee mug onto the floor. Splatters of hot coffee cover Kris's apron. Kate is full of apologies. Luke gets up quickly, helping Kris untie her apron.

"I'm good. I'm good." Kris, unfazed, balls up the apron. "Let me get a broom."

"I'll help," Kate adds.

"It's okay. No big deal."

And then it descends. The heaviness of scrutiny, his unerring, almost clinical observation. It's as though Jeff's suddenly there, watching, noticing every misstep, taking pleasure in it, with the knowledge that her own judgement, turned inward, would be enough fuel to undo her, and that this, in turn, would power him further. Kate begins to hyperventilate, her chest hollow and excruciating. While part of her body has already left the café, she can barely hold herself together long enough to walk out the door.

SHE PICKS UP HER MOTHER from the seven a.m. ferry. Nora tells her she's grateful to escape what she calls "the masses," which makes Kate snicker. Her hometown, with the moniker North Wailaish clumsily anglicized from its Indigenous origins, is on a much bigger island, but the population still only hovers around forty thousand. They go straight to Kate's cabin, where Nora begins tidying the living room and bringing her up to speed on events back home. Dad still can't find his keys, even though she's installed a small rack with the word "keys" embossed on it. And, the neighbour is growing a small slice of hedge on the city side of their front yard, between the two houses, in protest of the chaos of Ed's garden, the one that Nora refuses to tend. Rachel calls it "the garden of his discontent." Nora yawns.

"It's so pretty here. Fresh air makes me sleepy, though."

"You get used to it. It gives me energy."

"You're not too lonely?" She pinches her eyebrows into the expression she uses when commencing an inquisition.

"No. There are lots of people to talk to when I want."

"What did you do last night?"

Kate shrugs. "Not much, just hung out at the coffee shop.

Talked to a guy who lives on a sailboat. Listened to a poetry reading, sort of."

"Interesting. What's his name?"

"Who?"

"The sailboat guy."

"Luke. But no, Mom."

"Just making conversation."

"I need to see Ivy for a few hours today."

"The old lady in the wheelchair?"

Kate feels a poke of affront on Ivy's behalf, but remembers that this was how she'd initially described her to Nora when they first met.

"Ivy. Yes."

"Okay. I'll spend some time in the village while you do that. You sure you can't get a day off?"

Kate ignores her. She doesn't want a day off.

SHE DROPS HER MOTHER OFF at the market and watches for a moment as Nora approaches the woodturner's table, picking up bowls one by one, rotating them in her hands while squinting and frowning. Kate knows Nora wouldn't intend to disappoint anyone, but at the same time the hopeful vendors would be annoyed when, after they'd patiently answered all of her questions, she would walk away empty-handed.

Ivy is listening to a recorded book when she arrives.

"Alice Munro. How does she do it every time? Just when you wonder what all this is about, just when it makes the least sense, it hits you like the word of God. Perfection."

Kate brushes her long dark hair aside and unloads flowers, bread, milk, and eggs. "Does perfection really exist?"

Ivy pauses. "It depends how you define it. Probably only in retrospect, after we've failed to recognize it. I'd even dare say it happens more than we realize."

"What do you mean?"

"It's a matter of how we tune in. Sometimes we're open to

it, but most of the time we let it pass right by. I think I've seen more perfection in seemingly flawed things."

"Like what?"

"Like my old dog's tooth marks on the coffee table leg. Or the way Nancy can't quite pronounce the letter 's.'"

"That's perfection?"

"Absolutely."

Ivy's long white braid hangs off to one side. Kate undoes the furls and shakes it out. She notices how much hair Ivy has, how it billows around her face, making her features diminutive, except for her eyes.

"Have you always had this much hair?"

"I had a lot more, at one time." She cranes her neck to look up at Kate. "On the Isle of Pines they called me *Rubia*. I never cut my hair, mostly because when I walked by the local salon, everyone looked at me as though they'd be afraid to even touch it. It was very blonde, almost white. And big and curly. I think it shocked a lot of people there." Not for the first time, Ivy's eyes vacate the present.

Kate tries to imagine the bewildered expressions on the hairdressers' faces. She'd never considered the challenges of cutting the hair of an unfamiliar ethnicity.

"I liked to ride my grandfather's white horse to town," Ivy continued. "People must have thought I was a ghost." She wears a distant, almost mischievous smile as Kate pours a stream of warm water over her leaning head. "Boys sure liked it, though."

"I'll bet. Tell me more about this place."

"The Isle of Pines. Cuba. Communists changed the name to something stupid now. Isla de la Juventud, The Isle of Youth."

"When were you there?"

"Roaring twenties, my lady."

Kate rubs shampoo into Ivy's endless locks. As she lathers, she imagines the hunched old woman living it up flapper-style in Cuba, of all places. *What becomes of us?*

IVY

PETER, MAUREEN, MARK, and Ivy are at the swimming hole as usual, the afternoon humidity having risen to the point where standing still feels like treading water, even if you're on land. It feels as though there's no oxygen in the air that does manage to enter her lungs.

Oma hates her coming here. "Full of crocodiles that eat small animals," she'd said. "The Freisens lost their poodle last year."

She'd told Ivy and Opa that they're putting themselves in danger and being unfair, making her worry so much. Opa had dismissed this with rolled eyes, taking care that it was only Ivy who saw. Ivy can see that this little lake is everything peaceful to him. She loves watching him immerse completely into the tiny oasis as he floats silently on his back, his eyes reaching up to the sky, to something only he seems able to appreciate. Although Oma's words unnerve her a little, over time Ivy comes to see her grandmother as nothing more than a worrywart and before long has dismissed her completely. Besides, she's yet to see a crocodile anywhere on the Isle of Pines. Still, she always makes sure there is someone in the water before her—preferably a slower swimmer.

Today, though, she hasn't yet gone into the water and instead finds herself suspended in a deep fetal sleep on her towel. They've all been lazily reclining on the riverbank, falling in and out of books and conversation. In her abyss of sleep, she doesn't notice the other three go down the bank to the water.

After an indeterminate amount of time, her body full of sun and rest, Ivy awakes, surprised to find a Cuban boy perched next to her, holding a book.

"Hello," she says, flustered, sitting up and wiping the bit of drool escaping one corner of her mouth. It's a busy time on most of the farms, so she hadn't expected to see any Cuban workers today.

"Good morning," he says. Very dark eyes.

She reaches for a towel to cover herself, her cheeks becoming warmer, if that's possible. "Sorry. I'm being lazy today."

"It's good to sleep when you need to."

"Where did you learn to speak English?" Ivy tries not to look surprised, not wanting to insult him. He speaks slowly, but with a cautious, earnest sort of lilt. Most of the Cubans working on the farm speak only Spanish, and in shouts over the farm cacophony.

He shrugs, holding up his book. "Mostly this way, but I stayed in Havana for a while, and worked for some Americans. I also have friends from Cayman."

"I'm Ivy," she tells him, hand outstretched.

"Emilio," he says, his smile carving a dimple deep into his right cheek. He takes her hand loosely. Her first Cuban friend. And not too terrible-looking, either.

They talk about what he's reading, *The Great Gatsby.* One of his employers had passed it along.

"Is it like this where you come from?" he asks her, and she's not completely sure if he is joking. She read the book when it came out about a year ago, but nothing in it relates to her experience as a high school student.

"I'm from Vancouver."

He looks at her blankly.

"It's on the west coast of Canada," she explains. She's never considered that someone might have no concept of where that is.

"What do you think of Isla de Piños?"

"It's beautiful. So different from home."

"Your home is not beautiful?"

"Well, yes, very much so, but in a wetter, colder way."

"I imagine the air is very fresh." Something about the way he pronounces the last two letters of that word stirs the lower part of her a little.

"I suppose."

They talk about books for a while. She finds herself telling him things she hasn't even gotten into with Maureen and Mark, or her grandparents for that matter; things about her intent to study literature despite her father's insistence on business or medicine.

"Next time I will bring you something Cuban to read."

She feels an unexpected leap in her chest at the prospect of a next time, but then she sees her three friends climbing up the bank. They pick up their towels and start drying themselves off more quickly than usual, making noises about getting back home and helping with chores. Ivy knows instantly that this has something to do with Emilio. Emilio also seems to sense their discomfort. Without waiting for introductions, he stands up and says goodbye, then walks down to the water's edge, and dives in.

"Who is that?" Mark asks.

"His name is Emilio." She's still staring after him.

"He seems interested in you." Maureen looks at her, a slickened curl adhered to one cheek.

Ivy shrugs, lays back down, and covers her eyes with a towel.

"You ought to be careful," she says.

"Mmm-hmm."

When she gets home, a rose-coloured light insists on making its way through the cracks in Oma's drapery, lifting the shadows of the dark sitting room. Oma sits with Stefan Freisen, Peter's father from next door. She catches just the last few words of their conversation as she walks in. They are in German, but Ivy has always recognized the curse words—they've carried down a generation, to her mother's lips.

"Hello Mr. Freisen," she calls from the doorway.

"Hello, Ivy. How was the swimming?"

"Great."

Oma looks at her, one brow up. "Mr. Freisen's chickens have been disappearing. Do you know anything?"

"No. I'm sorry."

"We lose one almost every night. I'm staying up tonight, with my rifle."

"Have you seen anything suspicious with the Cuban workers?" Oma asks.

"No. Nothing."

"Good luck," Ivy calls, and excuses herself to get changed.

"I need help with the rice, Ivy...." Oma calls as her wet swimsuit hits the floor with a splat.

KATE

KATE WATCHES NORA, observing. She marvels at her mother's ability to digest and summarize instantaneously, no matter what she's taking in. Of course Nora loves to talk too, but most interactions with her typically involve the sort of scrutiny more often reserved for military situations. In her function as mother, this both annoys and endears Nora to Kate. Regardless of whether her persistence provokes or irritates though, it is at the same time a familiar comfort to feel Nora's concern. Kate dunks a corner of crusty sourdough into her soup, her mother's eyes following every movement.

"I love your beef barley," Kate says, reaching for distractions, hoping that flattery might offset a potential interrogation.

"You have the recipe, right?"

"It's better when you make it."

Nora smiles. Kate feels the unspoken, mutual nourishment.

"There's lots more at home."

Here we go.

"I talked to Mona at the paper the other day."

Kate picks at something gelatinous that's adhered itself to the table. "How is she?"

"Good. They miss you."

"Right."

"I don't know what sort of idiot is doing your job right now, but I've never seen so many spelling mistakes in the *Free Press*."

Kate gets up and collects Ann's gold-veined raku bowls from

the rutted table. Nora continues to watch, leaning forward on her elbows, hands steepled in the way the Women of the Loyal Order of the Moose were taught, when they wanted to look more trustworthy during their speeches.

"She said she'd take you back anytime."

Kate shakes her head.

"Sometimes it's easier to move on when you're busy, around other people."

"Have I told you how much I detest the words 'move on?'"

Nora sighs, shoulders drooping in defeat or possibly feigned exhaustion. Kate isn't sure which. "I just worry," she says.

"Well, stop."

For the rest of the evening, Kate makes chopped attempts at superficial conversation. She feels guilty rebuffing her mother, but can sense in her body, in the clench of her throat and the tightness in her shoulders, that there is no convincing Nora that *here* is the best place for her to be. After so many long, confusing months, she's finally beginning to relax, and to allow herself to think about what *she* might want to do next. So many voices, so many opinions, as though everyone is afraid of leaving her to her own devices, as though her circumstances had rendered her fragile. She already knows death doesn't make you fragile.

Inevitably their conversation comes around to the subject of the funeral.

"Who comes uninvited to this sort of thing?" Nora throws her hands up in the air, her mouth curled in disgust.

"Did you talk to Edgar? He seemed to know about it. A few others too, sounds like."

"He's avoiding me."

"I probably would too," Kate says, wide-eyed.

"Not funny. Respect your mother."

"Sorry, mom. I know you hate being left in the dark, but maybe people were just afraid of how you'd react."

"Since when did you become so direct?" Nora looks hurt.

"I'm too tired to tell lies to make people feel better, to be honest."

Nora's expression changes to surprise. Even Kate is a bit bewildered at how truthful this feels.

Nora pauses for a moment, then rallies her indignation. "How I might react is none of their goddamn business. They have a duty to tell me what's going on. I've been the director at the Moose Hall for as long as anyone can remember."

"I know. I know. Just go talk to Edgar. He'll come out of hiding eventually."

Kate's relieved that the subject doesn't veer into moral righteousness this time around, although she's sure it's coming eventually. Seeing her mother's yawn, she takes the opportunity to invite her to the guest room.

IN THE MORNING AT THE FERRY TERMINAL, Kate walks her mother down the dock toward the waiting room. Before she can do anything about it, a plop of seagull shit splats on Nora's forehead and begins to drip down her nose.

"Mother of Christ," says Nora.

It is Kate's first laugh in so many months.

IVY

STEFAN FREISEN FINDS OUT who is stealing his chickens. Although it's not the human perpetrator he suspects, he has the nationality correct. It is a very large, very dark, very Cuban boa. Mr. Freisen claims that the night before, while he was sitting on his porch watching the coop, he heard the chickens start to make a "big racket." He took out a lantern and glimpsed a flash of curving serpent in front of the pen, swaying and staring at a doomed, hapless hen. (Josephine it was, perhaps, for he'd named all of his chickens). He tells Ivy that the hypnotized fowl walked straight into the snake's mouth and he was so stunned and frightened that he simply watched it slide away, an enormous lump bulging its girth.

"Do you believe him?" she asked Oma.

"Course not." She waved the air. "He's full of *scheiss*."

However, not one week later work in the fields stops abruptly as hordes of farmers, labourers, and others run out of their homes and off their properties, down to the road, churning puffs of red dust into the sticky air. Mr. Freisen parades and shouts triumphant German, half-shouldering, half-dragging none other than the carcass of a ten-foot-long snake. The proof is a good thing for him, as the neighbours had begun to talk.

Ivy stands and stares. It begins to impress upon her that La Isla *is* speaking more clearly now, attempting to reveal something a little wilder than what she's seen up to this point. She discerns a shifting quality to the atmosphere. Things are emerging, but what? Locals assert that the novel *Treasure Island* was inspired by La Isla, and a history of pirates permeates the local folklore. Hidden things arouse her. Later that afternoon, at the swimming hole, she finally begins to give Oma's worries a chance to root more fully in reality.

She hasn't yet experienced the sensation of undisturbed waters enveloping her body. She tells herself she's been on the island and swum here often enough to know without doubt that the little lake is benign. It's a delicious discovery to find no one there.

The lack of movement and talk permits her to see how arresting the little pond is. It whispers invitations to her, as though part of it has evaporated and transported itself over to her, releasing and replacing itself as it washes over and throughout her body, leaving no difference between the lake and the waters that compose her own being. Late afternoon sun reflects itself in broken shards that dance across the enticing ripples as a small trade wind plies the surface. The surrounding grasses have been tamped down into amorphous hints of bodies, and it is so silent—the kind of silence that feels as though the entire world has inhaled and then paused. Even the birds sleep.

She takes off her dress and doesn't even put on a bathing cap. In seconds, her body splits the surface of the smooth, delicious water. She floats a bit on her back before turning over and heading to the middle of the lake, where she stops to tread water. She thinks about her sister Eve back home, how transformative it would be for her to come here too, to find out that people live so differently, that not everything back home matters like they always thought it did. That perhaps they have too much to worry about. She'll never be able to explain it fully.

Noticing a large log floating by, she swims closer and reaches out, intending to lean on it for awhile. Her hand grazes the rough bark, which feels oddly leathery. To her surprise the log lifts its head and looks straight at her. Eye to eye.

She'll tell her grandfather later that there was a small moment of species-to-species communication in that ancient glance, but truthfully this is embellishment. Realization in fact comes quickly, and she lets out a scream, swimming toward shore with all the strength she's endowed with, for all one knows she may be flying. After scrambling out of the water and onto the grass, she turns back to glimpse the scaly tail of the thing wiggling behind it as it hurries down the waterfalls.

"I think you scared it more." There is a voice, she's not sure where it's coming from at first, but as she rallies her senses she sees Emilio, standing uphill next to her blanket, grinning.

Her cheeks flush. Pulling the towel around her waist she forces herself to do whatever might be appropriate to the moment. Laughter? When she tries, the sound that comes out quivers along with the rest of her. She's mortified to feel tears brimming.

"He was big," Emilio offers.

She pants and gasps. "I. Swam. With. A. Crocodile." She begins to laugh. Hard, and a little maniacally.

"Something to tell your friends at home."

"No one would believe it. Oh my god. That was close."

"We feed the crocodiles very well here, so I think you are safe."

"My grandmother would disagree with you."

"She is not a *Piñero*."

"Definitely not." She wipes droplets of sweat and lake from her face, peels a cloying strand of weed from her arm.

"Your voice. It's a good defence." He points to his throat.

She collapses on her blanket then and continues to laugh and shake in a fitful, relieved-yet-still shocked kind of way. Emilio stares at her with a half-grin. He doesn't seem to blink much, as a rule. She pulls on a shirt and tries to compose a coherent thought. "I should go. I have to work tonight."

"You should stay inside. There's a storm of electricity coming."

"Not my choice, really."

He sits next to her. Something like a question swells in the air between them.

He hands her a book. "José Marti."

"Thank you."

"Enjoy," he says. He gets up and smiles, then walks away toward the far side of the lake, a place Ivy hasn't been to yet. .

NORA

HE'S TAKEN THE BEST SEAT in the place, the one next to the window that catches the late afternoon light, the one with the best view of the photo of the breeching orca that Nora likes to stare at when she's attempting to relax. She wishes she could be like Barb, happy with any seat in the place, but when you've been a client of the Mud Puddle for fifteen years, and when you're Nora, you like to sit where you like to sit.

It's muffin day. Two for one, and Steven-with-the-ponytail always has a warm one ready for her, messy with blueberries. Nora likes being known in this way. She reassures herself that there are still lots of folks in North Wailaish who know who she is, know what she likes. She puffs her chest a little, making space for the idea to settle in.

She squints at the man in her seat, but can't place him. He wears a tan trench coat and dark pants. His hair is mostly dark and well-groomed, the style a little finicky for her liking. He's greying at the temples, a place that works well for men, but not so much if you're female. Nora can't even remember when she'd started putting in the *Fanci Full* mousse to cover her own grey. She still uses it for touch-ups between salon visits. Not that she's vain, it's just that there are expectations for the Women of the Moose to keep up decent appearances. At least in their chapter. Come to think of it, this might even have been something she herself had instituted.

Something about him is familiar, but Nora can't figure it out. He isn't local, at least not a long-timer. His gestures are elegant. Even from where she sits Nora can see that his fingers apply just the right amount of pressure to allow the butter to leave his knife and find the perfect crevasses in his muffin. It's sort of mesmerizing.

He looks up at her and smiles. Nora flushes, realizing she's been staring. She manages the smile she reserves for strangers and moves her eyes back to her muffin. *Best eat it while it's warm.*

The testy weather has relaxed a bit today. While you can't say it's sunny, the clouds sit high enough to allow for a pale bit of yellow to show through—like the margarine she makes Ed eat, while she sneaks out to smear butter on her own muffin once or twice a week. Nora chortles a little to herself. Sometimes a woman just needs her secrets. It isn't like she has a whole lot of vices for him to complain about.

She squints, trying to see the title of the book he's reading, but she can't make it out. He puts it down and leans back in his chair, hands folded in his lap, looking around the room.

"Nice day." He smiles at her, his clothes the shade of a camel.

"Not bad for this time of year."

Now she's forced to talk to him. Her own fault for staring. But it's hard to engage in idle chitchat when you need to put your full attention on the muffin at hand, otherwise it won't taste as good. She tries to look beyond him, out the window, but can already feel his curiosity.

"Have you lived here long?" he asks.

"Most of my life. Born in Vancouver, but who wants to stay there?"

He looks at his hands. Nora sees the wedding band. Silver-coloured, but more expensive-looking, engraved with Coast Salish designs. He looks up at her. "You have a point."

"Where are you from?" she asks.

He gives a little chuckle. "Vancouver."

Nora blushes. She'd figured he was an easterner. He looks like Toronto.

"I'm teasing you. I live there now, but I'm originally from Boston, years ago."

She takes a moment to congratulate her powers of perception. *Boston, Toronto, same thing.* "What brings you to our town?"

"A friend. But then I got caught up in this cult story." He shows her the cover of his book: *The History of the Aquarian Society in the Southern Gulf Islands.*

"Oh yeah, I've heard of that. Strange stuff."

"It's kind of interesting though, mostly because of how the ringleader disappeared."

Nora isn't interested. All sorts of crazies make their way to these islands, especially the small ones. Nothing special about any of them. Nothing original about running away to an island. *Cowards.*

"I've become too intrigued to go back home just yet. Now, I know you're probably a very busy person, but would it be at all possible to meet with you again? I'd love to know more about the history of this place."

Nora is taken aback, feels she should be affronted. *What if he's a psychopath, fond of depositing body parts in forests?* She knows she shouldn't, but he looks so damned familiar, and once Nora's curiosity has been piqued, there isn't any way back.

"Why not," she offers. "You might be disappointed, though."

He laughs. "I'm sure I won't be. Can we meet here tomorrow?"

"Okay, how's lunchtime?"

"Perfect, thank you, um…" He extends a hand.

"Nora."

"Nora, I'm Neville." They shake. "Lovely to meet you."

KATE

GHOSTS WERE RETURNING to the small cabin in the woods to claim their belongings. What other explanation could account for the disappearances? Kate doesn't know every item in the place, of course, but she remembers the stack of papers—its existence, not so much what is in it—now two thirds of its original size. *And where is Jeff's old baseball?* She begins to lock her doors. The locals look harmless for the most part, but the thick forest surrounding the cabin evokes its own sort of creepiness in the night. She distracts herself for a moment, thinking about how Mike and Ann would react to her accidental ownership of their vacation home, which they'd left to Jeff so as to avoid the interests of a wayward uncle.

As soon as her mother leaves the island, the fall begins to move in. The midday air bites, so she brings in wood for the stove. Now for the real challenge. She hasn't spent much time here in the fall or winter. Little gnawings of awareness that she is very much alone make her uneasy. She thinks about Nora, genuinely distraught over the funeral, and then of her own refusal to go back home. Nora has relished her identity as a sort of town matriarch for a long time, but she fails to realize that the Moose Hall is no longer the centre of everything and that their hometown is going through not just a growth spurt, but a redefining. Nora seems to be the embodiment of the growing pains—Kate can't think of anyone more resistant to change.

She finds herself staring out the window and into a long-displaced memory: Lounging on the sofa, Jeff's familiar arm around her shoulders. He smells of sweat and beer, and from a radio somewhere close by "South City Midnight Lady" plays. *Who sings that?*

It's an easy memory, one she hasn't sought out this time. It saturates her body with summer. But it isn't long before a sharp void takes its place, as though Jeff, both his body and soul, has been violently severed. She spends more evenings softly grieving now, allowing herself to stay longer with the idea of so much gone, so quickly. She tells herself that this absence is real, that three people, always present in her life, can just vanish instantaneously. But what does this mean for her? How does she continue to exist without these people to perceive her? What is she if not a wife, a daughter-in-law? We're so fond of applying labels, as if they answer everything.

Will it always be like this? Should I get rid of the place? Are people right? Is this healthy?

Doubt blankets everything.

Small-craft season is pretty much done, so she winterizes the kayak in the dry boathouse up the path, patting its hull. She glances at the double hammock that's remained strung up in storage all summer. She thinks back to one of her and Jeff's first trips to the island, curling up together in this hammock, whispering, his parents periodically coming by with a number of invented chores for him, which he'd pointedly ignored. She recalls the sense of complete focus he had for her then, the alternate world that seemed to wrap the two of them in its protective folds. A very long time ago.

She spends the increasingly dark mornings sleeping later than usual and then walking the path to the beach or along other trails that veer into forest. She takes pictures. While she doesn't know what she's doing, she loves how the things she photographs show the hidden parts of themselves when transposed into black and white, or sepia. Summer is really a protected time, she thinks, deceptive with its temporary offerings. Then fall comes in and exposes everything, all the empty promises. As she walks the small trails around her cabin, the rain gets heavier, poking accusing needles at her skull. She wonders if snow will come to soften the island this year.

With this thought, she remembers New Year's. The scene inevitably replays, as it has so many times before: the impatience of the Coquihalla highway, heavy fog consuming the road while snow hurtles toward them in the darkness, she, half-expecting Jack Nicholson's crazed face to come looming out of the creeping darkness. Trees having long ago disappeared into what the locals call "snow ghosts"—Seussian renditions of a half-familiar landscape.

Ice clunking on the hood of the car, a hail of pebbles kicked up by a sanding truck and then a semi, a swerve, the over-correction, and then spinning and silence. Waking up later in the hospital, alone. Breathing hard with the effort of this memory, she pushes away its invasion and walks back to the cabin, shutting the door behind her, her heart pounding out the revisited shock.

Knocking bridges the distance between her mind and body. Strange, though. Nobody ever drops by. Her dark brow furrows, but there isn't anywhere to hide—the whole front of the cabin is almost completely windowed. And there is a window in the door, too, through which the head of Luke, the bearded sailor, bobbles disembodied, wearing a contrite yet urgent expression. He is talking even before she opens the door.

"...so sorry. Beached my kayak just down the shore. Too choppy. I don't know what I was thinking."

Kate stands in the doorway, fixes him with an uncomprehending glare. "It's October."

"Look, Kate, isn't it? I'm soaking wet. Can I just come in and warm up for a minute? I saw the smoke coming from your chimney. I don't want to bother you, but I'm kind of in dire straits here."

"Literally."

He laughs. A deep laugh, slightly froglike. Almost everything in her wants him to go away. She's spent too much time distracting herself and is only just beginning to hear her own thoughts, the ones that had been reduced to whispers amongst everyone else's noise. She doesn't need any additional commotion in her brain. But he's shivering, and she is not unkind. She leads him over to the kitchen and lets him drip there while she gathers towels. Then a clenching thought: *I'll have to give him some of Jeff's clothes, or Mike's.*

He doesn't ask for anything, just stands dripping miserably on her kitchen floor until she shows him the washroom and invites him to shower. Then she goes to her room and opens the drawer. She chooses a pair of cargo pants and a sweatshirt, holding them to her nose and breathing in. His scent is almost gone now. She'd done this a lot when he first vanished, and the immediacy of his return via her nostrils made it all seem bitterly impossible. Now he is evaporating. She has to work hard to remember his voice.

"Your boyfriend's?" Luke asks, receiving the pile of clothes with an expression of gratitude.

"They were my husband's," Kate says.

"Oh." Luke looks at her, something at the back of his eyes. His silence softens her irritation a little. Something in his look pauses to take her news and hold it for a moment, rather than search for a way to another topic or for trite words to release the discomfort. For one mortifying second, she thinks that he's going to reach out and pull her to his chest as he stands there in his towel-skirt.

"I'm sorry, Kate."

She takes a step back and gestures toward the second bedroom.

"Go ahead. You can change in there."

She makes a pot of tea and he flops on the sofa. Kate sits cross-legged in the big old chair that Mike used to claim. The room looks different with a strange person in it, cozy with wood stove warmth and liberated from the stifling expectations it used to hold. She tosses him a quizzical look.

"So now you owe me an explanation. What were you doing out there in a kayak?"

"I don't know if you'll understand."

"You can try."

"It's hard to explain this, but I feel strongly…. I guess I just don't like the idea of 'seasons' for doing things. You know, people telling you what to do and when to do it. It looked fine out there this morning."

"But it's about more than what you can see," Kate says. "The currents change quickly in the fall. You have to know about intertidal zones, boat traffic, and so much more before you go out there."

"I guess you've figured out my secret, then." He sighs with feigned drama and looks out the window with a distant gaze. "I'm not the old sea dog I appear to be."

Kate laughs. A not entirely unfamiliar sound, but still remote to her. "Where do you come from?"

"Colorado."

Now she's really laughing, at his expense. It feels at first static and unnatural, as though it were coming from somewhere else, but a familiar warmth soon settles in her chest, relaxing the contours of her face.

"This isn't the first time I've gotten myself into a predicament like this. I hate to say."

"Oh? Tell me."

He looks at her, appears to size her up for trustworthiness. "I used to teach English in Japan, and, like everyone, from the moment I arrived all I wanted to do was climb Mount Fuji. Unfortunately, I couldn't get any time off until November, and by then it was closed. I thought it was a joke. I mean, you can close a store, or an office, but a mountain? Ridiculous. Besides, I thought my students were being way too cautious."

"And what happened?"

"There was snow, and these little mini-tornadoes that kept tearing my tent down. I finally propped it up with sticks and huddled there until morning. I think I had the whole mountain to myself though, which is unheard of, so I suppose in retrospect it was worth it."

"You say that because you survived."

"There's an obvious truth to that."

Luke stretches his long legs out over the rug while Kate busies herself making sandwiches. As she works, her attention is split between the voice that entreats her to let him stay awhile and the one that insists she find a way to get him out as quickly as possible. In the end, she decides he is safe, and over lunch, as she listens to his stories, a forgetting of sorts begins to settle in.

"Let's get your boat inside." Kate gets up and walks to the door.

They head down to the beach. Kate grabs the front of the kayak. Luke lifts the back end and they carry it up and into the dry boathouse.

"Thanks, Kate. I really appreciate the rescue."

"I may have to hold the kayak hostage. I don't trust you'll keep away from it."

"You have my solemn promise. I'll pick it up tomorrow and put it straight into storage, if that's okay?"

"Sure, I'm here after six."

NORA

NORA FINISHES HER EGGS BENEDICT, crumples her napkin, and drops it onto her plate. She pushes it aside and brings her coffee centre stage. Getting cold. She stares into the middle distance, where a server ought to be. She sips and grimaces. Nothing is working out right this morning.

"Did you need some more coffee?" Barbara looks up from her cottage cheese and fruit salad. Nora takes a moment to sneer at her low-fat choices.

"Of course. You know I'm not human till I've got at least three cups in me. Where is that waitress? Service is usually better here."

"How was the visit with Kate?"

"Fine. I just don't know why she won't come back. It's been long enough."

"We all grieve in our own way, Nor."

"I know that, Barbara, but she's thirty-two. She has a life to get on with. They won't hold her job at the paper forever."

"What's she doing over there anyway?"

"Most of the summer she just drifted around in that canoe, but now it's too rough and windy." Nora sighs. "She reads, walks around, and helps out with an old handicapped woman."

"Kayak."

"Same thing"

A server catches Nora's agitated, caffeine-deprived look, and within seconds of the wordless exchange the steamy brew is being poured into her mug. Nora lets her shoulders sink and wraps her hands around the warmth.

"Seen Edgar these days?"

Barbara sniffs. "If I did I'd never say so. I'm sure he'll hide from you forever if he has to."

"It's not funny, Barb. I need to talk to him. There are rules that were completely disregarded." She leans into the table and glowers, unblinking.

"Nora, there isn't a single person in this town who doesn't know how you feel about that funeral. Can't we just move past it and let poor Mr. Clark lie in his grave?"

"He was cremated."

"You know what I'm talking about." Barbara wags a finger. She is the only one who can talk to Nora this way, apart from Nora's daughters—on select occasions.

"Hi Nora, Barb." A slender woman, bunned and perfumed, passes by their table.

"How are you, Ellen?"

"Good, good. Can't complain.

"How's the library?"

"Quiet." Ellen lets out a breathy laugh. "I suppose that's a good thing. How's Kate?"

"Doing fine. She's over on Brittania right now."

"Ah. Must be a nice place to be, especially after everything."

"Yeah. We're hoping she comes back soon."

Ellen sighs and rolls her eyes. "Well, I'm sure it won't be easy, given the way people talk."

"There's not much to say now. It's been a while." Nora tosses her words over her shoulder, not caring to meet Ellen's sharp eyes. She has a way of getting information out of you without you realizing you'd given it.

"I know, but the circumstances…"

"I'm not sure what you mean, Ellen."

Ellen mouths a word Nora can't hear.

"What?"

She looks as though she is trying to speak the words back into herself rather than out loud. "I just meant, you know, what happened with Shannon."

Nora gives an exasperated sigh. "Ellen, I don't know what the hell you're trying to say."

Wide eyes. "I'm really sorry Nora, I've got to run. Opening early today. Bye now."

"What?"

"See you at the pool, Barbara."

"Ellen!"

Nora drinks her last sip of coffee and slaps a couple of bills on the table. She pulls her sweater from the back of her seat, pushes her heavy arms into the sleeves, and throws a fiery look at Barbara.

"Sorry, Barb. Can't stick around today."

"You okay?"

Nora shakes her head and walks to the door. She is rarely caught off guard, but these recent days have pulled the rug swiftly out. She needs to walk.

THE RESTAURANT ISN'T FAR from the water. A few people dot the seawall. As she passes over the arched bridge with its white railings she notices the regulars: Jimmy, the foot-stomping, harmonica-playing busker; the man who sells Indigenous art; and the psychic.

"It's okay to be sad," the psychic, a woman with a pink hairband and cut-off lace gloves calls out as Nora passes.

She looks around, but there isn't anyone else there. "Things will change; they always do," the woman says.

"No shit. I hope you're not going to ask for money for that brilliance."

She squirms a little, forces a smile. "It's free."

"Can I return it?"

The woman looks down, her expression fallen. She pulls out

a cross-stitch and starts to embroider, glancing up just once as Nora huffs away.

KATE

IVY IS NOT WELL. Her normally rosy cheeks are pallid and she's making the unusual complaint of being tired. Kate stayed late with her yesterday, following Luke's unexpected visit, and made sure some nutrition drained slowly into her blood. She put together the proverbial chicken soup, and it appears to be having an effect. Ivy's cheeks are beginning to pinken. Kate gets busy chopping fruit for dessert.

"You're a bit of an enigma, you know, Kate." Ivy applies her goat's milk cream, pushing thin, crêpe-like skin around her arms. She pauses a moment to inhale its fragrance, then turns to fix her owl eyes on Kate.

"What do you mean?"

"I'm not sure what I mean, really, but you have a bit of mystique about you. I suppose it's because you genuinely don't like to talk about yourself; some people make a show of that. Protest too much."

"It's a boring topic."

"If you don't mind, I'm going to disregard that. You and I both know better. I suspect it has a little more to do with timing."

Kate brushes a swath of black hair that's resisting its pony-tailed confines behind her ear. "You're very perceptive, Ivy."

"No." She gives a rattling chuckle. "I just have a lot of time to sit around and think. Some people might consider that a dangerous thing, those who know me, at least."

Kate pauses a moment, her knife poised over an assaulted cantaloupe, its seed-filled mucus splayed over the butcher block.

"Who would you say knows you best, here on the island?"

"Why? Are you a journalist? Are you looking for my sordid past?"

Kate pulls the elastic out of her protesting hair. "I'd love to know your sordid past. And actually I am, or was, a journalist of sorts. If you count *The North Wailaish Free Press* as a valid publication."

"Well then, might I suggest an exchange?

"I wish I had something remotely interesting to tell you."

"Don't you worry, dear. I'll dig it up. But I'd rather hear it from you."

"Glad to see you're feeling better, Ivy."

"Are you changing the subject?"

"Of course."

"What was this husband to you?"

Kate stops. With one question her body shrinks, morphs into the posture of a scolded child. The sound of firecrackers haunts her perception and immediately she's back at the lake, with Jeff and his cousin at water's edge. The campground is full of families with young kids, but the two grown men throw firecrackers out into the lake, laughing at the explosions before they hit water, stopping only to pull long swigs out of beer bottles.

She'd wanted to run up to the highway, even though she was in her pyjamas. Anything to get away. She'd hitch a ride with the next truck driver who happened by. But then what? Fear stole the more daring of her thoughts, and she returned to the camper, climbed into their bed, and pulled the curtains closed behind her.

Jeff and his cousin barged in a while later and continued to drink. Jeff's voice was loud as he replayed his solo trip to Europe, and all of his female conquests during that trip, when he and Kate were engaged. The worst part of it was that he didn't care at all if she heard him. In fact, he probably wanted her to. But why?

"We loved each other in the beginning," she manages.

Ivy closes her bottle of lotion and settles it carefully on the warped table. Kate watches unarticulated thoughts shift around like shadows in Ivy's eyes.

"You don't see yourself yet," she tells Kate.

IVY

I have a white rose to tend
In July as in January;
I give it to the true friend
Who offers his frank hand to me.
And for the cruel one whose blows
Break the heart by which I live,
Thistle nor thorn do I give:
For him, too, I have a white rose.

                    —José Marti

SHE PERCHES ON the backless stool facing the switchboard, floating the poet's words around her brainspace, trying to see what familiar things they might attach to. It only took her a day to finish the book, but she continues to carry it with her. Reading it feels like a clandestine meeting with Emilio, intimate and sensual, unlike anything she is used to. She wants to know which lines stand out to him, what makes him love this book so much.

He is right about the "storm of electricity." Outside the skies are inked with early loss of light, and everything is filled with buzzing tension. Inside the phone lines go crazy. She is careful to place each call correctly, because Mrs. Freisen told Oma she suspected Ivy of listening in on her calls. Really, Ivy just has no idea what she's doing.

"She's worried someone will hear her complain about her

son-in-law." Oma had added absentmindedly. "Maybe she's gossiping about you too."

Ivy frets about Bonita, waiting outside in the oncoming storm. She must be scared, but there isn't a moment to go out and comfort her. The other operators flit around the room, apparently knowing what to do. She continues to plug and unplug the connections, willing herself to focus.

She's been taking some of her breaks with the supervisor, Señor Canton, who gives her Spanish lessons whenever he is free. She told him that she can no longer handle not knowing what the girls are talking about in the staff room. After their lessons, she practises rolling the words around her mouth. English makes the tongue so lazy.

Earlier in the week, he translated the poetry that Emilio gave to her. "A little like Shakespeare, like the sonnets," she tells him.

"I don't know poetry, just Spanish." He shrugs.

Just before dinner, when it's almost time for her to go home, the thunder starts to come at more regular intervals. She can hardly hear who wants to talk to whom on the lines, and before long she is connecting the wrong people again. It's a mess. Beads of sweat trickle down her back as she tries to concentrate on finding the right connections. It gets busier. She doesn't notice that the room has emptied.

Then a loud *crash!* and the next thing she is aware of is the concrete floor and an unfathomable headache.

"What were you doing on the lines?" Ivy wakes up to her coworker, Luisa's voice.

The question is confusing. "Working," she tells her.

"Didn't you hear the storm?"

"Of course."

"We ignore the lines when there's a storm."

"Somebody could have told me that."

She offers to take Ivy home. Bonita chuffs and prances, but she's still where Ivy left her, so Luisa takes her halter and they walk.

"Did I get hit by lightning?"

"Sort of. Not really. The electricity pushed you to the other side of the room." Then she adds, "You should probably see a doctor."

Oma hurries her inside. She lets Luisa ride Bonita home and wraps Ivy in one of her hand-crocheted blankets. Green and white squares. She puts her hands all over her head. Opa hovers at the edges of the activity.

"*Ésta bien,*" Ivy says to her, half-wanting to impress. Before she knows what is happening Oma's palm strikes Ivy's face.

"Greta!" Opa shouts, pulling her back.

"Don't speak that language to me," she says, and leaves the room. Opa casts a deflated glance at Ivy. He brushes her cheek with one hand, then makes noises about shutting things down for the night.

In the kitchen, she eats soup in silence while Oma plunders the pantry, looking for something. Opa plods outside around the barn and its surroundings. Ivy is baffled, but then again, she has never understood her grandmother. A surge of bitterness floats into her chest. For the first time on the Isle of Pines, Ivy feels a hollow loneliness.

KATE

THE WELLSPRING HAS REDUCED its hours to accommodate the shorter days, the dearth of customers. Kris is cloyingly attentive, drawing an elaborate *fleur de lis* in the foam on Kate's cappuccino.

"How are you keeping busy these days?" she asks.

Kate knocks over the tip mug, spreading nickels and dimes over the counter. She uses the edge of her hand to push the coins off the counter and back into the mug. "Nothing much. Helping at Ivy's, reading."

"How's your photography?"

"I wouldn't call it that. I'm just fooling around."

Kris looks down, appearing to disguise a grin. "Bring some photos by next time. I told you I'd put them up."

Kate wants to, in a way, but it doesn't yet feel like the right time. "I don't know."

"I won't even put your name on them, if that's what you want."

She looks down at the rough-hewn floorboards. "Maybe."

"Friday at the latest would be good. Then, switching gears, "Do you think you'll stay on the island? Become a local?"

Kate shrugs. "Maybe I already am."

She takes her travel mug and starts walking to Ivy's. Ivy now wants to see her three times a week. It's Tuesday, so almost nothing else is open. The baker—whose bread, made from hand-milled flour, is good competition for Nora's—has closed his shop for the winter and taken his sailboat to the Caribbean. There will be no more Saturday markets until May.

Day after day, fog creeps in and around the treetops, leaving cottony wisps between clutching branches. Kate feels locked away, hidden and alone. This isn't always a bad feeling, but there is the guilt, always pulling at her. The nagging thought that she is a coward.

Ivy wants to re-read classics, so Kate sits next to her at the kitchen table as they drift and bob in the ethereal prose of *To the Lighthouse*. "I like the idea of the dead never really leaving," Ivy says, staring out the window.

"What do you mean?"

"I'm thinking about the remnants people leave behind. Like with the mother here, her clothes in the closet at the beach house, animating her in a sort of negative space, even though she's gone."

"You don't find it creepy?"

"Darling, if you find death creepy at my age you'd best get yourself a good psychiatrist."

"But you're healthy."

"Oh, I know you want to make me feel better. That's very sweet, but you must know that I'm beyond that now. And it's okay."

"I don't understand."

"You're not meant to. Just consider yourself lucky if you get to see as many parts of the world and read as many fantastic books as I have by the time you're closing in on ninety-three. The sad thing would be running out of books before you ran out of life."

"Have you always loved reading this much?"

Ivy clears her grainy throat. "I think so. I remember my cousin Jane. Her family was wealthy, had a wall full of shelves stuffed with books. Always complaining about her father making her read them. I was practically salivating. Stole one once and she didn't even notice."

"You're terrible."

"Indeed. Listen, Kate. I'm at the Wellspring with my book group once a month. You really must join us."

"I don't know."

"Trust me, we're more fun than those ridiculous women back home you talk about."

Kate picks a piece of fluff off her sweater. "I know. I'm just not good with people right now."

"Oh but you are. You just need the right *kind* of people, if I'm not mistaken."

She sits silently. Surprisingly, for someone she's known such a short time, Ivy comes closer than anyone she's known to actually seeing her. What's also surprising is that when she probes Kate's inner workings like this, she doesn't seem to find it as sad or off-putting a place as Kate does—and perhaps others do as well.

"You must find it nice and peaceful here," she muses.

"Now that's where you're mistaken. I socialize more here than I ever did in the city. I mean, this can be as sleepy a place as you want it to be, and I obviously can't go out as much anymore, but I love to hear live music, see art shows, argue over books. In the city, just getting to the places to do these things eats up half the night. Transportation is a non-starter here."

Kate thinks about this. She's never been one to go out very often, but maybe if it were easier she would. If she could pick up and leave whenever she wanted.... She can't believe she's considering this, but even just a small moment among others might do her some good.

NORA

ALONE AT THE MOOSE HALL, Nora prepares for the Girl Guide group that's coming in at six. *Spoiled little brats from the valley.* She sets up the tables in two rows for whatever useless, messy craft they're planning to work on. Nora will be long gone by the time they get there, trailing skinny moms in yoga pants. She's happy to have taken a leave from the board.

If there is one thing Nora can't stand it's a secret, unless of course she's the one keeping it. In her mind she replays the conversation with Ellen more times than she's reviewed the events of the funeral, which feels like old news now, much less important. Now she has yet another reason to worry about Kate, who once again is occupying the majority of Nora's allotted worry-space. After Ellen's comment yesterday about Jeff and Shannon, Nora's funeral-obsessed thoughts had skidded fully to a stop and reversed direction. *Which Shannon is she talking about?* It seems like the whole town is full of nothing but Shannons, Jennifers, Lisas, and Nicoles.

Obviously Ellen is insinuating that Kate's husband was having an affair, but why the hell does she want to stir up trouble almost a year after the guy died? Once again, Nora feels a protective surge, somewhere below her ribcage. She thinks back to when Kate was small, in grade three maybe. For years she could never get to sleep. Nora would lie next to her and listen to the small puffs of her whispers in the dark, talking about things like all of them dying, about where they would all go—things someone so young should never worry about. Then she'd review all the events of her day at school, getting hung up on the stupidity of boys and the false friendships of girls. Shadows moved and tormented her throughout the night. Sometimes Nora would wake up in the wee hours, still in Kate's bed. Ed thought they should just leave Kate be, let her sort things out on her own, but to Nora that felt cruel. Even though Kate is now so distant from them all, still no one knows her better than her mother.

Nora brings herself back to the present, spreading out the plastic tablecloths and smoothing the wrinkles. Static alternately holds the coverings to the tables and also makes them cling annoyingly to Nora's wool sweater. She thinks about the time the family travelled to Disneyland. Rachel was the one who wanted to go on every ride. Kate only got as far as "It's a Small World." On other rides, when the little car or boat ventured inside, the darkness and disturbingly real-looking characters made her cry and cling so tightly to Nora she was practically climbing up her body. On the second day of their trip Kate refused to do anything at all and Ed swore a blue streak about the "goddamned three-day pass" and how they'd broken the bank to get to California. It ended up being Ed and Rachel on all the rides, while Kate cowered timidly behind Nora's legs at the exits, working away at a lollipop the size of her head. "Waste of money," Ed had grumbled more than once both during the trip and after it was over.

What he fails to understand is how much Kate *feels*. Not like most kids who are able to brush things off. Everything bothers Kate. Things are too loud, too itchy, too hot, too cold. It's as if her senses are in overdrive. Funny though—although he'll never admit it, he is just like her. Take that man into any crowded store and he'll lose his mind. Send him to a movie that has something to do with relationships instead of robots and guns and she'll catch him wiping his eyes. He could never see his own self clearly. What separates him from Kate is the thing that makes them most alike.

Somewhere along the way Rachel became less of a daredevil and more practical, plotting out each category of her life. Kate however, after a communications degree she'd hemmed and hawed over committing to, answered an ad in the local paper and wandered into an entry-level editing job. With Kate, things are never thought through in a way that would ever satisfy Nora or Rachel, and when Jeff asked her to get married so young, Nora imagines Kate shrugging and saying "sure." Maybe she'd even misheard the question, thinking she was agreeing to a ski trip. Nora shakes her head.

At four o'clock Barbara comes in to set up the snacks. She casts a wary glance at Nora and stuffs her umbrella into a stand. "Disgusting out there," she ventures.

Nora is not interested in small talk. "What do *you* think about Ellen?"

"Nora, don't listen to her. She's always stirring up drama. I'm sure she's jealous of you still having your kids close by."

"True. She's browbeaten hers all the way to the other side of the country." Nora allows herself a smug sort of grin.

"What if it's true, though?"

"What if?"

Barbara can be so aggravatingly obtuse. "What do you mean, 'what if?' Do I tell Kate? Ed?"

Barbara pulls out a cutting board and starts in on some cucumbers. "I don't see the point in opening this up now. Do you?"

"I don't know what I think anymore."

"Ellen's been trying to get to you since high school; this isn't new."

"How does she always find my weak spots? What is it about people like her?"

"Honestly, I think she's just bored. Leave her alone and she'll find someone else to annoy. Some people spend too much time thinking, mostly about their own supposed position in society, not so much about how they affect other people."

Nora snorts. "Society. What does she think this is? Manhattan?"

"Her version of it, I guess."

"Sometimes I just want to get the hell out of this town, Barb."

"Now you're making sense."

SHE ALMOST FORGETS HER DATE with Neville. *It's not a date, ridiculous woman.* Still, she wonders why her? Why not one of the lawyers or real estate agents that come to the Mud Puddle every day? They seem more his type. What can she tell him about North Wailaish? If he's interested in reading about it, then she doubts the kind of information he wants is something Nora can offer. But what else is she going to do with her extra time, now that she's stepped back from most of her Moose Hall duties?

He's already there when she pushes the metal door open. Same table.

"Neville. You've stolen my favourite spot."

He stands up and pulls out a chair for her. "Good thing we're friends now."

"Don't go getting ahead of yourself."

He throws his head back and laughs louder than Nora thinks is necessary. No one ever thinks she's that funny. "I can tell you like me already."

Steven-with-the-ponytail is already getting her coffee. At the counter, Neville lurches from one side of Nora to the other, trying to pay. "Don't even think about it," she warns.

"Please? I'm the one making demands on your time."

"I've got more than enough time now. Don't you worry, sit." Neville sits.

The previous night Nora tried to look up the history of North Wailaish on the internet, but soon became distracted by email. She opened the ones from the Moose Hall council, only because she needed to keep up with everything, but didn't reply to any. After doing this for an hour she'd gotten bored and gone to bed.

"I'm afraid I have nothing interesting to tell you, Neville."

He looks amused. "I doubt that, Nora."

"No really. My history is terrible. I'm just not that interested."

"Why don't we chat? Get to know each other?"

"What about the research?"

"I'm sorry if I misled you. I'm not really doing formal research, Nora. I just want to get a feel for the place."

"Why the hell would you want to do that?"

He takes a gulp of his coffee. "I don't really know. I'm just drawn to it."

She intuits a lie. "If you say so."

KATE

IT RAINS ALMOST EVERY DAY now, the sky a soaked, grey cotton. Thermometers drop, but not low enough for snowfall. A sharp chill works its way through Kate's skin and into her core. Usually, the only way to warm up during a coastal winter is to take a bath, but since she doesn't have a tub, a shower will have to suffice. The cabin is on a septic system though, so she can't stay in for too long. The second best way to handle it is with a couple of knit layers and an almost constant fire in the wood stove. Fortunately, the shed is full of cedar that Mike and Jeff had spent last summer chopping. They'd set her up well, not that that was their intention. She'll have to prepare everything herself next summer, if she decides to stay.

Luke still hasn't picked up his kayak. She'd run into him at the grocery store last week and he apologized and made a bunch of excuses. Then he invited her to have coffee. Today.

At the time it seemed okay. Kate doesn't feel lonely; in fact she's getting used to her own company and is actually starting to enjoy it. When she wants to talk, she has Ivy and Nancy, and even Kris at the Wellspring. Ivy and Nancy are easy people to be around. They don't seem to want anything from her. Why do we pin so much hope on potential friendships? she wonders. They never seem to pan out. It's easier with the older people, at least the ones on the island who are above the calculations of Kate's friends back home. It's easier with the ones who have steeped a little more in life, and who understand the way it lives them, not the other way around.

Luke sits at a corner table, squinting at charts. He gives a curled, perplexed sort of smile when he finally looks up and sees her.

"Getting ready for spring," he says. "Have a seat."

"Studying?"

"Yes. I'm taking your advice."

"I know nothing about the tides. I just wait for nice weather. No wind."

"And you were lecturing me?"

She looks down. "Just a little."

"I'll go up. What do you want?"

"Americano."

He comes back with two mugs, placing one in front of her. She gives him a once over, determines him too skinny, and that his beard is a bit much, then shakes her head for even thinking this way in the first place.

"I forgot to ask if you wanted something to eat."

"I'm fine," she says.

"Thank you, again, for helping me out the other day."

"It would have been cruel to turn you away dripping wet."

"That is one damn cold ocean."

"You're surprised?"

"No. Well, yeah. I mean, you know I grew up in the mountains. And this is the west coast."

"Not southern California, though." After a beat, she asks, "What do you do for work?"

"Environmental consulting. But I'm on a bit of a leave."

She wants to ask him why, but doesn't want the responsibility of knowing.

He tells her anyway. "My mom thinks I'm unfocused. I just wanted unstructured time, though. Not forever. I guess I'm looking for something. Something you can find on an island but not the mainland."

Kate shakes her head. "There's nothing more here. It's all the same, just at a slower pace." Even as she says this, she knows she doesn't believe it.

"At least with a slower pace you can actually hear what's going on, and spend time thinking about it instead of moving on to the next distraction."

"I wonder if that's a good thing."

He watches her take sips of coffee and look out the window. She can't get comfortable meeting his eyes. She can sense that he wants to know things. It feels uncomfortable, this wanting, and his restraint from asking makes it even more so.

They shift to the benign. Her job, her family. Luke finds most of Nora's antics funny, as do most people who have never had to live with her.

"I'd love to meet her someday."

Kate can't help but smile, imagining. Nora would be disgusted with Luke's 'softness.' "She'd put you straight to work."

"That's okay. Maybe I'd learn something."

"If you don't mind learning the hard way."

"I'd like to see you again, at least. Is that possible?"

"It's hard to avoid people here."

His face falls a little. "That's not what I mean."

Kate begins to feel herself yielding. As it is with her mother, curiosity always wins out over most of her other instincts. But then Kris approaches their table, lingering too long over the tidying of mugs.

"Give me a call," Kate manages, then looks at her watch. "I have to go to Ivy's."

She shifts her hips, preparing to get up, and can't help but notice that the glossy, wooden chair has grown warm with her own heat, returning it to her body. Momentarily repelled by the oiled, distorted attributes of lacquered wood, she recalls a room lined with coffins and the absurdity of choosing one for her young husband. The funeral director had treated it like a trip to the furniture store, invoking in his voice a "shopping" sort of tone as he compared various sorts of wood composition, interior cushioning, and quality of embellishment. Since then, to her, all bed frames have looked like coffins. Time to leave.

IVY SEEMS TO THINK IT WAS A DATE. "Tell me how it went."

Kate, her back to Ivy, pours tendrils of fusilli into a boiling pot. "He's nice, but no."

"Nancy and I saw him at the coffee shop last week and we both thought he was attractive, even though Nancy's a lesbian."

"You're worse than my mother."

"Why shouldn't you have a little fun?"

"Fun? Why?"

"Because you deserve to. Everyone does."

Kate thinks about this for a moment, then turns to stir the sauce. *Deserve* is a funny word. But if she really looks at herself, she'll have to say that no, she doesn't feel she deserves fun, or whatever Ivy is getting at. Not right now. Not yet.

"Why does anyone think they deserve anything at all?"

"Simple birthright, my dear."

"I disagree. Wouldn't we all just be entitled assholes if we spent the majority of our time contemplating all the things we deserved?"

"Not if those things are as simple as trees, water, mountains, the company of good people.... I'm not talking about a Mercedes here. You keep your priorities straight. At the very least, you deserve much more than this." Ivy lifts Kate's left arm and feathers her fingers over the swollen lines running along the inside of her wrist, disrupting the smooth, inner skin.

Kate recoils. She'd forgotten. Long sleeves always. With Ivy she'd assumed clouded vision.

"You'll tell me about it when you're ready?" Ivy says.

Her throat is taut. She can barely get the words out. "He never touched me."

"I know."

Kate holds her right hand over the scars, remembers the neat split of skin, blood hastening to fill white space, the release of something too big to hold in her body, something that would have come out of its own accord, eventually. Better this, better her own way.

Not ready for *deserve*. Almost ready for breath. Not quite. Only this—a small cabin, a kayak, fading birdsong. Nothing more.

IVY

I T'S AN OPPORTUNITY. She can't stay in tonight; the world will surely turn on its side without her there to breathe the perfumed night. Three months of hanging around her grandparents' place. While she feels a mild stab of guilt for misleading them, she's restless and knows that there will never be another opportunity like this once she's left the island. She'd have no chance at any sort of freedom if her parents were here. She silently thanks the brilliant gods who've stocked the Cuban waters so abundantly with tuna—the blessed silvery shoals thickening the emerald waters, imparting the need to stay late at her shift. She feels an almost religious "thanks be to God" rise up in her head—a result of too many weeks of church. An avid fisherman, Señor Canton requires all of his staff on the lines so that he can take advantage of this prime season. All Ivy had to do was exaggerate her working hours when disclosing them to her grandparents.

A few curls pop out of alignment, but she licks her fingers and slicks them back against her temples, adding a headband with a large gardenia. She's brought extra beads from back home and strings them around her neck. A dab of Oma's long-neglected Chanel and she is ready. She'd said her goodbyes at the office before sneaking into a washroom to prepare. No one need notice the effort.

The night welcomes her, sultry and full of energy; it's impatient she's taken so long. The rising, syncopated buzz of cicadas has long given way to the kindling intoxication of a clear, tropical night. *How could anyone stay inside?* By this time back home, a humid chill would be penetrating every pore, cloistering everyone in their houses for months and months. Even summer nights would be chilly.

Ivy hastens toward her bicycle, her steps taking a little longer in the white dress, clingy at the bodice and flared at the hips. *Will Emilio be there?* She wouldn't be honest if she didn't admit that much of the effort had been made with him in mind. She checks for the observant eyes of her colleagues, hikes up her dress, and flings her leg over the seat. Pedalling, she pushes through the warm, thick air and into the trees—*jungle*, her parents would call it, making it sound so primitive.

Twenty minutes later she finds the narrow trail, altered by darkness, but discernible still. Night creatures, whatever they are, are deafening and obnoxious—she remembers a friend saying once that North Americans are calmer and more conservative because their forests are quiet, while people with Latin blood reflect in their spirit the warm cacophony of the tropical rainforest. A generalization, but it seems true tonight. Even the tiniest of creatures celebrate.

It takes fifteen more minutes to get to the clearing. The swimming hole at its centre looks as though it has stolen the moon and hidden it there, grasping and pulling it down into a viney embrace. Everyone Ivy knows is there, along with several people she's not yet met. A layer of sweet cigar smoke hovers over the moon-filled lake, and everything pulses and teems with creatures—human and other.

Peter Freisen offers her a cigarette and a light. The excitement is palpable—rebellious friends joining together after having made it past the gauntlet of parental obstacle. Someone is playing drums.

"Oy, Rubia. Come dance." Her heart leaps, looking for Emilio, but instead it's a spindly Dutch boy, a friend of Peter's. Down by the water, he bounces and shakes in a group of sweaty bodies. Ivy joins them, closing her eyes and feeling her own body sway with delight, as though she's shaking off ten coils of heavy rope. Mark and Maureen are there, as are the German twins from up the street, and a lot more Americans. She moves as sensuously as she knows how, in hopes of becoming magnetizing. Her eyes closed, imagining Emilio. Three songs later there is still no sign. She chides herself, knowing that it would not be likely for any Cubans to turn up at this sort of event. She decides to socialize, heading back toward Peter and a few of his friends as they squat with drinks a few yards up the bank. Peter pours a glass of pungent rum and offers it to her.

"You enjoy your time here, Rubia? He spreads a blanket for them all to settle on.

She leans back, observing the night sky, which is perforated by what looks to be the glow of heaven. "God, yes. Where have I been all this time?"

"In the wrong places, I think." The two men and women laugh. A girl Ivy hasn't met before with an equine face and short, black bangs gives a throaty, cigarette-infused chuckle. "It takes a while to find a party in the middle of the jungle."

Ivy sips her rum and looks out at the lake. No local would ever dream of doing this. There is some kind of distancing from oneself that comes solely with the expat experience, as if this isn't really happening. None of them are really here in totality. Just parts of themselves, living a parallel existence.

The last glug of fiery rum pulses through her veins, while the group on the blanket descends into a mellow, philosophical mood. She reaches her arms up, stretching, then makes her way back to the haze and rising pulse of the dancers. Drums continue to punctuate the stillness and humidity.

She'd almost given up hope of seeing Emilio when over on the far side of the lake she sees him. Kate watches as he winds around the path. *Who does he know here?* Not in the least bit tentative, he strides across the flattened grasses and finds Ivy with his eyes. She continues to dance, allowing him to come closer to her. His wavy brown hair looks a little messy, and she notices for the first time that his dark eyes have the webbed beginnings of laugh lines radiating outward. She's never asked his age, still doesn't really know him.

"Do you like to dance?"

They make their way into the crowd, and Emilio pulls Ivy tightly against his chest, closer to him than she's ever been to any man, subtracting all remaining space between them.

His dance is unfamiliar, more insistent and directive than she's used to. He smells of soap, and she begins to feel webbed within a sort of net, like a sticky spider's web, although she's not sure who the spider is. It's getting crowded, and most people are up and dancing now, trampling the grasses further into submission. Emilio is tall, but she's able to stretch her arms up around his shoulders and join his rhythm. Before long he has her hips and is gently moving them with his large hands.

"This is how to dance if you go to Havana."

Ivy laughs at his line, but the lesson continues and she is an attentive, if not slightly drunken, participant. Drumbeats melt into one another until Ivy and Emilio become a single swaying branch, hips fused, bodies liquefying.

"I'd like to go to Havana." She looks up at him.

He responds by taking her hand and pulling her away from the others, heading toward the thickness of trees.

She stops, pulls him back. "What are you doing?"

He takes off his shirt and wraps it around her shoulders. His answer is a smile. She's intrigued enough to follow.

They find a clearing where they can still hear the music and continue to dance, which before long leads to his mouth finding hers. This is all new to Ivy, but within a few minutes she dispenses all her well thought-out boundaries as they move into rapid exploration of one another. Ivy pushes away the warning voices in her inebriated head, most of whom sound like Oma, as she threads her fingers through wavy hair, her mouth moving instinctively to his neck. Before long he lifts her up and she swings her legs around his waist, as though she's done this many times before. He pushes her against a tree and brushes his mouth softly against her ear. The bark of the pine is rough through his shirt and the cushion of his mouth travels over her, hands everywhere. *Is this happening?* She feels a surge of euphoric fear. *I can stop him.* But then her mind travels away. *Just one moment more.* But she's standing again, and he is removing her clothes, laying them on the ground.

In what seems to take very little time and effort he's taken off everything, opening her skin to the moonlight. He cradles her back and lowers her slowly onto the pile of clothes, continuing to search her mouth, hands finding their way to more intimate places, releasing gasps. Then in one fluid motion he pushes into a place where pain and pleasure tear simultaneously and a new dance continues as his body works, slowly, pressing itself into this task alone, lifting her. She asks him to slow even more as the pain begins to transform. He meets the clumsiness of her rhythm and brings her into his with slow caresses and a hungry mouth, and it's too late now. Despite knowing better, she allows everything. Lungs, long, thin limbs, the deepest of places. Alive.

DID IT HAPPEN? She feels the solid pew beneath her hips and squirms. The hawklike minister is exceptionally agitated this morning; it seems that he himself possesses the all-knowing, damning power. Ivy searches for the remorseful side of herself, but it hasn't surfaced yet. Oma casts sidelong glances. Ivy doesn't want to give her grandparents reason to send her back to Canada, so so she'll have to be extra cautious for the next week or so. Perfect granddaughter, no trouble at all. Her head pounds.

"How late did Señor Canton keep you last night?" Opa asks on the walk home, from beneath an arched eyebrow.

"I don't remember. Must've been around midnight."

She'd scrambled in clumsily around three a.m., folding herself beneath the window sash. The dogs were cooperative; the treats in her pocket helped with that.

"Glad he's not fool enough to suggest the Lord's Day. I think he's taking advantage." Oma shuffles along the dirt road. "What do the other parents think?"

"It's just temporary, for the tuna run. I'm sure they don't like it, but it'll be over soon enough."

Her grandparents always take Sunday off from the bakery. On Saturday night they bring home whatever hasn't sold that week—heavy German loaves with the odd sweet danish thrown in. Oma sets the percolator and Ivy thinks she might slide with exhaustion beneath the table before it burbles its way to fruition. Her Sunday saviour. She watches Oma's hands spread out sausages and other cured meats and cheeses along with the breads, noting that her chubby fingers resemble the very foods they are preparing. Oma is a practical woman.

Soon Mrs. Freisen joins them. Conversation switches to German and Ivy inhales large gulps of coffee, fades into the deliciousness of last night. Emilio had accompanied her home as far as the trailhead. A pause there as he leaned his bicycle against a tree and kissed her, hands in her hair. She'd wanted to throw her bike down and continue, but he stopped and told her she should get home.

"I think we need to find a way to meet again."

"Oh yes."

She hasn't intended any of this. She knows as soon as Mark and Maureen find her they'll be full of questions she doesn't feel equipped to answer. She can almost see their expressions, watch them reframing their opinions of her, for better or worse. It doesn't really matter, though. They haven't known her that long to begin with, and she'll likely never see them again after she leaves. Besides, this new thing in her—this thing that *is* her, that wants to live, talk, read, feel what a body can do —has its own driving intentions. Not her decision, really. She'll go back to her old self when she's back home. But not before then.

She replaces thought with sensation: the excitement of drumbeat and how it sounded in the trees—permeating, amaranthine, unfading, inviting her body to forget, to dissolve into dance. And then Emilio. She's never known anyone like him, so without hesitation, so present in mind and body. Not that she's ever known anyone in this way before. She thinks of his soft Spanish words and checks again—still no remorse. The only worry in her mind is the forgotten condom, but he'd sworn his intentions at the outset of the night were not to seduce her. She respects him for this, tells herself they'll remember if it happens again.

Vibrating with coffee and the remnants of last night, Ivy excuses herself from the breakfast table and heads to the kitchen to clean. Best to avoid the swimming hole today.

NORA

THE CLASS, "Fundamentals of the Internet," wasn't captivating enough to keep Nora and Barb from gossiping. Although she's come late to the party that is the World Wide Web, Nora likes the recipes, and the home decor and organizing sites. Barbara likes that she can find all sorts of free patterns for her knitting.

"Remember when we used to take the kids mushroom picking?"

Barbara snickers. "How could I forget? Kate used to pull her own hair and scream that we were torturing her. Nora, don't write down that recipe. Just print it out."

"Right. I remember how she'd sit on the path and wouldn't move until we promised her ice cream. Good god, there's about a million recipes on here for chanterelles."

"It's endless. You can spend forever looking for things and find way more than you ever thought you wanted. And then you forget what you were looking for in the first place."

"Can you find me an article on how to get your husband off his ass and start fixing things?" Nora quips.

"That's probably the one they don't have."

The teacher glares. They are supposed to be doing a guided search, but Nora doesn't care. She's not some schoolgirl. Besides, this isn't even a real sort of school, just an adult-ed evening class. It's supposed to be more for fun than anything, but some of these women and men take themselves far too seriously, wanting the teacher's attention every five minutes. You'd think they were hoping for an 'A' or something.

"There's an ad here for a trip to Mexico. Think I could get Ed to go?"

"Always worth a try." Barb doesn't look up.

Later at home Nora floats the idea while Ed is in the middle of checking his hockey pool stats at the kitchen table.

"Are you out of your mind? We haven't even visited my folks in Regina in a year. How could I explain that I'm going off to Mexico instead?"

"People take holidays, Ed," she says.

"It's not safe in Mexico. You ever watch the news?"

"They only report the bad stuff. It's not safe here, sometimes. Anywhere for that matter."

"Can't see it happening. The food would make me sick."

Nora tries to picture Ed in a swimsuit, but instead conjures pursed lips, a wrinkled brow, and scrawny, pasty legs. He'd complain about anything that wasn't exactly the way it was at home. If Nora looked in the mirror, she wonders, would she see that same expression on her own face?

What if she just bought the tickets? Ed's been working at the Foundry for more than thirty years. They wouldn't bat an eye if he asked for a holiday, and of course he'd have no choice but to go if the money's already been spent. She is beginning to surprise herself. There was a time, not long ago, when travel outside this town was the last thing she wanted to do. She opens her laptop and types, *travel agents North Wailaish* into the search bar.

NEVILLE WAITS FOR HER AT THE MUD PUDDLE. He always gets there before her, and she is always early.

"How about a walk?"

Nora pauses. She was getting used to hanging out at the café with Neville, where he'd bring books and old photos dug up from the library. Nora had told him to watch for Ellen when he was there, and to torment her whenever possible. Neville, happy to do so, sneakily rearranged books just moments after Ellen had re-shelved them. Nora likes his playful side. Like a little boy. She's stopped worrying about his intentions. The fact that one of Nora's arch enemies is now Neville's too makes them fast friends.

"It's cold. Where do you want to go?"

"Let's do the seawall."

"Only if you stop calling it that."

She curls her scarf more tightly around her neck and hides her hands in her pockets. Neville dawdles, arranging items in his man-bag and putting on his jacket in a manner more meticulous than Nora can comprehend. "Hurry up before I change my mind."

They circle around the place where the ice rink used to be and walk over toward the eastern point of the park, where in the summer small ferries take folks to neighbouring islands for the day. On one of those islands is a small pub built right on the dock. It has a hole in the floor so that kids can fish for bullheads while their parents drink beer. The island next to it, across a narrow channel, is a provincial park with a camp-ground and an old dance pavilion.

"I can just see the old 1930s steamships arriving with their guests," Neville says, gazing across to the grassy embankment on the island.

"I forgot about that."

"It's a fascinating place, isn't it? I mean, apart from the old parties in the pavilion there's thousands of years of First Nations history."

"I never think about that either."

"When was the last time you were there?" he asks.

"I don't know. I think Kate was twelve."

"We should go."

"Neville, I don't know what motivates you sometimes. And how come I'm learning more about this place from you than the other way around? I thought I was supposed to be helping you."

"You are. The books only have information. You bring it to life."

Nora stares at him. He doesn't make a lot of sense most of the time, but still, she is flattered. And after all, few people really know this town as well as she does. Neville can get what she wants out of her because he seems to have figured out that she can never hear enough compliments. She sees this, but still thinks he's a good guy.

KATE

IVY GRIMACES EACH TIME the spoon comes near her mouth. Kate feels terrible that she has to feed her, but Ivy broke her index finger two days ago, not wanting to bother Nancy with the pull-tab on her beer.

A glob of spit from Ivy's lower lip attaches itself to the upper and forms a string whenever she speaks. Kate feels a wave of nausea. She's always been prone to vomiting at the slightest provocation and is horrified to feel her throat beginning to convulse. She tries to sit as still as possible, mortified that Ivy might notice. It's not always easy to work with a ninety-two-year-old.

"Jesus, Kate. Go to the bathroom."

"I'm so sorry."

Three prescriptions sit on the vanity. Kate remembers the one that Ivy takes after her meal. For pain. She's been in the wheelchair for ten years now, following the Vancouver accident. It's no small wonder Ivy never goes there anymore. Nancy has been working with her ever since.

When she returns, she sees Ivy's used her one good hand to toss the bowl of soup down the sink.

"Ivy, I'm sorry. It's me. I have this problem."

Her back is turned away. Kate walks around the wheelchair, finds Ivy staring out the window.

"There are times when I'm ready to go."

"Please don't talk like that."

Her blue eyes flash. "Kate, grow up. I'm ninety-two. Don't say things you think you have to say. You're smarter than that."

Kate can't breathe. Ivy can bite like a vicious dog. She feels tears pressing against the backs of her eyes.

"I'd rather hear you read right now."

Kate's whole body is tight. "I can't."

"Are you sulking?"

She feels a sudden, hot surge of resistance. "No. I mean I'd rather not. I'm a volunteer. Doesn't mean I have to do things I don't want to do."

"Good girl." Ivy smiles and pats her on the shoulder.

What the fuck? Kate is totally confused. *How can someone be an adversary and a cheerleader at the same time?* She wonders if Ivy's mind is beginning to go.

"It's nice to see you thinking more about what you want."

She doesn't want this conversation. She's still angry with Ivy.

Ivy continues. "Who would you be if he hadn't told you you were shit?"

Kate reels. "He never told me that."

"You don't always need words to tell people things."

Kate forces her brain to remain with Ivy, not to focus on herself, but her thoughts are muddled. What would it be like to be Ivy, strong and vital in so many ways, yet stuck in a body that didn't even work well enough to eat independently? Usually when Kate's around Ivy she isn't thinking about her own stuff. Around Ivy, if she's not completely present to what she needs, things can go very wrong. She can't afford to take advice from Ivy, to be distracted. She's so infuriating, though. Part of her wants to push the old woman right out of her wheelchair.

"You don't need to answer that question *for me*, but you do need to answer it."

Kate shakes her head. She isn't sure anymore who is supposed to be helping whom.

BACK AT HER CABIN, SHE SITS WITH IVY'S WORDS. It was true

that near the end Jeff never told her outright what he thought of her, but it was also true that the air surrounding the two of them had become toxic. The physical pain was of her own doing, she'd convinced herself.

IVY

SHE SEES EMILIO three times that week. The tuna run is finished so the office is no longer the excuse, but she becomes the world's most helpful granddaughter, running errands the moment there is a hint of need. When she doesn't have the horse, she goes on foot or takes her bicycle into town, grabs what is needed, and rushes to find Emilio in ever-changing hiding places. She wonders if her grandparents can smell him on her. If they find out she will surely be on the next ship home.

But she can't stop, despite the risk. They are always furtive, she and Emilio, always with a nod to time and the lack of it, but still their moments together have an air of the divine. It is as though she has no choice but to continue what they've started. She feels so very alive, and he has become a sort of conduit, filling every part of her body with rushing blood and energy. He is so strong. She becomes greedy for him, increasingly so. She draws an illusory world around the two of them, fancying herself like the liberated women in *Gatsby*. She is strong, in control. She twins herself, cloned into something she never gets to be back home—something that *feels*.

Opa still likes to hike on his day off. After church Oma shuffles home to take care of the cooking and laundry while Opa points at one of the hills rounding out toward ocean and says, "Let's try over there today." Ivy, companion and navigator, has come to know the island well. Oma throws her arms up and complains she never knows whether or not they'll make it back for dinner. They take a picnic lunch and Ivy follows him uphill.

Partway to the top, they stop for a sip of water. She asks him again why he chose to come here, to a little island so far from Germany.

"I had a bad case of *fernweh*," he answers. Ivy arches a brow in confusion.

"Longing to travel. Missing a place you've never been. Do you know this?"

"I think I had it but didn't know until I got here."

"It's peaceful here." He closes his eyes. "Funny to think I wasn't originally headed here."

"Where were you planning to go?"

"You know this story."

"Tell me again."

"Guatemala, where my friend Gerhard had gone. But there were too many problems. The dictator had been overthrown just three years earlier. Things were unstable, so we stayed here. It's good, though."

"Do you ever wonder what Guatemala would have been like? Or Germany, if you'd stayed?"

He shakes his head. "I don't have time to think like that. Things were changing so much. I had an opportunity to do what I do and see something different. And it's warm. I like to swim, you know. Simple as that. Your Oma, though, she felt differently."

"How so?"

"I guess I didn't realize how sad she was to leave. When the ship left port, a band played a song, 'Muss Ich Denn,' and your grandmother cried."

"Oma?" Ivy can't imagine a single tear from that woman.

"She is tough, though. Never complained once," adds Opa. "And it is a very pretty, very sad song. I give her that."

Ivy realizes she's come to think of her grandparents more as Cuban than German, in many ways—well, Opa at least. She's never known them in another place. Her family never visits Germany, and her grandparents have never been to Canada. It is good to begin to know them now.

Opa leans into the incline, giving himself over to the climb. He is strong but Ivy has noticed a recent slowing. So many years of very early mornings, perhaps. Climbing is easier for her today—her thin legs have gotten muscular from all the running and biking, among other things. Her mind switches briefly to Emilio, to how well they fit together. *How would it feel to sleep next to him all night long?*

When they arrive at the summit they look out to where the rainforest ends, the treeline giving way to a few farms, then their small town, and finally the black sand beach, Bibijagua. The afternoon sun bleaches everything, slits their eyes. They eat crusty bread, cheeses, and cured meats that Opa had imported from home. And beans and rice, as they do every day. *Either beans and rice or rice and beans*, Oma is fond of saying. Ivy can't get enough into her mouth at once. Opa looks at her and laughs.

"You are good at being young."

KATE

KATE DOESN'T SLEEP on windy nights. The clunk of branches against decking, the non-human slamming of doors, the sheer notion that a thing like air, normally silent and unnoticeable, now churns in mercurial ways, are not conducive.

On Brittania, she's learned that fall and winter mean power blackouts. Tonight, she's up well past midnight, surrounded by candles, inviting ghosts.

The thing is, she still isn't sure whether or not she owes Jeff an apology. When she asks herself, *what for?* she thinks she might say for not trying harder, for not always listening or understanding the undercurrents of his complaints, for not knowing how to be a wife. For everything that had disappeared. For the way she flinched whenever he touched her, toward the end. But he could have told her the same.

It's true that what we remember most is not what a person says but what feelings take shape in their absence. *Wooden,* she thinks, remembering how she felt around Mike and Ann. As though composed of only stiff things. Like a stranger in her own body when she was here at the cabin with them. She couldn't ever figure out where to sit, or even *how* to sit for that matter. She felt as though constant judgement swirled in their minds as they watched her—that she had done something wrong—but what? Maybe it was more in her head than theirs. Still, she'd always felt as though her soul needed to vacate her body in their presence, that she had to conjure herself up as something *other*, a daughter-in-law that would make them proud. But was this really true? Was she reading their minds or was she totally off base? Was she really so inferior in their eyes? Would they have been prouder of her if she'd joined them at the real estate agency, become a part of of the family business, as they'd asked her to do? But how could they possibly have accepted someone who had capitulated entirely, who had left their own talents, abilities, and desires behind to focus entirely on what they wanted? Would they really have liked that? What was beneath this guilt? Had it originated with her? Had they detected something deficient in her that she herself was unable to see?

Something clunks against the side of the house. A branch? Pine cone? Kate knows that whatever it is, it's probably smaller than it seems. Little things can sound very loud when they fall on a wooden roof with no insulation. The windows heave somnolently, groaning with the burden of external pressures, as a few more objects bang against the roof and bounce over the gutters. Ann kept a list of things to put away in case of bad weather, but shortly after she arrived at the cabin, Kate tore it up in a moment of resentment. But it didn't matter. She knew the routines, and most of these things she's already secured for the season: the kayak, the tarps, various tools. Her phone startles the night. Instinctively she knows it's Nora.

"Mom?"

"You all right in all that wind?"

"Why are you up? Is everything okay?"

"I'm like you on windy nights."

"Wouldn't you feel bad if you'd woken me up?"

Nora laughs. "I know better."

"Why is that?"

"Family gift. You can thank your grandmother."

"Why did you call?"

"I just had a feeling."

"About what?"

"That you'd be up, thinking."

"True enough."

"It's not your fault, you know."

Kate bristles a little. This is abrupt. She hates when Nora gets into her head. "I know that."

"What I'm saying is you don't have to do penance."

"Again, that's not what this is."

"All right. You still don't want to talk. But you know where I am if you change your mind."

"I know that, Mom. It's okay."

"I love you."

Kate finds her way back to her bed and rolls over on her side, somewhat comforted by Nora's concern, by the way she knows her so well. She loves her mother too, although it's the kind of love that sometimes feels more like the wind outside her door.

IVY

"I WOULD LOVE A COCONUT. We don't have those back home."

"Could I get one for the lady?"

"Oh, I don't think you could." She twirls a white plumeria flirtatiously between her fingers while perched on the bank by the swimming hole. Mark and Maureen are in the water, pretending to ignore them.

Emilio grins and sets to the challenge immediately. Ivy feels the potency of her feminine charm as his legs grip and shimmy up the slender trunk of the palm. She allows herself the pleasure of watching his thigh muscles tighten against the resistance of bark. Despite his distance her body responds as though it is all for her. He returns and presses the smooth green oval up against her chest. She kisses him with more than her mouth.

Ivy wonders about love, if what she feels now is the thing they all speak of. She craves Emilio constantly, and she supposes that if she's doing what she's doing with him, then inevitably she should be in love. That would make things acceptable, or at least understandable to others, and to her own fretting mind. She could be the tragic heroine of a romantic affair, just like Juliet. She might even be given a little sympathy, or a pass to act outside the norm at the very least. Truthfully though, there isn't a soul on the Isle of Pines that she can explain herself to. Her grandparents' community is a religious one, where most of the time even the young seem old, and Mark, Maureen, and Peter clearly have their own ideas about Cuban people. She tells herself she can stop at any time, and Emilio doesn't consider any of it to be much of a problem. They do what they need in order to avoid pregnancy, although she admits that it's somewhat haphazard. When not busy consuming one another, they spend a good deal of time laughing. He has a great sense of humour. Ivy loves that he can indulge his masculinity without any self-consciousness. Proudly, even. His manners would be considered regressive, or too overt back home. Within Ivy though, they produced the desired effect.

"I want to leave the Americans," he tells her, nodding his head toward Mark and Maureen. "They watch."

They ride their horses along the path until the forest is far behind, and emerge into farmland. Emilio leads her across a large field and along an imposing-looking road lined impressively with royal palms.

"Are you sure this is okay?" she asks.

He continues on. At the end of the road they round a corner and come upon a huge, columned house. Ivy recognizes it as an American home, the only sort that would flaunt colonialism so obviously. Emilio exchanges a few words in Spanish with a woman sitting on the front porch, knitting.

"I work for this family, but they are away now. She is their maid."

Ivy gapes at the magnitude of the structure, but Emilio seems unimpressed. They dismount and tether their horses. He leads her around the house until they stand gazing downhill at a clearing, in the middle of which sits a rectangular pool surrounded by more groves of royal palms. A tiny hut sits right in the water, off to one corner of the pool.

"San Rosario Aguas Minerales," he tells her.

"A spring?"

"*Si*. Here you can cure anything. My father, he likes smoking, but since he comes here, he doesn't cough"

"I had no idea this was here."

"There are more, here and in Santa Barbara. They are the best in the world. Scientists from Havana tested the waters and they are full with calcium, magnesium, salt, and other minerals."

Ivy is already peeling off her dress. She walks down the hill and slips into the warm, silken waters. They seem comprised of the same elements that flow through her body when she and Emilio make love. He follows her in, proud of sharing this secret place. In the water, she finds herself once again held within the circle of his arms and chest. Their mouths and tongues explore each other roughly. His hands find the folds of her beneath her swimsuit and he brings her quickly to the shuddering point, rippling the surface of the healing springs. She doesn't even care who's watching.

A slice of sun lands on the little blanketed portion of the clearing where they lie afterward, heat-exhausted. Emilio hacks open the coconut and they chew on its flesh. He turns his face to the sky and soaks in it, hands behind his head, his dark torso stretching upward and in, chest expanding. Ivy considers placing a hand on his stomach, fanlike, and tanning the outline of it onto his skin. Instead, she picks up a fallen needle. It still gives her an unexpected start to find conifers on a tropical island—startling little reminders of home—and brushes it gently over his arm.

Emilio releases a smile. "That tickles."

"Darling, how many girlfriends have you had?"

He stays where he is, rather than rolling over to take in the intensity of her stare. "I think too many to count."

She pokes his chest with the needle. "No jokes."

"*Ay.* I don't know. Is this important?"

"Just curious."

"Five. Maybe six."

"Did you sleep with all of them?"

He is looking at her now. "Why do women always ask questions they don't want answers to?"

"I can handle it. And the question will come up again so you might as well answer it now and save yourself some measure of irritation."

He sighs. "All right then. I think most of them, yes." And then, "It's just a natural thing, not so big as some people make it."

He doesn't ask about her past. With Emilio, there is always an unspoken sense of their intentions. Mutual respect—yes. Admiration and a desire to protect each other and what they have—most definitely. Perhaps the ease of their union has something to do with this—it simply felt right to be together. Nothing more. No sweeping melodrama. Just adventure. She still struggles, though, when she thinks of how to make sense of it to others. What brings them together feels beyond them, uncomplicated and physical.

On some level, though, they are gradually connecting, forming sticky invisible bonds. How could they not? Nevertheless, Ivy fancies herself coolly detached, capable of stopping whenever she wants.

His chestnut eyes, losing interest in conversation, speak of another intention as he rises from the blanket, stretches, and holds out a hand. He pulls her up and scoops up the blanket with the other hand. Her thoughts begin to evaporate as he leads her toward the trees, to a more private place. She only glances back once to see if there are any eyes following them. She tries to ignore the small tightening in her chest, a tiny but insistent indicator that some kind of storm is beginning to gather.

AT HOME IN HER ROOM, Oma's frantic knocking startles her out of her book. Without waiting for Ivy to answer, she barges in through the door.

"Say nothing," she tells Ivy.

"What?"

"I said, say nothing. You will listen."

Ivy listens.

"You are a naive, young girl and you are smarter than you act. Did you think no one would see you? Didn't I tell you

Mrs. Freisen is always watching? And she's only one of many others. This is a very small island, Ivy. What are you thinking?"

"I don't…"

"Shhhh! Don't even think about trying to make things up. I know better than you think I do. I didn't think I would have to spell this out for you, but you are causing trouble for your grandfather and me. And I won't have it."

Ivy sits silently, watching her grandmother's chest rise and fall. Her face is flushed with anger. Of course, she knew she couldn't get away with this forever. *Please don't let them send me home,* she silently implores.

She's blown it. Her grandparents have given Ivy far more freedom than her parents had ever allowed, but she's abused it and betrayed their trust. She pushed it too far. This is a small island, and Santa Barbara is a very small town. She could hardly think herself inconspicuous to neighbours like Mrs. Freisen and the network of merchants in town who watch her trot by, a white woman with white hair on a white horse. From Oma, she learns that for some time now they've wondered aloud to her grandparents about where Ivy is going, and who the young Cuban stranger is. And her grandparents made excuses, telling them that it must be one of their farm workers. At first Ivy was so wrapped up in her body, his body, that she wasn't aware of how they looked, Emilio and her, even when they talked casually in town. Even now she has to step a little outside herself to consider what the others see. If she really thinks about it she can admit to herself how stupidly she's behaved.

As the result of a few well-meaning "conversations with neighbours" her errands now have time limits and social outings, while still permitted, are to be always chaperoned by groups of friends. Ivy knows she should probably stop, but the trouble is, the situation has gotten too far ahead of her now; it has long embarked on its own trajectory. Instead of disabling her, the new limitations inspire a frantic necessity, serving only to fuel Ivy's hunger and awaken her resourcefulness.

But she doesn't really think she's in love, despite how strong this feels. It isn't as though he's just an 'umbrella'—there for anyone who wants such company—She can see that she is outside of Emilio's ordinary realm of experience, that he cares about her in a way he doesn't normally reserve for outsiders. But she doesn't feel love from him, either. Does this make it unworthy?

She asks herself if love might come in different sorts of arrangements. Everyone—the minister at church, and the women of the ladies' guild—always speaks of love as something pure and sacrificial, at least if you're a woman. A woman loved is an untouchable thing, garlanded and placed on a pedestal. This is not Ivy's experience. She wants the unclean things. She wants the smells, sensations, and fluids of another body surrounding hers. She wants to devour Emilio, to have all of him inside of her. This is far from the definitions of love that she has been taught.

Could this be another form of love, a distant cousin or hybrid of some sort? She honestly doesn't think so. She'd had only a small but painful reference point, last year, as she watched Philip Tremblay walk the corridors of their high school. In his presence, it had felt as though she was swallowing her heart, but she knew she could never disclose this to anyone. Because of this, she conceives of romantic love as more of a searing, serious thing, something that steals reason and concentration and perhaps a small part of oneself. But she was very young then, and maybe that hadn't been love at all either.

She's heard the island minister, as well as their own priest back home speak about *lust*, always using terms like fire and heat and burning. Why is it that the most dangerous of religious matters appear to be the most compelling? Nevertheless, these are most emphatically words that apply to her and Emilio. She feels that she is experiencing an awakening, not of her heart, but of her body—tall, slim, strong, and covered in a billion sense receptors. Though she continues to search for it, she

KATE

SHE RUNS FROM THE CABIN, legs straining, adrenaline shooting through her blood. It isn't like how it is in her dreams, where she stumbles and falls, unable to get up as a pursuer's inevitable approach draws closer. This time she leaps, lifted and buoyed by the cooling air until she comes to a spot in the forest where she's sure there's nobody behind her. She stops for a moment, catches her breath, and runs the remainder of the five kilometres into town. She has the flawed vision that dusk always brings, but not a single root or branch trips her. By now nothing on the path is unfamiliar, but still, it is darkening, and this fact alone makes her flight impressive, at least to herself. She's never run so fast.

The Wellspring isn't so busy. She stops a few metres away, leans over, and presses her palms into her thighs. She can't go running in, wheezing and sputtering that she saw him—her? A figure edged in shadow, walking out her front door. But she can't go home, either. All along she's known something is happening. Some of Jeff's things have been disappearing: the striped rugby jersey that she used to sleep in, the photo album with the yellow cover. She's convinced herself that it's absent-mindedness, pushing aside the chills that stream throughout her network of veins. There isn't room for anything else in the landscape of her body.

She walks slowly toward the café and takes deeper breaths to slow her heart, hammering high in her chest, dispensing adrenaline to the rest of her body. Night settles, cold and sharp. She can see her breath forming clouds around her body in the Hallowe'en-like evening air. At the same time, she wonders why she's come here, guessing it's a place where there would be enough people to intervene, should her pursuer—who hasn't pursued her at all—have made it this far. She begins to feel daft and unbalanced, considers turning back, but the idea that someone has breached the only safe place she knows and might potentially return keeps her moving toward some semblance of safety. And when she opens the door, the relief at seeing Ivy sends tears, immediate and hot, tumbling down her cheeks.

"I didn't know you'd be here," Kate says, brushing her face with the back of a hand. Nancy sits opposite Ivy, who occupies a spot at the table where a chair has been removed for her "wheels," as she calls them.

"What's happened?"

Ivy's concern touches a button. More tears. Nancy digs in her purse and hands her some tissue. She wipes her eyes, looking down.

"Sit down. Take your time."

Kate pulls out the chair next to Ivy, who takes her hand with a shockingly firm grasp and keeps her eyes locked on Kate's.

"Someone was in my house," she manages to say, too quiet to hear. Ivy looks to Nancy who repeats Kate's words.

"Did you talk to the police?"

"No. I just ran."

"You ran all the way here? Now catch your breath. Nancy, call Jack; tell him to come here now."

Kate begins to feel ridiculous. She is making a scene. Maybe it's her mind. Something's gone off since the accident. She tells herself that maybe she didn't see anyone. But Ivy, removing her sweater and circling it around Kate's shoulders, holds her shaken composure for her. She fixes Kate's wretched face with her keen eyes, in which Kate can see peace, and the kind of sharpness that can coexist with kindness. Kate is suddenly aware that nothing can shake up Ivy.

The rest of the evening is a confused blur, within which Kate begins to question her own perceptions, and at times her lucidity.

Jack is leaning forward, a sympathetic cast to his expression. "Can you tell me what this person looked like?"

"Not too tall. I couldn't really see them though."

He scratches behind his ear. "Why couldn't you see them?"

"The sun was going down. I just saw a silhouette. I don't even know if it was a man or a woman."

"What do you think they want?"

She leans away from him. "No idea."

Jack turns to Ivy. "I can go take a look, but other than that there's not much to go on."

Ivy sneers at him. "I'm sure there's enough."

Jack sighs and leans his chair backward, stretching out his legs. Kate resents having to give him any information about herself and tries to remain removed, detached and factual. All she feels is exhaustion.

He tries again. "Did Mike and Ann have anything valuable in there?"

"No." If it weren't for fear of the stranger's return she would gladly go home and pretend it hadn't happened.

Ivy turns toward Jack. "That's enough now."

"I'll need a bit more information about the cabin."

"You can come by tomorrow. She'll stay with me."

Kate's whole body sinks into relief. She slumps into her chair and drinks the tea that Nancy had pressed into her hands at Ivy's request. She thinks about how Ivy immediately took charge, how steady she is, how much force there is to this woman. *We are truly not our bodies,* she thinks. Before long she is hidden beneath a lofty eiderdown that Ivy had long ago brought back from Europe. It floats above and around her in a cloudlike embrace, and finally she lets her mind go as her body releases into dark, bottomless sleep.

THE DREAM IS OF THE BOY down the street, Vince. Her best friend. They were children on whizzing bikes, evading large dogs with hollow barks, finding their way beyond what the adults in their lives considered the perimeter of safety. She watches their dream-selves as he sticks his hand up into the pop machine at the new strip mall, crosses railroad tracks to the corner store, and tramples hay in the off-limits field. He is fearless.

In summers, they would crush her grandmother's rose petals into "perfume" and try to sell it by the side of the road. They'd make jam out of smashed thimbleberries. They'd hide in the apple tree with a tape recorder making radio advertisements. Back then everything was for sale.

Looking back, she sees that the boundaries were for her alone.

Vince would find treasures in a dumpster—coils of pricing stickers for bartered playthings. Kate feared his basement, the stale remnants of Christmas stacked high in one corner, piles of laundry below the chute, a half-burned glove box resting inexplicably on the cement floor.

The dream shifts and she and Vince play in a group with toy cars, as they often did, while the wind grows stronger, eventually stirring the dust into tiny vortexes. One by one other friends are called home, but Vince and Kate jump and catch longer and longer spans of time midair; the time is stolen for her while he is outside of it, unencumbered by guilt. No one expecting him home until the streetlights come on. But the scene turns, as invisible currents claim them and mock their bravery, lifting their bodies ever higher until they are pulled beyond the grasp of gravity, and dangled over rooftops. Kate awakens with a sucking breath. As her eyes adjust to the light entering Ivy's guest room, she thinks she can still see the forgotten children, herself among them, drifting in an empty field now covered by a shopping plaza. Her dreams have hardly changed since childhood.

SHE WAKES TO SOFT KNOCKING. Nancy at the door. "Kate, do you want breakfast?"

It takes a moment to figure out her surroundings. The clock claims it's nine-thirty. In the morning? There is a solid, confused pause before she tethers herself to Nancy's voice and pulls herself back from oblivion. "Yes, please. Be right there."

"There's coffee too."

Ivy drinks from a bone china cup with the words *Mother Fucker* written in feminine cursive below a painted forget-me-not.

"Birthday gift from my book club," she says, noting Kate's befuddled expression. She wears a blousy, smocked nightgown that makes her look almost like a little girl, and clutches a book, *God on the Rocks*, while squinting at the cover.

"Have you ever read Jane Gardam, Kate? Ivy doesn't even look up. She moves the large-print book to arm's length and proceeds to read. Nancy bustles about assembling eggs and toast on a plate. She hands it to Kate.

"Not sure," she responds, distracted.

"Shame," Ivy says. "Wickedly brilliant. Funny as shit."

"Sounds like someone I know," Nancy says.

"I think that was a compliment. Books aside though, we have some real drama to deal with, but I'll let you wake up first. Coffee?"

"Oh, yes."

Ivy motions to Nancy, but Kate is already up and pouring. The last thing she wants is to be any sort of burden. She sits down again and sips the invigorating brew. Gratitude seeps into her body while Ivy takes over the practicalities.

"Now I don't want you worrying about how long you're staying here; obviously I'm not going anywhere," Ivy laughs. "Kate, is there anyone you want me to call, anyone you want to know where you are?"

She thinks immediately, strangely, of Luke. Then her mother, then Rachel.

"Let's just leave it for now. Thank you, Ivy."

"It's my pleasure. You don't need to say a word, to me or to anyone."

The next few days pass by in half-wakefulness. Kate muses that having her house broken into has caused a reaction in her almost worse than the shock and sudden grief of ten months ago. At the time of the accident it was as though part of her, an unseen part, had been thrown from the car too. This was the part that could feel things, unlike most of the time ever since. What remains now is ragged and older, but emotionally numb. Shortly after the accident, she'd wandered the frame of her life in a fog that was irregularly punctuated by piercing shocks of realization. Gradually, her brain settled into a form of understanding that her husband was gone, as were his parents, and every tangible form of the life they had begun to piece together. Everyone else's life then began to seem like a pretence. She wanted to laugh anytime a friend told her about "plans."

She'd never been one of those people who had scheduled her life according to a master plan drawn up in adolescence, like her sister. To Kate, the apparent uselessness of that activity had differentiated them early on, even though Kate was supposed to be the older one. Her little sister took life very seriously, and up to now had lived out every step that she had imagined. Kate was a self-proclaimed "cautious bohemian," who allowed for the changing of plans as time drew in different people and unanticipated interests. She supposed it was a good thing that this hadn't happened to Rachel, who is currently surprised and annoyed at the lack of a potential husband in her immediate realm of possibilities, during the precise time when he was expected to arrive. To lose everything in the way that Kate did would send Rachel to an institution. In Kate's case, she just continues to wander out her questions, albeit with an elephantine pain in her chest.

Jack stops by and asks her to write out a report. She manages to appease him with a few more details about the cabin and gives him her fingerprints. He promises to install some extra deadbolts at no cost to her. He agrees to watch the place for a few more days. She's almost ready to go home. If it wasn't for the constant threat of someone intruding into all that remained of her peace, she'd be back already. She loves Ivy and Nancy, but she's also come to love silence, and the idea that she doesn't have to talk to a soul unless she wants to.

ON THE DAY OF HER RETURN she walks from Ivy's place into town. Taking in the empty field, she finds herself missing the market. She picks up a few staples at the grocery store, and as she leaves she puts on her hood to escape the drizzle.

She doesn't notice Luke at first, and she gives a small start when she sees him waving and walking toward her from the other side of the parking lot. He's wearing red Gore-Tex and carrying a mug of coffee. Kate is surprised at her own reaction to seeing him. With the exception of Ivy, she usually braces herself when she runs into anyone, but something warm accompanies the vision of Luke. She smiles and simultaneously slips in a patch of mud, almost falling on her rear, then catches her balance and returns to stability.

"That was impressive," Luke says. "You okay?"

Her face burns. "Guess I should stick to concrete."

He cocks his head. "Where've you been? I dropped by to give your clothes back and got accosted by the local police force."

"It's a long story."

"Coffee?"

"Why not."

They walk back to the café. As soon as she opens the door Kate feels an immediate rush of appreciation for the steamy interior. Not so much for the barrage of questions that is waiting for her, however.

"Kate! Did they find him? Are you okay?" Kris is working as a barista today. She typically fills whatever role has been recently vacated by a transient or oversleeping staff member.

As soon as she speaks, heads in both the bookstore and café turn in Kate's direction.

"No. I'm fine. Jack's looking out for me. It might have been nothing."

She then has a dozen offers to refuse. First Norm, the grocer, asks if she wants him to deliver her things, then Claire wants to know if she should come out and stay with her. Kate reminds herself that this is kindness, but the focus on her, even the knowledge that so many people know who she is now, makes her slightly ill. Eventually she and Luke find their way to a table. He brings her a coffee and croissant, and she stares at the slow, jerking movements in paths of rain creeping down the steamy window.

"I'm glad to see you." Luke's voice breaks into her hazy mind.

Kate looks at his green eyes and beard. Scruffy. She hates the beard.

"It's good to see you too. How's the boat?"

"Oh, I had to put her in drydock. The rocking. Just thinking about it makes me nauseous."

Kate laughs. She appreciates his efforts at self-effacement. She can't help but contrast this with Jeff, how he never laughed at himself and how angry he'd get if she laughed at him, even affectionately. Eventually she'd stopped teasing. It was impossible to predict what action or nonaction of hers, would call forth a startling surge of his intimidating anger.

"So what have you been doing, then?"

"Decided to stay put and work for the marina. I have a bit to learn before I set out again, and it's not so bad. The coffee makes it worth the stay."

He waves at a couple of locals passing by their table. The woman smiles at him and the man grabs Luke's hand, simultaneously slapping his shoulder as if he's an old friend. They exchange a few words as Kate realizes how many more people Luke already knows here than she does. But then, she'd made a point of trying to remain as invisible as possible.

"So can I ask where you've been staying?" his look is one of concern—caring, not meddling.

"At Ivy Lanwick's. I work with her a few times a week, as a relief aide."

"I know Ivy. So you take over for Nancy then."

"Yes. Although Ivy and Nancy have been doing more taking care of me in the last few days."

"What exactly happened?"

She describes the night she saw the shadowy silhouette of a person leaving her cabin with an armful of something. She shivers and is startled to feel tears threaten the corners of her eyes again. Has she spent more time crying this last week than she did after the accident? Just when it seemed like a sense of normalcy was setting in. But maybe it isn't normalcy. Maybe it's just another sort of death, another separation.

"Are you sure you're ready to go back?" His eyes show nothing of the gossipy interest the others in the café had. One of the gifts of her loss has been the acute ability to discern sincerity, or lack thereof.

"I have to. I can't impose on Ivy any longer. And it feels like it's time to go home."

"You know, you're welcome to stay at my place." He holds up a hand to halt forthcoming protests. "I'm not trying to be inappropriate. I rented a place and there's a couch. You can stay as long as you want."

"That's kind of you, Luke, but I don't think so."

"Or I can stay in your place for a bit, and you can stay in mine."

"It's not that. I just really want to go home."

"Are you sure you're okay?"

"I've got the entire Brittania police force looking out for me." She brushes away his concern and laughs. He stares at her. Green eyes.

"Jack is going to be watching the place. I'm sure he's happy to have something else to do apart from breaking up bush parties. And actually, it seems so unreal now that I'm beginning to feel stupid. Maybe I didn't see anything."

He pulls out a pen and a small notepad from his pocket and starts to write, then pushes over a paper with his number on it.

"Just in case."

They leave the cafe and walk down to the docks. There is a bite in the air and the only people around are busy doing chores to prepare for winter. Kate hugs her thick jacket as she negotiates the placement of her feet on the sloshing dock, which jolts in protest—a stiff thing, unable to accommodate the unpredictable, relentless movements of sea. Luke walks to the end of the dock and stands with his hands at his hips. He strikes the appearance of a commanding figure in his red Gore-Tex, but Kate, of course, knows better.

"I keep coming down here. At first I forget and have to remind myself that the boat hasn't been stolen," Luke says.

"You were starting to feel at home."

"It's hard to let go of intentions, especially with the things you really want."

"Yeah."

Kate continues to walk toward him. He opens his arms and lets her in. There is something like home in his embrace, even though she's never really been there.

IVY

THE ROADS ARE RED DUST. A warm quiver of wind releases fine particles from the calla lilies lining the way to her Cuban neighbours' home. Today she walks instead of taking the horse or her bicycle, forcing herself to find something time consuming to do instead of looking for Emilio.

Nalda's husband Cédro works on her grandparents' farm. He owns two oxen, which he brings over during the week to work the fields. Ivy likes to sit and listen to him and the others shouting to each other in Spanish. She, a solitary white-haired girl who doesn't interest them at all, is enthralled by their warm jokes and laughter. She wants to feel what it is like to enjoy mango juice after a long day's labour in the heat. She knows nothing of what it is like to earn refreshment.

Every day Nalda comes at noon to deliver lunch, usually trailed by her two smallest children, Atalon and Elisa. They sit and eat together with the other workers, Nalda stroking Cédro's hair or massaging his shoulders. A couple weeks ago Ivy brought them some of Opa's day-old rolls and danishes.

"*Gracias.*" Nalda's smile was bright. The children began to jump around, speaking too quickly for Ivy to understand.

"*Como?*" She fumbled, pointing to the bread.

"*Pan,*" Nalda said.

She follows them home. Oma would kill her if she saw Ivy embarrassing her like this. When the family arrives at a small shack she waits outside, sitting in tall grasses. Eventually Nalda emerges with a stout barrel and begins to fill it with well water. She goes back inside and returns with a pile of laundry. Ivy decides then to say hello.

"*Me sorprendiste!*" Nalda says, a hand against her chest.

"*Lo siente,*" Ivy stammers. She realizes she can't carry the conversation any further, so begins pointing again. "*Qué es?*"

"*Lavandaria.*" Nalda seems amused. Ivy takes this as an invitation.

She begins to show up at their home more often in the afternoons. She gets to know the children, who sit on her knee and laugh at her Spanish.

"*Soy una maestra de escuela primaria,*" Nalda tells her one day. Ivy knows *escuela*, can parse together the meaning of the sentence. She invites Ivy to her classroom.

One week later, she sits in a class full of children. She ought to be embarrassed, but instead she feels driven, excited to get inside the language that surrounds her, to know the emotions that seem so plaintive in the music that is constantly expressed, everywhere. What the locals call *sucu-sucu*. Why this drive? It might be Emilio, or maybe it's just how lonely she is when he isn't around. Nalda has informed her via gesture that if anyone official-looking shows up, she is to run out the back door.

With the exception of Luisa, the Cuban girls at the telephone lines don't pay her much attention. To her entwined delight and dismay, Ivy begins to understand what they are talking about, but since Oma's slap she has had to keep her understanding of Spanish covert.

But understanding is not always a good thing. She soon figures out exactly what her coworkers think of her, not that she'd learned the word *puta* in primary school. Whispers always intensify the focus of the listener, even if she isn't supposed to be listening. A short conversation with Señor Canton confirms her suspicions, and although it stings, she is unsurprised.

She begins to occupy a liminal space, neither here nor there, no longer knowing who she is. There is a part of her, the part that comes from somewhere else, who stands with the others in judgment over what she's been getting up to with Emilio, but there's another girl inside, a girl who defies them, who is stronger, who knows that everything is temporary, and who cares very little about what these people think, with the exception of her grandparents. She wonders if she will remain forever split after she returns to Canada.

ONE SUNDAY AFTER CHURCH Oma, Opa, and the Freisens pack a picnic and pile into Opa's pickup truck bound for Bibijagua beach. They have to bring blankets with them because the black sand has absorbed half of the day's sun. To place a foot on it would be akin to walking on hot coals. Peter carries Oma's giant basket of bread. He holds the hand of his three-year-old nephew Hannes, as Hannes' mother, his sister Sonia—a quiet woman who speaks only German and never comes to the swimming hole— trails behind them, walking next to her husband.

Peter dumps the basket at the base of a white-trunked, skinny palm, scoops up Hannes, and runs toward the ocean, the boy squealing in delighted protest. At the water's edge he stops, puts Hannes down, and encourages him to take his hand and walk into the waves. Ivy watches them submerge. Hannes' grip moves higher and higher up Peter's arm the deeper they go, and he climbs his uncle like a monkey that doesn't want its armpits wet.

"*Ein, Zwei, Drei!*" Peter, up to his chest now, peels Hannes off and hurls him into the ocean. He then grabs the boy's torso and flips him on his back, his big hands securely tucked under him. Sonia shouts something in German, to which Peter responds, "*Ja, ja.*" Opa smiles broadly, his expression reflecting the idea that everything might be perfect in his world. Either he isn't as aware of Ivy's misdeeds as Oma is, or he has chosen not to join her in her brooding.

"Ivy, come and make sandwiches," Oma calls. Ivy sighs,

wanting to run into the waves with the boys. Instead she dutifully joins her grandmother at a picnic table and begins to stuff stacks of cheese and meat into puffed buns.

"What does your mother think of you and boys?" Oma is looking directly at her, her fingers coated with butter.

Ivy plays dumb. "She allowed me to bring a date to my graduation."

"And what about now? Did she give you advice for your travels?"

"Not really."

Oma puts the butter knife down and takes Ivy's wrist. "I want you to think not just about yourself, but about the others who are here, the people who look after you."

Ivy doesn't make eye contact, just stares at Oma's generous belly, at the apron that is a part of her wardrobe—even at the beach—as she continues. "There are things you don't understand about living in strange places, problems you bring. Do you understand?"

"Yes," Ivy lies.

"You don't know anything about this place. We didn't come here to change things, to intrude on people's lives."

"What do you mean?"

"Stop pretending you don't know what I'm talking about. We have our lives and your friend, he has his."

Ivy knows better than to keep pretending, but she stubbornly thinks that there might be a way to change Oma's mind. The world is changing and she is such an old bird. "Oma, it's good to have friends from different places."

"Stupid girl! You and I know we are not talking about friends. Now listen to me, before you ruin your life and get us into trouble here. Leave him alone."

Ivy nods agreement, but inside she knows. Impossible.

NORA

RACHEL'S APARTMENT is a wonder of tidiness. Nora congratulates herself for this—they are peas in a pod in that sense, but at the same time she has to admit that Rachel had pretty much left the womb that way. The Hallowe'en candies neatly ordered by category, the colour-coordinated closet, everything on identical hangers. Rachel likes to keep things organized, just like her mother.

Nora's eyes move along the spines of Rachel's book collection. She only recognizes two of them, *To Kill a Mockingbird* and *East of Eden*. She'd studied those in high school, but she'd be hard-pressed to remember anything about them now. Never mind. She's better with numbers. There's one more title she recognizes, but she'll go right on telling herself she hasn't seen *The Joy of Sex* on her youngest daughter's bookshelf.

She'd taken the bus into town because Rachel liked to stay at the school until five. Unfortunately, she didn't have to test the theory about whether or not she was still a weirdo magnet. She hadn't been in her seat for more than five seconds before the world's smelliest man chose the empty spot next to her. Reeking of mildew and deli meat, he pulled off his boots and started clipping his toenails. Nora cast him as many disgusted glances as she could, but he was oblivious, and there was nothing more she could do, squeezed into the cattle-car as they were.

These days it's been getting harder for her to stay in North Wailaish. It isn't just the nosiness. Nora feels a restlessness in her bones. It's as though she can predict every word to come out of everyone's gaping maw. Nothing ever changes. Not that she figures herself to be any less predictable, she just wants to learn how not to be. Neville has been nice company—he always has interesting things to say, and makes her see her hometown in a completely different way—but he, like everything now, is a distraction. She wants something new, but she isn't sure what it is.

Rachel was keen to give her mother a key so she could let herself in, as opposed to Kate, who still "felt funny" about giving out one for the cabin, even though it was legally hers now. It wasn't helping things much that she still kept everything in the same place it was in before the accident. The family photo collage in the hallway, Ann's endless stacks of books. Kate even keeps her mother-in-law's last to-do list next to the phone. *Is she really that afraid of ghosts?* Nora shakes her head. Last time she was there she'd furtively thrown a few things away.

The lock clicks and Rachel pushes open the door with her hip, a gigantic bag stuffed full of papers slung over one shoulder. She notes her mother's frown. "Marking," she says, plopping the bag down on a chair and giving Nora a squeeze.

"I'm starving. You?"

"Getting there. Let's go out."

"There's a good sushi place around the corner."

Nora hesitates. "Isn't that raw fish?"

"Not just. There's other stuff too. And the fish is really amazing, if you try it."

"You know I'm fussy."

"I promise you'll like it."

NORA IS TERRIFIED OF THE TINY DISHES that arrive one by one, in no apparent logical order, the only recognizable thing being rice. She remembers the headlines of articles she'd sent to Rachel back when she was travelling: "E Coli Poisoning

Prompts Beef Recall" and "Family Hospitalized with Salmo-nella." She dissects the tiny rice rolls, points to every visible ingredient, asking "what's that?" If she didn't know any better, she could swear Rachel was laughing at her, even though her face wore patience.

"*Tamago, tonkatsu, tekka maki, ebi nigiri.*"

"English, please."

"Egg, pork, tuna roll, shrimp."

"Is it cooked?"

"The only thing that's not is the tuna. Just try it, though, it's delicious. And it's just a small piece of fish."

"I have no intention of dying today."

"I come here at least twice a month. I'm not dead."

Nora pokes at the raw fish. "I can't."

"Suit yourself then. More for me."

NORA PICKS UP A HOT DOG on their way to the movie theatre. Best thing she's had all day. It's going to take more work than she thought to get the North Wailaish out of her system. Later, when Rachel asks her opinion on the movie, she has to admit that she couldn't see well enough to read the subtitles.

"Why didn't you tell me, Mom? We could have moved."

"I was sleeping."

Rachel shakes her shiny black head and unfolds the pull-out couch.

"Hope I'm not cramping your style," Nora says.

"Sadly, I have very little 'style,' as you put it."

"Come on. Guys must be breaking down the door."

"Hardly, Mom. This city isn't an easy place to find friends, let alone dates."

"I'm sad to hear that. Must be better than the island, though."

Rachel shrugs. "My social life consists of little more than hanging out with other teachers on pub night. Everyone seems to already have a set group of friends. I'm too late to the party."

"That's not like you." Nora remembers sleepovers, giggling,

KATE

WHEN SHE RUNS she is a body of breath, unarticulated, head lifted to cloud. She is mystery pain, the kind that disappears if you don't pay attention to it. She is pricked sea air; she is away.

The island is all hills. In the forest, these are obscured so you can forget that that you're climbing, but out here on the road the topography has been shaved to expose its random rises and falls, and then later coated with concrete on the main routes. Kate likes the spots where trees wall both sides of the street. They remind her of the posters of Terry Fox that hung in her seventh-grade classroom, photos taken from behind while he climbed the impossible, his one-legged marathon full of something more inclusive of pain and determination than she or any other runner would ever know. These roads are silent, unless you are out with the munching deer at dusk or the diesel truck that steals your moment as it confronts a hill, its beer rattle belch stealing your brain as you run, as you try to release the stubborn habit of thought.

She pauses at the hill by the grocery store where Jeff once stopped the car, got out, and told her to drive. *You're going to learn how to handle a stick shift. I can't believe you don't know this already. It's embarrassing.*

Kate, an icicle of fear. *What about starting somewhere flat? No, now. Right here.*

His hands didn't do anything when she stalled for the fourth time, when she cried, called herself an idiot, sided with him against herself. Failing again to make him happy. His hands never did anything, but what came out of him was equally pernicious, maybe more so. She sank still lower into his assessment of her insufficiency, believing in it wholeheartedly. No one in her life has ever made her so hollow and purposeless.

A pop of anger shoots her burning quads rapidly upward. At the hill's crest she stops to walk, checking her watch. If she allows the thought that Jeff had woken something dark in her … an excuse to remain unmoving…. She is five kilometres from home and an hour from book club. If I don't go…? She turns and lets gravity pull her downhill.

IVY IS RIGHT ABOUT THE PEOPLE in her book club. While most of them are younger than Ivy herself, she is always more than able to keep up with their analysis of whatever book is under discussion. A cluster of intellectuals, they are unassuming and joyful, yet sharp and empathic. Theirs is a hard-won kind of joy, one that's absorbed all kinds of experience and, instead of rejecting anything, has digested it into something more comprehensive and articulate. They are not the kind of people you often run into in town, but when they do show up they are always greeted with respect. It is also this way with Ivy herself.

Nina, a former lawyer, has family roots on Brittania, like Ivy, but Maura is newly retired, having spent a forty-year career in publishing. Lila spent most of her life as a waitress in North Wailaish and is the most potent observer of human behaviour and nuance that Kate has ever met. When it comes time to choose the next book, the four of them go into lockdown negotiations so heated that it sometimes takes days. Maura whispers to Kate that a glass was once thrown, but she will not disclose the thrower.

But tonight is not about books. Not really. It's the annual year-end party. "Don't say 'Merry Christmas,' dear Kate. We do this early enough to avoid that sort of nonsense, and besides, Nina's Japanese and Maura is Jewish. Wouldn't make much sense, would it?" Ivy says, as Nancy thrusts a martini into Kate's hand.

Normally the club meets at the Wellspring, but parties are always held at Ivy's place. "We can't give the town gossips too much fodder," Lila tells her without lifting her eyes from the Scrabble game she and Maura are locked into. "Sorry I can't look up. This one cheats," she says, pointing across the table.

"Bye, all," Nancy calls on her way out.

Kate joins Ivy and Nina at the other end of the table, where Nancy has left a platter of mini quiches and smoked salmon spirals. "How was your run?" Ivy asks.

"How did you know I was running?" Kate replies, stuffing a quiche into her mouth.

"Your face is bright red."

"Still?"

"You're pale like me. Whenever I exercise ... or, used to, it took a good half an hour to lose the tomato face."

Kate appreciates the connection. "It was good. It's the only sport where I don't trip over my own feet, and everybody else's."

Nina laughs. "You're a mental athlete, Kate. It's the best kind."

"I don't know about that. It gave me a lot of grief in high school. I think I was the only kid in my town who didn't play soccer."

"North Wailaish is hardly the centre of the universe, even for athletics." Ivy winks. "When I taught phys. ed in the U.K. we did more than team sports. We taught orienteering—if you like running, you'd like that. Gymnastics, dance. And track and field, of course."

"I stopped trying to fit in a long time ago," Kate says. "Not that I was fooling anyone."

"That's wonderful," says Nina. "Doesn't sound like the kind of place where you'd want to blend in."

"No. Not anymore."

An hour later and everyone is drunk and shouting. These women could hurl insults like nobody's business. Kate makes the mistake of asking them to give her book recommendations.

"Don't listen to Maura, she reads too many men."

"Up yours, Lila, you sentimentalist."

"Ivy will only give you classics."

"Nina likes it young and glib."

"Why don't you ask Kate what she's interested in?"

Kate shrugs. Ivy scratches her head. "Some books, when you read them, you know you're reading a story," she says. "With others, though, you *are* the story, you go inside it and inhabit the characters. It's not so much the characters who change as it is you. This is what art is, and this is what it does, no matter who wrote it."

"Unless you've had as many cocktails as we've had. Then even Danielle Steel reads like Shakespeare," Maura adds.

Kate, nervous, doesn't feel like she has much to offer these women. Soon enough they will see her for who she is, a frightened, unworldly child. She can almost predict the onset of their disappointment once she's revealed enough of herself. She can see that these are the types of women who know how valuable time is and insist that none of it is wasted on people who are less than fascinating.

She sends her eyes to the corners of the room. They fall on a hairy clot of dust against the baseboard, and suddenly she is back in their apartment, Jeff cupping a dust bunny in his hands, his expression a completely articulate, albeit wordless demonstration of disgust. She doesn't remember his words; they'd been laughing only moments earlier. Shame lifts from her hidden places and envelopes her body. There is no breath. She feels blood rising to just below the surface of her skin, heated, wanting escape. Her fingernails press into flesh, knife edges, looking for places to create release.

"Kate? What's wrong?" Ivy's voice is barely discernible

outside the blood rushing in her ears. She has to get out. She is exploding. There isn't enough space in her to contain the mounting agony. She doesn't even remember where it comes from. His anger, hot groundwater, always beneath them. She will never be safe.

She is screaming.

IVY

THE NEWS HITS like a medicine ball to her chest. Her parents are coming. Five months have passed since her arrival, and she'd kept putting them off whenever they asked if she'd applied to schools, put money away. If she thinks about it, she has to admit that their letters had been taking on more of a frantic or demanding tone, but Ivy was still so far away that it had been so easy to dismiss them.

She can't even imagine them here. It's too hot for her father's rage. He'll simply combust. She shudders to think about that rage, directed toward her. And her mother's disappointment. They'd always put so much faith in her, which is why they'd even allowed her to come here in the first place, and now she'd shamed her family, let them down completely. She could run away. If she wanted to spend the rest of her life with Emilio, that would be a logical choice, but it wasn't what she wanted, and La Isla is much too small a place in which to hide. She'd have to go to the main island, figure out a way to travel the sixty kilometres to Batabanó and get a bus to Havana. And they'd likely find her there. She could confront them. After all, she is an adult, capable of making decisions. Has her time away given her such confidence? She doubts it. Fortunately, though, boats are slow. She has time to think.

She doesn't want anyone to break the spell of her sojourn, so she simply and conveniently casts aside what isn't immediately, directly in front of her. Back in Vancouver, the weather would have turned by now and there would be a collective, albeit unarticulated sense of "that's enough, now." Everyone would shut down their enjoyment like a carnival closing down its stalls for the season, and return to a singular focus. Live to work, never the opposite. There would be a clear sense of finality in the air. Some would push the limits and continue to go for a morning swim before work or school; others would smile regretfully and lament the brevity of summer. These emotions and behaviours all seemed natural back home—everyone follows the dictates of season. But here the sparkling sun, sand, and heat continue, giving full permission for things to go on as they always have. Ivy is only too happy to oblige, even though her time has suddenly become limited.

Perhaps the Piñeros can see some change as the seasons give way, something subtle that she can't detect. Although there aren't any real seasons here. It seems incredible to her that her whole life seems to have been governed by what the leaves were doing. Looking back though, maybe this inability to see change involves a sort of denial on her part. There had been a natural break in her progression through school, enough to make coming here a reasonable choice, and neither her friends nor her family are enough to compel her back.

She guesses there is a little more rain. Not too much, but enough to spoil a few plans. Emilio has gotten braver. Ivy is sure that her grandparents have merely reached a state of exasperated resignation—let her parents deal with it. She and Emilio remain stealthy, but there is the odd Saturday morning when her grandparents are busy at the bakery and they are brazen enough to meet in the house. These meetings were at first furtive and hasty; they groped each other clumsily, casting frequent glances at the door. Emilio's body had become so familiar to her, but there were a million peaks and valleys she still needed to traverse again each time she touched him. After they'd gotten their explorations out of the way it was a comfort to lie in her bed and either drift in a pseudo-sleep or start all over again. Sometimes they talked. Her grandparents were never home until after lunch.

"My parents are coming," she tells him one sweltering, breathless day, long after they'd come together in the usual way, not wanting to spoil the mood.

He raises himself sideways on one arm, looking a little ridiculous in her tiny bed, like a sort of grotesque doll. "What does this mean?"

She squints. "I'm not really sure. To begin with, it means two more sets of eyes on me. Three if you count my sister."

He takes this in, rolling on his back and looking up at the ceiling. "Okay."

"Truth is, I don't know how long I'll be on the island. They expect me to make some decisions about college."

"Things aren't so simple for you, are they, Rubia?" His tone annoys her. Something like contrived wistfulness. Or sarcasm.

"And they are for you?"

"Mostly."

"How?"

"Expectations, I guess. I am expected to find my own way. There isn't the same kind of ... how do you say it? Push?" He brushes a piece of her hair back and kisses her neck.

"Pressure. Well, I guess at some point I need to think about my future. Don't you?"

"Of course. But not so that it takes away from right now. Especially when things are, hmmmm, very pleasant." He traces an invisible line over her breast, but for once her head outpaces the rest of her.

She juts her lower jaw. "It's not like this can go on forever."

"Nothing is forever. What are you hoping for?"

Outside the window a buzz of cicadas begins to fill the dusk with a sudden, deafening chorus.

She turns away from him. "For now, I just want to stay here as long as I can, even though I can feel it ending soon. It feels like my choices are disappearing."

"Your parents hope you become well educated, make money, make them proud of themselves?"

She sits up and glares at him. "They're giving me opportunities."

"Giving *themselves* opportunities. What if you didn't want to do what they ask? What if this 'security' makes you unhappy? What if it is not what you really want?"

"It's just a foundation. After that I have more choices." Even as she says this, she can't figure out why she is defending them; she only feels that she has to.

"You have so few choices. You can't see this?"

"Emilio, I know your life is different, but having a good job and a good income means I can do other things."

"Not when your life becomes so complicated with this."

"You think making money makes things more complicated?"

Emilio looks down and laughs without any joy. "People with money make themselves more complicated. And maybe less happy."

"Seems a bit simple, don't you think?"

He shrugs. "Exactly my point." He tries to kiss her again, pushing his weight over her body, but the mood has evaporated.

"What do you make of this, Emilio? Who am I? Someone with no consequences for you because I'll eventually leave? Of course it's simple for you."

Emilio raises his eyebrows and shoulders at the same time. "To me this feels right, and I know it does to you too. We don't need to pretend anything. We are young and so we should enjoy it."

"I don't know anyone who feels as little guilt as you do."

"This is probably why I'm here."

"I think maybe you should leave."

"When are your parents coming?"

"They leave Canada tomorrow. A few weeks, I guess."

He pauses to consider this, scratches his arm. "That still gives us some time."

"For what? More sneaking around?"

"What else?"

Ivy has to get out of bed. The room is airless. "I don't know what I'm doing with you."

He sits up, his dark eyes painted with something not quite like anger, but close. "Who is this talking? I've known you for many months now, but I don't know this person."

"Maybe this is who I am."

"I think this is your parents. They're not even here yet, but they're *here*." He points a finger at her forehead. "And even worse. I feel like I've already met them."

"I can't expect you to understand. Things were simple before this, before I found out, before anyone knew anything. We had time."

"Rubia, there is nothing wrong here. There is still time."

She looks at him. Everything is fading so quickly, and she hasn't even left the island yet. "Not really. My grandparents know. They must have written to my parents."

"But they're busy. Your parents won't be here for several weeks, and even then they won't take you back right away."

"You have no idea."

"What then? Why do things have to change right now?"

"I'm trying to tell you that I already have an alarm clock. All the time, somebody is watching me. Nobody understands. It's not going to be the same."

"What is this clock?"

"My grandparents. Their friends. I am never alone."

"Why do you suddenly care so much about what people think? You've been with me at the lake, in town, and you never cared before."

"I know, I just felt like everything real was so far away. Until now."

Emilio thrusts his arm above his head, exasperated. "You're so afraid of your family you can't even figure out what you really want."

"That's not true."

"This isn't really even happening for you, is it? It's like you're in a dream. I could be anyone."

"No," she says, shaking her head. "That's not what I mean."

"You're trying to accuse me because you're still a child."

"That is totally unfair. I'm trying to be an adult about this."

"You're no different from the others who come here and think this is some sort of ... playground. Just an extension of America. I am sorry for you." He gets up and begins to dress.

"Emilio, it's not that way at all. Stay for a minute. I can explain this better."

"I can't. You're confirming prejudices I don't want to have."
He picks up his bag and walks out the door.

SHE TAKES THE HORSE ALL THE WAY to the beach and rides her up and down the firm sand, looking out at the surf and the ghostly mangroves, engaging in imaginary conversations with her parents, each time attempting to make herself sound more convincing. But the parents who arise in Ivy's imagination must be someone else's. Hers are rigid; they will never understand that she is already living a life, not waiting in limbo or running away. It is 1926 and they've not yet caught up with modernity. Funny how she's come to find a sense of it on a tiny, secluded, tropical island. Far from home. And just as she's begun to hold it so dear, it's beginning to vanish. Again. Emilio is right, she has no freedom.

KATE

KATE IS IN THE FAMILIAR half-asleep, half-awake place that she's frequented since Jeff died. She pretends he is still here— it's how she protects herself in the emptiest moments. It's only the known things that comfort. But tonight is different. Normally when she allows memory she goes back to the early days with Jeff, the ones that were new, full of unanswered questions. She has a harder and harder time remembering the days that had changed, turning slowly, like spoiled milk. This is odd to her, since most of their last year together they'd been like strangers. She rolls over and sees herself that one night, watching his back, almost touching the place between his shoulder blades, where she knew he felt. The rolling was itself a strain, as the lump in the middle of their mattress rose to impede her reach. Two a.m. She'd thought he called her name.

She remembers what they'd called each other earlier that night. The first time she'd thrown dishes to the floor. Such a ridiculous thing to do, but each of his criticisms had, up to this point, wormed their way into her, and the cumulative effect was not that she couldn't stand him so much as she could hardly stand herself. She should be washing the dishes before loading them into the dishwasher, and then loading them back to front; she didn't fold his pants properly; every meal had at least one small imperfection. The house was a mess, and what was she doing renting expensive new releases when they hadn't yet seen all of the old movies on offer? They were small things, to be sure, but over time they replaced almost all affection, forming a slow, incremental assault on her consciousness until it had become unbearable.

He hadn't always been like this. She remembered laughing with him—a lot in the beginning—and how they had the same ideas for the future. It had seemed natural to plan one with him.

But that night she'd used the word *hate*. That night he wondered aloud why he'd married her. That night they stepped a little further into their disintegration.

Fifteen years. Some of it remembered, some shadow. She feels like the poetry of Leonard Cohen—smooth and echoic, resonating low. *There is a crack in everything, that's how the light gets in.* She can't recall the origin of the crack, was it in their mutual truth-telling, or had it begun to form before then? And she couldn't yet see the light that was meant to come in and replace the darkness and misery that the cracks revealed. Her mind prickles with awareness, the beginnings of a sleepless night. She sinks back into the memory of that last conversation, the one that had changed everything. She recalls looking back to what they had been prior to this, on the other side of their words.

They'd ended up talking more that one night than they'd done in the previous six months. Within Kate these months had given birth to a duality—a stoic and a gypsy, warring, but never aloud. A few evenings before this one she'd walked out the door and down the street into night, wondering if the walking could gradually sink her into pavement. To stay, to go. No talk of children. Time wasted.

He slept.

The conversational divide that night was brief, but it separated one span of their relationship from another. She marvelled at the decisiveness that was almost inarticulate. Rhetoric offered no path of return. Too much was already said, other potentials addressed.

By morning they would no longer be as they were. They had torn into wordless places and released what was cowering there. They swayed in the balance of beginnings and endings indiscernible from one another. Individually they were dormant seeds in frozen soil, waiting to be planted elsewhere, but as yet unable to uproot.

He's gone now. In retrospect, the effort of that conversation seems pointless, although it wouldn't have been if he were still here. Kate wishes for a script to walk her along the inside channel of this new passage, where even the pumping of her blood feels unfamiliar. She marvels at how, for so long, she has stood slightly to the left of herself, without enough breath to assert a presence. She had forgotten herself alive, and the reminder was like a night in a strange alley, where she perceived threat in the presence of benign shadows.

Her thoughts wander to Luke, and something fills new spaces she didn't even know were there. *We outgrow the skins of our affairs*, she thinks, *these amorphous things we're so certain we understand.* It is a marvel how, after so many years of attempting to fly under the radar, she had effectively ghosted herself. How could Luke even see her now? Ivy was right, she can't even see herself.

She shifts her thoughts to Luke's embrace on the dock. The shadow of it warms her in the tiny cabin, but along with it comes a host of conflict, most of it having to do with everyone but herself. Her relationship with Jeff had died along with him and his family, even before their physical deaths, but the unresolved is no longer their shared responsibility. It stays with Kate, alone, like crusty residue at the bottom of a wine glass left too long, the kind you need to scrub to remove.

In the morning, she goes to the dresser and one by one she opens each drawer and removes the clothes. She takes a garbage bag and places it all inside. Her chest begins to tear itself in two the way it always does when she starts to confront the remains of his presence, the things they'd hoped for in the beginning and the mess they'd made out of it in the end, the disappointment now hers alone. She heaves the heavy bag out to the dry boathouse. She'll let herself be parted from the clothes, from him to some extent, for a few days at least, then drop them off at the Free Store. She takes advantage of the energy while she has it and continues the purge, emptying first Ann's, then Mike's drawers as well. There are a million memories attached to each item, but she puts them in bags regardless. All of the thoughts that come up are of happy events, and Kate figures that this probably has something to do with survival. Who would want to keep going if they could only remember the bad? She forces herself to recognize the not-so-lovely things, but at the same time there is something to be honoured about a completed life, and it seems pointless to shroud these people in the emotional torment that made up the last year or so before their death. It's all much too heavy. Literally.

The phone breaks her thoughts and her focus on the task.

"Kate. It's Nancy. How's everything at home?"

"It's fine. I might be going crazy. How's Ivy doing today?"

"She's good. Worried about you. She's having a good rant about Luke not coming to stay with you."

"She knows I'd never let him."

"Yeah, I don't think she sees how alike you two are."

Kate is surprised at this observation. "Oh?"

"You want to come for dinner?"

"Is it just you two?"

"Just us."

Kate closes her eyes, relieved. It feels so good to be cared for in such an expectation-free way. "I'd love to."

IVY IS ABSOLUTELY INTOXICATED, but mentions nothing about what happened at the book club. Kate can't even talk about it. How gracious they all were, how they held her, unflinching, as the torment worked its way through and then out. Because of them, it happened without the need for her to release it physically this time. Because she knew for once that she was safe, that she was seen and cared for. And she sensed there was no need to apologize for her behaviour, had the feeling those women had seen so much that they were unfazed by her outburst. In the end, she was left with a kind of calm that was completely unfamiliar. And on some level, she knew that their gift enabled a return to herself, but to a new place this time.

Kate worries about the damage that Ivy, so recently recovered from a flu, might be doing to herself, but she doesn't dare attempt to dissuade her from drinking. That's Nancy's job.

"Quite a girlfriend you've got there, Nancy."

Nancy blushes. "Too much for me, maybe."

"Nonsense," Ivy slurs. "She should be so lucky."

"She's a little young, but it's fun for now."

"As long as the sex is good. Enjoy yourself." She turns to Kate. "And what about you? Any prospects? I know the island is brimming with possibilities," she says sarcastically, widening her eyes.

"You're so nosy," Nancy intervenes.

"Yes. And what of it?" Ivy's gaze remains on Kate.

Kate frowns. "It's too soon, Ivy."

"Maybe for some things, but not for others."

"Are you talking about sex, *again?*" Nancy rolls her eyes.

"Not necessarily." She cocks her head and looks closely at Kate. "What do you need right now?"

Kate pauses to think about the question. She hasn't really contemplated it. She'd behaved more primally when she first came here, like a frightened rodent scurrying back to its burrow. Only now is she beginning to settle, to poke her head out and look for the things that might swoop down on her.

"I honestly don't know. Friendship, maybe. Time."

"What about the pseudo-sailor? He seems nice in a bumbling sort of way."

Kate looks to Nancy for reprieve, but she is busily lifting things off the counter and dusting underneath them, looking

happy enough to have the focus shift away from her. "He seems
fine. He could be a friend."

"It's a start. But you might just want to fuck him anyway."

Nancy throws her cloth down. "Jesus, Ivy! That's it. No
more Anaïs Nin for you."

Ivy throws her head back, roaring.

Nancy and Kate have to carry Ivy back to her room. She is
like a husk of a person when sleeping, as though her soul has
already lifted off. Although Ivy has been tall most of her life,
she seems to have shrunk to fit the frame of her wheelchair,
which now seems like an extension of her body. Kate wonders
how such a thin frame can house a person as grand as Ivy.
Maybe this is the ideal form of aging: you simply grow too
large for your body to contain you. Ivy has lived so much, read
so much, and is nowhere near finished with either. There are
moments when she seems to forget she isn't a contemporary of
Kate and Nancy's. Admittedly there are moments when Kate
forgets this too. Time rolls itself into confused waves of present
and past. Some waves have further to travel before releasing
their mysteries onto beach, or broken rock. Kate sleeps at
Ivy's again that night. She is beginning to forget where and to
whom she belongs.

NORA

NORA'S WORRY SETTLES in thicker than coastal fog. It menaces, encircling her forehead and robbing her of sleep, particularly between the hours of two and four a.m. In those hours, her mind pops and prickles with alarm about things she can't identify clearly, usually something to do with the kids. Ed is of no help.

"What do you think about Christmas?" she asks him, facing a sink full of dishes.

"What about it?" Ed squints at his cereal, doesn't look up.

"Do you think we can get both of them here?"

"The kids? They're always here."

"I'm sure Rachel will come, but I don't know about Kate this year."

"Of course she'll come."

Nora holds her breath. She doesn't want to remind Ed again. In his mind, nothing ever changes with the kids. His world is a static one—at least to his perception.

She pulls on her coat and starts down the hill from their home. Today she feels faster and in better shape. At her last visit the doctor was pleased with her blood pressure. Ed usually pisses her off enough to fuel a couple miles, at the very least. She stops at the bottom and looks at the boarded-up windows of Clark's grocery. It looks so insignificant, an anachronism. Ready for the wrecking-ball—she's even heard locals complain about how long it is taking. Nora is sentimental, though. She can still feel the heavy glass door against the shove of her body, the scent of fresh bread, the crisp paper bags stuffed with the ingredients of that night's dinner, the familiar faces. In her mind, Nora returns to the days when she came here for baby food and diapers, pushing a stroller over the hills, stopping in the store to talk to no less than five or six people, usually, a simple errand that could expand to an hour and a half or even two hours. It made her feel less alone when she was keeping company with two babies all day long. *And how do those strangers at the funeral fit into all this wholesomeness?* Nora doesn't have the answer to that, and Mr. Clark has clearly left the building without a word. There is no lingering spirit that might guide her to understand. How sad he'd be to see this place now.

She hustles on, past the homes of families she's known most of her life: the Shepherds, whose four boys are all away at university now; the Livingtons, who'd never had any kids; and the Morris's, whose son and daughter have taken up the local hobby of drinking and bar-hopping, continuing their high school years long after they should have ended. She thinks of her own daughters, always so different from each other, even when they were little. Rachel always off to soccer, or lining up her stuffed animals in military formation. Funny, Nora often has to remind herself that Rachel is the younger one. Kate was always much less sure of herself; she talked less, and had what Nora liked to call an "artistic temperament." From as long ago as she can remember there's been something sad and disarmingly strange inside Kate. She remembers her at three, looking up at her with large brown eyes and whispering, "You are made of meat." Nora had turned vegetarian for a good two weeks after that. She can't think of a time when she and Ed had done anything differently in raising the girls—no, they came the way they were, their personalities encoded from day one.

She'd already decided to check in at the Moose Hall. It's been almost a month since she's shown her face at a board meeting.

There had been lots of phone calls from the executive, but Nora needed the time away to show everyone just how put out she was. She was aggravated that no one felt as slighted as she did; everyone just wanted to get on with things and pretend that that insult of a funeral had never happened. For the last few weeks she's been drumming up her own agenda, though. Her lips purse when she thinks about Edgar and Evan, and how they insulted her authority. She has other plans for them. Neville has been a nice distraction, but now she's started to worry that the council members will all forget her. It's taken everything she has in her to stay away this long, even though she's occasionally shown up to do grunt work that someone else had set up. Nora is, if anything, a proud woman.

At first the hall looks empty. Nothing out of place. The local girl guide chapter photo is still hanging in the small hallway where she enters—Nora always makes sure the photo is up to date even though she hates most of the brats in it, and their snotty families. Then there's the photo of Her Majesty, a requirement of the organization, and the display cases flaunting photos and trophies that go back to the early years, when the hall smelled of new cedar instead of must, even before Nora's time. No one would dare touch those. She walks the perimeter of the main hall lost in thought, and almost bumps into Marian.

"Nora! I was starting to wonder if I'd ever see you here again." She reaches out and squashes Nora into the pillow of her ample chest.

Nora tries to keep her cool, but she is awfully glad to see Marian. Anyone, really. Her life alone with Ed is pretty small in comparison to the one she has here. She feels a small wave of relief that at least one person is happy to see her back.

"How are you doing, Mar?"

"Aw, same old. But I can't tell you how good it is to see you back here." She moves closer and whispers, "Ada's been annoying as shit these last few weeks, trying to imitate you, but she can't pull it off."

Nora chuckles, spitting glee onto Marian's floral-print blouse.

"Would you believe she's got some kind of talking feather that she wants us to use at the meetings now—problem is, no one can keep up with the topic if we can't cut in with an important thought when it happens. We're a bunch of old ladies with no memory—we all forget what we wanted to say by the time that ridiculous feather comes our way and by the end of it, nothing gets done. We just sit and stare at each other. And eat."

"Hmmmm. Not a bad idea, though. There is a lot of interrupting that goes on here."

"Oh Nora, you know we don't work that way. We tossed Robert's Rules out the window long ago and everything goes just as smooth as pudding when you're around. Takes a good leader, though."

Nora beams, then demurs. "Well I don't know if anyone wants that anymore, to be honest. I still don't know what happened at that fiasco of a funeral."

Marian sighs. "Nobody does, Nora. As soon as it was over we all just pretended everything was normal. No one knows how to talk about these things."

"We have to talk about it."

"The meeting's tonight. Are you coming?"

"I don't know."

"Nora, we need you. Truly."

Music to her ears. Of course Nora is well aware that the meeting is tonight. She's been waiting for it, but she needs to make a few things clear if they are going to move ahead with the vision she has in mind.

WORD MUST HAVE GOTTEN OUT that Nora would be at the meeting, because everyone has gone all out—Marian's made her special butter tarts, Loni has on her best ruffled blouse, and Ada even brought that godawful expensive coffee that her niece brings in from the city—tastes like burnt mud. Anyway, on some level Nora is relieved. She sets out her notes and makes neat little piles in order of importance. She has a month of talking points she's busied herself with writing down, and she intends to be here until every last item is addressed.

She faces the group. "I'd like to call this meeting to order."

They all turn her way. Barbara rushes in and flops her coat onto the back of a seat. "Sorry... bloody cat took off again."

"Since Ada has been filling in for the past month I think it's appropriate she start us off."

Ada smiles and grows a few inches taller with the recognition. She has a tidy stack of notes written in perfect cursive, ever proud of her elementary school penmanship awards. She announces the profits from a recent bake sale, and asks Loni to give the secretary's update. No talking feather yet. Nora sits back and listens. When Ada is finished with the upcoming events schedule, listing who is to do what, there is a bit of silence. Nora takes the opportunity.

"I'd like to talk about the funeral."

Barbara pushes back from the table. "Here we go."

Ada: "Not much to say, Nora. We never saw those folks again."

Loni: "Hold on. I'd like to talk about a few things, too. We have a respectable town."

Marian: "...can't hear a goddamn thing."

A roomful of chickens, everyone talking at the same time as usual, no one hearing what the other is saying.

"Alright. Enough. I'm starting." Nora takes a breath and reads out item number one. By the time she's reached item thirty-four the room has fallen into its usual submission and the committee for funeral conduct has been formed. Nora is back.

KATE

SHE BORROWS KRIS'S TRUCK to take it all away, every last item boxed and marked "books," "clothing," or "misc." She removes them, finally. Now there won't be a reason for anyone to come back. This is her home now. She's figured out where her body lives; maybe now she can discover her place inside of it.

As the old pickup winds down the dirt road toward her home she's surprised to notice the flag is up on the mailbox. It's been awhile since anyone's written. She feels a chilled poke of alarm. Part of her has been waiting for the intruder to come back, she realizes. She parks the truck, slowly walks over, and slips a sleek envelope out of the mailbox. Inside, an invitation. Folded within it is a letter.

> Kate,
>   I have given you space. Rachel said this was what you needed. I have tried very hard to respect this. To be honest, I wasn't sure if I wanted to send this or not, but the thought of you not being at my wedding makes me feel horrible. If I can find it in myself to give you the respect you need, maybe you can find it in yourself to do the same for me. If not, I won't trouble you again.
>   Nicole

Artifice. How grand of Nicole to "give her space." Kate

crumples the letter and tosses it into the recycling. She leaves the invitation on the counter and continues to load boxes into the back of the truck.

At one time, there hadn't been a day's space between their calls, but over the last few months Kate has given very little thought to Nicole. When Jeff first died everything about her had become suddenly and inexplicably superficial: hair, restaurants, the latest device nobody else had. Kate couldn't even dredge up a morsel of concern about any of it, couldn't swim in waters so shallow when she was barely able to breathe on land. Now she's missed the flowering of Nicole's relationship to its inevitable climax and all of the conversations that would have happened in the meantime. This is what really angers Nicole, Kate figures, the lack of attention. She has other friends of course, but none of them were as readily available as Kate was.

This is an ultimatum, thoughtfully crafted with guilt-inducing words, as though their experiences were equivalent. Nicole is putting her in a place where she'll now have to grovel, apologize, make excuses for her abandonment. She picks up a box waiting on the front porch. No way will she go to that wedding.

The old Ford bumps over gravel and snapped twigs that had fallen during the nighttime windstorms. It's crisp and sunny, an Arctic front having swooped down through the coast, turning it into a refrigerator. It's dipped below zero, and although there's no sign of precipitation, snow is expected in the next few days. Waning sunlight pulls an orange hue out of the bark of the cedar trees as Kate pushes the gas pedal tentatively. The truck slowly obeys, moving up toward the main road. She turns left where the driveway meets pavement and continues along the upward curves.

Her head buzzes with the notion that soon so much of Jeff and his family will be gone. She's convinced that peoples' energies cling to their stuff, and has felt the slip of Jeff and his parents' presence in and out of the cabin since the day she arrived there. With this removal, she is exorcising them, and along with them, the spirits of other people she's unwittingly absorbed in through her pores. No wonder she's had trouble locating her own thoughts. Too much of other people in her, Nicole especially. But she had to admit that she'd invited her in, far enough to take up residence and authority over her choices and opinions. Kate wasn't just disillusioned with Nicole, she was most deeply disappointed in herself. *Fuck that. What is a friend supposed to be?* Kate doesn't even know where others end and she begins.

Luke said he'd meet her to help with the boxes. She'd seen him at the Wellspring when she'd asked Kris for the truck. For some reason Kate has begun to feel a bit of silly light-heartedness when she thinks of him. She chides herself for being adolescent, but some miniscule part of her deep inside is stretching and yawning, waking up—to what she isn't sure; it's just a stirring. She starts to reason herself out of it. Levity feels wrong— but there is no need for reason. Her old friend guilt is swift to arrive, a mud-coloured cloud that filters in, spreads itself out and settles into the upper part of her chest. It has a familiar home in her body, but Kate is beginning to realize that to continue this way is to continue in a kind of living death, to sentence herself to a form of purgatory she'd unwittingly shamed herself into.

He is already there, talking to James, the owner of the free store. James's concept is a sort of permanent swap meet that feeds the spirit of sustainability on the island. He'll take every-thing you bring, if it's in decent enough condition, and believes that every item will eventually find its rightful owner. Nothing costs a penny of course, and it's okay just to shop, even if you have nothing to exchange. For the papers, he has a shredder.

"Kate. Your hair is longer."

"Hi, James." She hugs him. She hasn't seen him since the summer before, when she helped Mike and Jeff lug a cord of firewood up to James's place. Mike had just taken down a spruce that was weakening, losing branches, and threatening to tumble down onto the cabin in the coming cold season.

James and his wife Leanne live off-grid. Their only income is what she brings home as a checkout clerk at the grocery store. They are always grateful for these kinds of donations.

"You doing okay?"

She wills a smile. "I'm fine. It's nice to be here."

"Come visit us sometime."

"I will."

Luke shows up, but gives her space, pretending to busy himself moving boxes around James's garage, making room for Kate's things.

"James, if there's anything you want…. There's a box of photos."

He points to his head. "I keep the memories here."

Kate is relieved. She hasn't taken the time to go through the items carefully. It's only occurred to her now that someone else might want them. She just wants them gone.

They grab boxes and walk them over to Luke, who takes Kate's and puts it on the floor, straightening up to enfold her in his arms, and then pulling back to study her face. His eyes are so bright today. A shade of green she's never seen before— almost amphibious. She marvels for a moment at how guileless he is, almost naïvely so for someone in his mid-thirties. It's all up-front with Luke; there is nothing lurking, murky and disturbed behind these eyes. But he's not simple-minded, either. He moves around her with careful intuition, makes space for her. This is all such bizarre terrain. Luke is not the kind of masculine she knows.

"Ready?" he asks.

Kate feels her previously pinched face soften. She goes back to offloading boxes. With each one she removes a stone from the pile that sits on top of her chest.

IT DOESN'T TAKE THEM LONG, but the light is already waning when they finish.

"Want to go for a spin?" Luke asks.

"Okay, but can you drive? I'm exhausted."

"Let's go up Porter Road."

Kate settles into the passenger seat as Luke wends the truck along the rising ribbon of road. Something soft and folky plays on the radio as the trees begin to thin and she looks out over the ocean. It is a beautiful place if you allow yourself to admit it, albeit rugged and unforgiving at times. She's lived on the west coast all her life, and yet has only recently caught a few glimpses of how extraordinary it is, especially on rare days when the sun shines through an approaching winter. Far below them, she can see the crags of rock that tumble out to meet splashing waves, and every now and then a beam of sun throws a spotlight onto one of them, allowing it to assert its presence, if only for a moment. They drive on in silence, Luke in earnest concentration, Kate trusting him, despite his dubious sailing skills.

At the top of the hill he parks the truck and jumps out to open her door. She stretches and slides down, taking his arm. She walks to the viewpoint and takes in the 360-degree expanse of island: hills of varying sizes appear carpeted in green, rumbling about the lower-lying areas. The ferry is docked at the terminal, loading passengers for the last run of the day. Islands both small and large scatter off in all directions, as though they'd been tossed like skipping rocks, following the coast until they lose track of themselves and continuing somewhere distant, out of sight. Each island looks like a different sort of possibility to Kate. Each island is its own distinct place, with its own people, plants, animals, culture. Islands can contain, hold, insulate, gestate.

"Want to walk a bit?" Luke kicks stones, looking around for a trail.

"Yeah."

The switchback meanders down along the face of a cliff. "I remember this spot." Kate pauses at a familiar plaque. Luke waits for her to continue.

"I came here with my dad and sister once. My mom was at a conference for the Women of the Moose."

"What's that?"

"Like a club. My mom likes to be a part of running things."

"Go on."

She laughs. "I don't think he had a clue what to do with us. I was eleven and Rachel was nine. We had a day off school. He drove south on the highway from North Wailaish and then all of a sudden he turned off toward the ferry terminal."

Luke continued to listen.

"We somehow made the boat and ended up here. We hardly said two words to each other most of the day..

"Do you get along with your dad?"

"For the most part, but he isn't a talkative guy, apart from the odd rant. Doesn't have much opportunity, I guess."

Luke sits down on a giant rock, grabs a nearby stick and starts drawing in the soil. Kate sits next to him. It looks as though, if they wanted to, they could lean forward and roll down the hill, plunge into ocean.

"Can I ask you something?"

"Sure."

He looks at her, then down again at the soil. "I don't want you to think I'm prying or anything, I just, well, have started to care about you—quite a bit, actually." He looks away again.

Kate wonders how it is possible to feel dread and elation at the same time. The question has already been articulated, even though he hasn't said a word.

"What happened to your husband?"

She's silent for a few heartbeats, then it comes in one breath. "He and his parents died together in a car accident."

He takes her hand, warming it. "I can't imagine."

"No."

"And then you came here?"

"Shortly after."

"How long has it been?"

"Almost a year now."

He is silent for what seems to be a long while. Then, "Where were you when it happened?"

"I was driving."

IVY

TWO WEEKS AFTER their argument, Ivy still hasn't seen Emilio. *That must be it*, she thinks, and strains her thoughts toward the future, counts herself lucky to have experienced what she has and having emerged relatively unscathed from it. But she can't stop thinking about what Emilio said, about how frivolous and cavalier she is, and how she's been so focused on herself she hasn't even considered his experience. It's all been about her, really. For the first time, she wonders about his everyday life and who is in it, feeling guilty for not having given much thought to it before. He isn't much older than she is, but Ivy senses he's seen a lot more. What she knows about him she knows through poetry, José Marti's, in particular. Like most Cubans, he is supportive of the independence movement. His sentiments are anticolonial. This is why the homes of outsiders constructed on Cuban soil fail to impress him. She chides herself for being so preoccupied with his body that she'd missed really looking into his mind, his soul—seeing him as a person, not just a partner for fun. While they both come from islands, she is far more isolated, far more naïve, as Oma had rightfully noted.

Two weeks later he turns up at the swimming hole. He walks over to where Ivy sits with Mark and Maureen and holds out a hand. "Ivy…" Mark begins.

"Just help me this once," Ivy asks, a slight whine in her voice. "Please."

"I hate lying."

"I'm not asking you to lie. Just please, don't say anything."

Maureen shoots Emilio a dark look, which he ignores. Ivy picks up her belongings, wraps a sarong around her waist, and follows him to his horse.

AS THEY RIDE TOWARD TOWN, she's careful not to bring up any of their previous conversation, supposing, or at least hoping he's gotten over it.

They are building an enormous prison just outside Nueva Gerona, and Emilio is enthralled by the construction. "The buildings are circles," he says, making rotating gestures with his arms. "And there is something in the middle of each one. I guess a watchtower. I think they will put the rooms, what do you call them..."

"Cells?"

"Yes, they will put the cells around the inside walls, and the guards will be able to see everyone, all the time."

They cross town on horseback, trying not to watch the turning heads and the expressions not just on the expats' faces but on the locals' as well. Ivy is being bold now; her parents could arrive anytime.

Oma and Opa had demanded that she not see Emilio anymore. They'd finally confronted her as a team one night at dinner. "We asked your parents to come here because you don't know what you're doing."

Ivy stiffened. "What do you mean?"

"You are here to work, to have an experience with your grandparents, not to run around with Cuban boys." Oma thumped a thick fist on the table.

"I'm not running around with boys. I have a friend."

"Again, you think I am stupid? You are making a big mistake."

"So, what's wrong here? What if I have a date or two?"

"This is not dating, this sneaking around. You'll end up in trouble, mark my words."

Ivy had become used to Oma's opinion, but Opa's support of it made it feel more potent, even though he had tried to soften the tension. His gentleness made her feel worse than Oma's calling her stupid had.

"Ivy, we are responsible for you. You are young and far from home. This is a small place, you don't understand the way things work around here," he'd told her.

But the rebellious pulse within her would not subside. "So you call my parents instead of having a reasonable, adult conversation with me?"

"I'm not a young man, Ivy. To be honest, I don't know how to deal with this."

"You don't have to deal with anything. I'm mature enough to handle my own life."

"That's exactly what concerns us."

Opa didn't speak to her much after that, he just slumped around looking defeated. She couldn't pretend it was all okay anymore—all she could do was get every experience, every desire that she could out of her system in the short time she had left. There wouldn't be another opportunity, she'd blown this one completely. She felt lucky Emilio still wanted to see her. It was at this point that she fully embodied her rebellion.

THE CONSTRUCTION WORKERS don't appear to like them around, but Ivy and Emilio stay far back enough to be out of their way. The prison is a massive undertaking at the foot of the hills outside of town, not too far from the beach. Emilio says that they are modelling the prison after an existing one in Illinois. Most of the buildings are circular, as he'd mentioned. Roads are also under construction.

"You see this?" Emilio points to some excavation going on around the periphery of the complex.

"What is it? Security?"

"No, my cousin is working here. He told me that it's to take away the...excretions?"

"A little river of shit."

"Exactly."

He changes the subject. "Do you know of Evangelina Cisneros?"

"No," she answers.

"She is my first love. The queen of the rebellion. She is the Joan of Arc of Cuba."

"What happened to her?"

"She was in prison. The newspapers of the United States tried to pressure the government to release her but she'd already done too much for the independence, for the rebels. They were going to try her."

"Did they?"

"No. It was very dramatic. Some Americans broke into prison and took her away to the United States. She became free, got married, lived a long life."

Ivy turns to look at him. "Why don't you hate me for being a part of what threatens the independence of Cuba?"

His eyes are downcast. "It is no use to hate. I am glad to know you, to know you are good. It is politicians and military that cause these problems."

"We don't have much time," she says.

She senses that they've said the things they needed to say, that the argument is not erased but understood, so they easily busy themselves with the thing that interests them most. They ride up into the forested mountains and put a blanket down in a clearing. Emilio helps Ivy down from the horse and brings her into his arms. They stand like that, devouring each other's mouths and moving their hands all over one another, teasing and teasing until they can no longer wait. Ivy doesn't think that it will be their last time, but they still come together as though their bodies know it is.

A WEEK LATER SHE ARRIVES HOME from work to the stony facade of her mother, father, and younger sister Eve sitting in the living room. Oma is with them, and all three stand up when Ivy walks in. She doesn't know that Opa has already been ousted from the conversation. Ivy is shocked, but at the same time unsurprised. She had felt them getting closer. Her mother moves first, puts her arms around her daughter.

"It's so good to see you."

Her father walks up behind them and places a hand on her mother's shoulder. "We have a great deal to talk about. Go wash your hands and come to the table."

Already she feels her defences crumbling. Does the dynamic of a parent and child always remain the same? Do the beginnings of adulthood not account for anything? She's spent weeks in imaginary conversations with her parents, and although she knew that she had idealized the outcome of these conversations and over-inflated her ability to deflect their arguments, she is surprised at how the mere presence of them, her father especially, pierces through almost all of the confidence she's attempted to cultivate. As always, he undoes her.

At the dinner table, Ivy listens. They speak.

Her father: "We will be here together for two months. During that time you will write your already late university applications under my guidance. We will work on getting you admitted for next year. When you are not working on those, you will be helping with chores on the farm. You will be under the constant supervision of either your mother or I. You will go nowhere without us, at any time."

Her mother: "You have given your grandparents enough trouble. For this month we will work on getting you back on track. You've wasted enough time and now you'll learn to behave like an adult."

The speeches have been well rehearsed. Ivy doesn't stand a chance. As it has always been, nothing real has ever come up in her conversations with them—nothing is mentioned of Emilio, of who he is or how either of them feels. Ivy wonders if indeed, outside of anger, self-righteousness, and the need to control, anyone here feels anything at all. She sends a hateful glare to her father and stomps off to her room.

Eve follows her, shuts the door behind them. "Ivy, what is going on?"

Ivy releases the anger, hands it all to her sister. "Am I owned? Am I his possession now, until I can be handed over to some other man, to be owned yet again? Am I a slave?"

Eve stands silent, knows better than to interrupt Ivy's anger.

Ivy pulls the pillows off her bed and throws them onto the floor. "He can follow me to the ends of the earth if he wants, but there is no goddamn way I'm living my life in his prison."

NORA

CHRISTMAS IS HER FAVOURITE time of year. Nora heaves box after box out of the garage while Ed barks instructions from his perch at the kitchen table. "That one doesn't go in the kitchen. Put it in the living room. And don't forget the extension cords. I'm not putting anything up until you find them all."

"Shut up, Ed."

"You want me to help you or not?

"Helping would involve getting out of your chair and actually carrying some of these boxes."

"This is your stuff. I have no idea which boxes have what in them."

"You would if you'd be more involved."

"You know what, Nora? I'm done." He storms out of the room, leaving Nora to decorate on her own. He won't feel any guilt or shame about his wife climbing all over the house stringing lights and plopping reindeer on the lawn. How can he be expected to do any of the work when she speaks to him so disrespectfully? It's a familiar pattern. He will feign injury and not speak to her for days. Nothing will be said, at least not by him, about how Nora does everything.

All of this is fine by her. Let him sulk. She gave up on trying to set things right between them a long, long time ago. In fact, she prefers it this way—on her own she can think clearly and arrange things just the way she likes them.

She turns on the all-Christmas music station and pulls the

decorations from the box. There's something inherently pleasant about this task alone. Everything she touches holds a memory, the faint warmth of small fingertips. The papier-maché snowman Kate made in grade two, the garland embellished with pinecones she and the girls had collected from the tree just down the road, the box of bedazzled Christmas sweatshirts with cavorting kittens on them—one for each member of the family. They have a tradition of taking an annual photo wearing these sweatshirts. The girls think they're incredibly tacky and always make a big show of posing in exaggerated ways. Nora doesn't mind them so much. They were made by her Aunt Charlotte who passed away three years ago.

She pulls out a few pinecones, wishing Ed was still in the room so she could throw them at his head. *Asshole. He's already ruining the first opportunity for all four of them to be together in a long time.* Last year Rachel was in Europe. It was the first time she'd missed Christmas at home and Nora could hardly stand it. Rachel had always been there, every year without fail. Kate was married at twenty-three and had been dating Jeff since high school, so Nora was used to sharing her with Jeff's family, but Rachel was on her own and it felt so wrong to not have her with them. She remembers her hollow little voice on the end of line, calling from some train station in Belgium. *Doesn't Ed feel any of this? Why can't he get excited too? Would a little nostalgia kill him?*

"Don't mind me, I'll just get the ladder myself!" she shouts to the vacant room.

Despite his curmudgeonliness, Nora knows that having both girls home will cheer Ed up. There is the shadow of Kate's loss to consider—it will be her first Christmas without Jeff and his family—but Nora feels sure that her attentiveness, her cooking, and visits to family and friends, will ease Kate's pain, or at the very least distract her. Nora doesn't know how to talk to Kate about Jeff. She'd always felt distanced from him, looked down on somehow. His parents were real-estate agents who

KATE

LATE IN THE EVENING Kate sits at the end of the dock, a thick, velour blanket coating her shoulders and torso, a mug of earthy green tea in her hands. Every now and again a chilly substance surges up her spine. She'd told him. Outside of her family and friends back home, he is the first to know.

She unfurls her legs and lets her feet fall into the frigid water. They feel weighted, gravity and water pulling them in and down. Sucking in her breath, she releases the blanket and slides the rest of her body into the ocean, letting go, submerging as far as her weight will carry her. She used to do this as a child, trusting the ocean to be wiser than her, trusting the creatures below to be benign and accommodating in the unseen depths that were beyond interpretation. She tries to close her mind, tries to feel everything, to expel the numbness, to welcome the stabs of cold and heavy darkness without resistance.

She imagines that down below her, the rocky ocean floor sees a white body plunge through the bubbled murk, falling. Its place will always be far below on the other side, in silence. Although the earth pulls, the water between them will be kind enough to raise her up again. If she wants it to.

Her lungs contract; her heart seems to stop for a moment and then begins to knock hard at her chest. Every pore screams. She shoots up out of the water and scrambles back onto the dock and into the embrace of her blanket, shaking. And *what of it?* she asks herself. Why shouldn't she let her body take some of the pain, instead of her mind for a change? She takes a big gulp of tea. Her shoulders and teeth begin to rattle, but she doesn't want to go back to the cabin. Every moment of torment feels deserved. Kate is seized with the urge to spread her mind's agony throughout her body. *It should feel like this.*

She heaves herself off the dock and whisks back into the cabin, moving as quickly as she can while peeling off drenched clothing, her body rigid with cold. She shuts the door and opens the woodstove to stoke the fire. She'd told him. He'd said nothing as she talked about that night. New Year's. How drunk Mike and Ann were, how warm and loving they'd been toward her, how she'd have done anything to please, to finally be enfolded, deserving. She'd caught the tossed keys easily. She'd had almost nothing to drink, ever watchful around Mike's raptor eyes.

It had taken a while to find Jeff. He was texting in a corner, agitated. He didn't hesitate when his parents said it was time. Kate remembers smelling the residue of pot.

She didn't try hard enough to get them to wait out the storm, to ask their hosts to let them crash on the couch. "I really need to get back to my hotel room," Ann had said. "I need my space."

Kate obliged and sat behind the wheel. The rest she still couldn't let her mind's eye watch. So little remembered, to be truthful. And memory is not a thing to be trusted, at least not hers.

It was an accident. Luke had finally said.

If things hadn't been so bad leading up to that moment, she might have believed him.

She isn't sure how long she sits with the unfathomable before falling asleep among the cushions of her sofa.

IN THE MORNING, SHE SETS OUT for Ivy's place. It's grey and damp. Nothing out of the ordinary, even though she felt otherworldly. It was a mistake to think that she had made progress with all of this. Rather, she finds herself sinking back into this sense of self-flagellation, that she's not yet been punished enough. She's not sure how she can get through the day. Has she revealed too much to someone she shouldn't have? How is Luke supposed to understand what it was like to grow up where she did? How could he relate to the culture, the expectations?

"There's some stuff in the freezer if you don't feel like cooking." Nancy makes trips to and from her bedroom to retrieve forgotten things. A small, overstuffed backpack perches on a chair in the kitchen. She tosses an apple into it and it falls on the floor.

"Have a great time," Kate says.

"Thanks. I'm a bit nervous."

"It'll be relaxing. And you don't need to worry about anything here."

"I know. She's asleep right now, but she'll want to read when she wakes up. In fact, that's all she wants to do when she's not sleeping. But I don't need to tell you that."

After Nancy leaves, Kate busies herself with keeping the fire going. She stuffs a Pres-To-Log into Ivy's fireplace, lighting and poking at it with a stick as it begins to pop and spit. She's always thought of fireplaces as portals. She wonders if she can see the outlines of Jeff's and his parents' faces in the licking flames, pointing their burning fingers at her.

IVY

EVE FINDS A SCORPION in her shoe. Fortunately, Opa taught the new arrivals about shaking their shoes out every morning, and the thing scuttles away in the wake of their screams.

Eve and Ivy fold laundry in the living room, while Oma and their mother prepare dinner. Out the window Ivy can see her father and Opa bringing the animals into the barn. This is as alone as she's been in a week and it feels like she's losing her mind, taking furtive refuge in corners, reading or drawing, her face tickled by cobwebs.

Where is Emilio?

Eve puts down a shirt and looks at Ivy, sitting backgrounded by Oma's collection of Hümmel dolls with their chubby, bloated, eternal blushes and leiderhosen.

"That *thing* this morning. It was the most disgusting creature I've ever seen."

"I think you're kind of lucky. I've been looking for one ever since I got here."

"You know they're dangerous, don't you?"

"Of course. But most supposedly 'dangerous' creatures think of us as more so."

"You must have been having quite a time, Ivy."

Ivy looks at Eve's querying eyes, so much bluer and softer than hers. Her features tiny and gentle; she is definitely the pretty one.

"What's on your mind?"

"I'm wondering why I'm here, for starters."

"I don't think you had much choice."

"You know what I mean. What have you been up to to make Papa so mad?"

"They didn't tell you anything?"

"No. Just whispering. The word 'judgment' comes up a lot."

Ivy grins, in spite of her annoyance. Of course. It's *her* judgment that's off. Theirs is completely intact.

"Let's just say I swam with a crocodile."

Eve sneers at her and brushes a drip of sweat from her forehead. The air itself is liquid. It's too hot for her here, but Ivy has acclimatized.

An idea. "Would you like to go swimming?" Ivy asks her.

"That would be so great. Papa will never let us, though."

"Maybe if he comes too…"

"Yes. Ask him."

"You know you're the one who has to ask," Ivy says.

"Right."

It is an even more sweltering day than usual, so it actually doesn't take much to convince Papa to go to the swimming hole. They all sit together on the high bank. Nobody else is there. Opa dives straight into the water.

"I make a big splash and scare the crocodiles," he shouts back to the group, grinning. Papa doesn't laugh, but Ivy loves her grandfather in that moment.

Eve looks wary. "They're scared of us, right?"

Opa laughs. "Only of your sister's voice!"

"Opa, be serious. We're talking about crocodiles."

"Don't worry."

Eve wears her internal conflict high on her forehead, which always seems deeply creased, even at sixteen. A gift from Oma. She slips off her dress and walks tentatively to the water's edge. Ivy resists the urge to scream and frighten her—she's in enough trouble. Instead she runs past Eve and cannonballs straight into the tiny lake.

"Don't be such a girl!" she shouts on the way in.

"You should be more of a girl, Ivy," Eve calls back, but Ivy is already underwater, transported by the waters that separate her from the rest of them.

KATE

SHE CIRCLES OLIVE OIL into a cast iron pan and flicks the ignitor. When it warms she adds pressed garlic, breathing in the aroma as the paste sizzles and turns white, seasoning the pan. To this she adds chopped shallots, celery, peppers, and finally mushrooms. When the vegetables begin to caramelize and stick to the bottom, she deglazes the pan with some sherry. Kate can make bolognese with her eyes closed.

Luke is coming for dinner, but Kate's mind is absent, already travelling home to North Wailaish. She knows that when she gets there more of her childhood will return, unbidden. She remembers the summers when she, Rachel, and a few friends would take the five-minute ferry ride over to Juniper Island, to the Mariner Pub, where the food consisted of unrecognizable deep-fried meat nuggets and you could fish through a hole in the dock while dining and drinking beer. Some days they'd hike around the island alone, find their favourite hidden bay, and sit watching diamonds scatter across the water's surface, eventually splitting its perfection as they entered the frigid shock. They'd walk in the cool forest, run along the lagoon, and eat ice cream. As a family, they'd sometimes visit Shipstead Beach, home to an annual sandcastle competition, where the tide retreated for miles, scattering sand dollars. A few years ago, Kate went back and couldn't find a single one. *Where they had gone—red tide?* The sand dollars may have disappeared, but here on Brittania she can still step on clam and geoduck airholes in the hope that they might squirt out a stream of water, tickling her feet in that strange way.

Ed always wanted them to watch him swim. Nora, Rachel, and Kate would marvel at how long he could hold his breath. Kate liked to be melodramatic and imagine how the trajectory of their lives would twist and turn tragically if he never resurfaced. He would disappear underwater for impossible lengths of time, eventually surfacing with a whale-like exhalation. While he plunged down into darkness, twelve-year-old Kate thought about how hard she'd cry at his funeral, wondered who would give the eulogy. Edgar, she supposed. She wondered how poor they'd be with only Nora's salary. Just as these thoughts began to lift bubbles of increasing panic in her chest, he would skim beneath their feet, his aqualine shape resembling something other than human as he'd tug at their legs, willing them to play underwater with him.

Nora would go to the beach, but she would never swim. She would eat chips and turkey sandwiches and take pictures of her daughters drenched in sea, sitting astride floating logs, pretending that they were riding horses in the bobbing waves. Together they would watch dusk cast thick golden beams over the water's surface and let their eyes follow kayaks as they disappeared across the inlet. Kate would jump from rock to rock looking for kelp. She would remember that the ocean was capricious and engulfing. She would sense its evasive rhythms and remain suspicious of its motives. And she'd wonder how she ever got herself into that water. It's much too cold now.

Despite her previous mood she admits that there is a buoyancy beginning to enter her. The absence of Jeff and his family's possessions has had the effect of expanding the space of the cabin, allowing breath and light into corners previously stacked with books, opening wall space that she covers with vivid abstracts she finds at the market and the free store. Most of what lingered in their clothing, in the drapes, the rug, on the walls, is gone, having flown out along with the dust motes she's pushed out the windows. She considers Ivy's comments about the invisible parts of themselves people leave in their belongings, and the ways in which everything they've touched seems altered. For someone to die completely there must be nothing left behind of their touch, their smell, their energy. No dust. She knows that this is impossible. *Maybe we never completely die. We are neither created nor destroyed....* Still, she is determined to scrub away as much spectral residue as possible.

Over the weeks she'd started moving the furniture around, and the place has begun to feel like a home of her own. Inviting Luke over even feels okay, rather like a seamless reciprocity of the generosity he's extended to her over the past few weeks. A thank you of sorts. She's not only stopped comparing Luke to Jeff, but, more importantly, she's also stopped looking for hints of similarity between the two. The past is beginning to leave. This is not replacement.

Luke is appreciative of her dormant culinary skills. As they sip glasses of cabernet on the sofa he stretches and moans a little. "Best sauce I've ever had. What's your secret?"

She pulls a hair off her sweater. "Attentiveness."

"Makes sense."

"You can't let the garlic burn. Ever."

His eyes look huge. He doesn't appear to be blinking. "No. Of course not."

She looks at his lanky legs stretched from the sofa into the middle of the small room. He looks as though he might slide right onto the floor and fall asleep.

"Do you have any objection to scented candles?" she asks him.

"I feel strongly about some things, but not so much scented candles."

She flicks a match and joins its flame to a stubby, wooden wick.

He slides onto the floor as predicted, and places his glass on the coffee table. "Come."

She feels something rise up between them, filling the room,

and hesitates. Slowly, she kneels on the floor and moves closer to him. The arm he places around her shoulders has the momentary effect of melting her conflicted mind, and kissing him is the closest she's come to forgetting.

But she pulls away, stiffening. "This feels wrong."

Luke looks hurt for a moment.

"I don't mean that," she says. "I'm ... sometimes I feel like I'm still married."

"I don't want to push you," he says.

"Can we just sit here?" she asks, moving back beneath his arm, resting her head on his shoulder.

"As long as you want."

He's still there the next morning. He'd spent the night in her bed, fully clothed. Kate slept peacefully in the crook of him until about four in the morning, when her mind began to dance with imaginary conversations. What others would think. Christmas was not far off, and she promised her mother she'd come home. She wants this little world to stay sealed away. But maybe she isn't being fair to Luke. Maybe she isn't emotionally available; maybe she's too complicated, too used up to burden him with her troubles. All of these excuses echo the vernacular of the many self-help books she's indulged in since Jeff died, clichés and all. She stares at Luke as he sleeps and he looks so impossibly *good*. He is patient with her; he seems capable of none of the anger she's seen in so many of the men in her life. It isn't that he doesn't have his own 'stuff' —in fact she realizes how little she knows about him—it's just that, even without saying anything, he calms the pointless chatter in her head. She trusts him.

He opens one eye and notices her staring. He smiles, seems to enjoy the attention. Kate feels a wash of embarrassment and takes her gaze to the window.

"How long have you been up?" he asks.

"Not long."

"I wasn't doing anything embarrassing, was I?"

"No, I'm just not sure who Isabel is."

"What?"

"You were calling her name."

He pauses, then notices her grin. "Was not."

He pulls her close and rolls over her, sinking deep kisses into her body until her mind finally lets go.

"I'VE ALWAYS FELT A KINSHIP with Virginia Woolf." Ivy picks at her chicken.

"How so?"

"Well, she wrote *To the Lighthouse* in 1926. That was a big year for me."

"In what way?"

"Have you ever known anyone that can inhabit the world of the living and that of the dead simultaneously?" Kate was getting used to Ivy's style of conversation. You have to wait for her thoughts to present themselves. Asking what she means is usually moot.

"Not really."

"But that's what she does, doesn't she? That's why people are afraid to read her books—they can sense this. She was unafraid of the things we refuse to talk about.

"Can't say I blame them."

"You have to get over that, Kate. The only literature worth reading is the kind that comes close to killing you a bit at a time. The kind that tells the truth. Life is a marriage of pain and happiness. Together they make joy, if you can see it."

"How do you know *truth*?"

"You feel it. It's a visceral thing."

Kate stabs a piece of broccoli. "Isn't it important to keep some things to yourself. Let the dead be dead?"

"Death is an inevitability. So what? Just be honest. You have to look straight into it. Life and death are better friends with each other than you think."

"Have you done this, Ivy?"

"A very long time ago."

"And you didn't get depressed?"

"Maybe. I'd still encourage it, though."

"I slept with Luke last night."

Ivy sprouts an enormous grin. "You have no idea how happy this makes me."

"Don't get too excited. I'm leaving for North Wailaish soon."

"You'll see him again? Before you go?"

"I guess so."

IVY

I T'S LIKE BEING STUCK between two worlds. In a way Ivy wishes she could have left the island quickly, instead of staying here and staring out at the dirt paths leading off into adventures she is no longer allowed to have, watching the grapefruit fall brown and sloppy from the trees, and the palms being tickled by invisible breezes, hearing snippets of the percussive churn of *son*, the Afro-Cuban music she's come to love, emanating from doors and windows not open to her. It isn't enough to be able to go swimming from time to time. Perturbed, she tries to fill her days as much as possible with reading, chores, anything. She finished her college applications, sent them off, and neither of her parents will talk about anything other than *plans* and what needs to be done around the farm. She asks if she can go with Opa to the bakery, but they quickly veto that idea as well.

And then one day she wakes up feeling as though she's been travelling on a boat all night long. The sensation is familiar but with a foreign flavour, an internal rocking, and she's horrified to have to run to the outhouse.

Of course, she'd known what might possibly happen. She'd thought of it many times, but when it didn't happen at first she figured that maybe she was one of those people who needn't worry about it, that there was something wrong. This was stupidity of course, with a hefty helping of denial, but Ivy's lease on denial is running short, and her new situation makes itself immediately clear. Eve somehow hears her, even though she's outside. When she comes back to the bed they share Eve stares at her. "Ivy, you're smarter than this."

Ivy gets back under the blankets and rolls over, her back to her sister. Apparently not.

LATER, OPA AND HER FATHER COME BACK from a fishing trip. Ivy sits in the living room with a book, eavesdropping as they shuffle around the kitchen.

"So, did you catch our dinner?" Oma asks.

"Not so much." Opa is chuckling.

Ivy cranes her neck and strains to make sense of her father's mutterings. She hears him pull a bottle out of the cabinet.

"Tell her what you caught," Opa tells her father.

"No need."

"Oh come on, lighten up."

Her father still isn't laughing. "Alright, if I must. It was a gull."

"A bird?" Oma asks.

By now Ivy's head has craned its way around the corner and into the kitchen, but they don't notice her. She sees Opa leaning on the counter, steadying himself against the laughter he can no longer hold in. "That's right.... It was this big." He stretches out his arms and strides past Papa, slapping him on the shoulder. "Let's do it again. Anytime you want to go fishing for birds...." And he continues down the hall to his bedroom, accompanied by what are now loud guffaws.

"It's fitting," Ivy's father says to Oma. "Nothing you go looking for here is as you'd expect it to be."

It is then that Ivy knows he's stopped watching.

Suddenly everything is for naught. Ivy slumps back into her chair, returns to the laundry. What is the point of even trying to resist the definitions already laid out for her? Something else owns her now; even her own body no longer belongs to her. First her father, now this. A chill runs through her. *What will he do when he finds out?* She sees herself cast out, adrift, a person of shame. Her life is ruined, just as Oma said it would be. There is no other way to see it. There will be no freedom for her. The rest of her days will be a struggle, and it's all her fault. She'd been given every opportunity. For the first time since she arrived on La Isla, the veil of unreality begins to lift. Behind it is something too terrifying to look at.

NORA

THEY ALL HOVER at the pocked and weathered pedestal table in Nora's kitchen. Outside, the sun must be sinking, but it's hard to tell beneath the shroud of winter. Nora looks at her husband, hunched over dinner with one eye on the newspaper. She can't remember when the four of them last sat together.

"Mom, I'm sorry but I don't think I can eat this." Rachel holds her fork midair, scrutinizing the meat.

"What's the problem?" Nora sighs. "You told me you weren't a vegetarian anymore. I saw you eat fish at that sushi place."

"It's not that, it's just, it's chicken."

"So?"

"In a quiche."

"Would you care to enlighten me?"

"Just think about it, Mom. The quiche is made with eggs. You know, laid by chickens, and there is chicken meat swimming around in it."

"It's not swimming. I cooked this thing a good fifty minutes, just like the recipe said."

"I'm not talking about the texture. I just can't eat both ends of the life cycle all mixed together in one pie."

"Technically a life cycle has no ends," Kate adds.

Ed throws his fork down. "Would you two just close your mouths and eat what your mother made for you?"

"Never mind." Nora's lips form a tight line. She picks up Rachel's plate and walks it over to the garbage can.

"Mom!"

The quiche slides easily from its plate, and in a quick flash Nora is out the door. She silences the shouted protests quickly, with a slam.

I am not going to cry. She shakes her head and wipes the corners of her eyes. It isn't raining, so unfortunately there are lots of nosy assholes out walking around with nothing better to do than speculate about other people's business. She wonders about the people behind the neighbourhood doors. *Are their kids this ungrateful?* She'll never know. *We all hold our secrets dear.*

It had taken weeks to figure out what to cook for them, and still—this. She thinks about the girls when they were little, how they respected their mother— she'd seen to that. Now neither of them knows how to talk to the other. And they are endlessly changing their minds about things, always on some soapbox or another, then switching to a completely different one in the space of as little as a day.

Is it possible to have nothing at all in common with your kids? she wonders.

As Nora trudges below the sky's deepening grey, an idea starts to squirm inside of her. It has something not unlike delight attached to it. This will not be a typical Christmas.

KATE

KATE AND RACHEL SHRUG their fleece and Gore-Tex wrapped bodies along the path at the lagoon. Kate looks out toward the ubiquitous dark clouds, sagging low over the ocean between here and Vancouver. She kicks an open, barnacle-encrusted oyster shell out of the way and digs her hands deep into her pockets.

"How are you doing these days?" Rachel cuts through the chilly, moist air, a tentative shudder in her voice.

"It's hard to answer that question, Rach."

"It's hard to know what questions to ask."

"Fair enough. I'm good, I suppose. I'm where I need to be."

"Mom thinks you're avoiding everything."

Kate stops to pet a Jack Russell sniffing at her leg. "Yeah, she's pretty obvious about that. She doesn't get it, though. Sometimes it's too much, being at home."

They reach the section of trail that leads up into the bluffs, to the Arbutus and Garry Oak groves that stand vigil above the ledges of rock shearing straight down to ocean. This is one of the first places that Kate and Jeff had snuck off to to have teenage sex. Kate can almost see the skinny apparitions of their bodies, entwined yet confused, suspended high above the surf. The same Arbutus still look on nonchalantly, exfoliating themselves with their incessantly peeling red bark, the occasional assist from a curious child or bored adolescent hastening the smooth display of naked green beneath the furls.

"What might help you move on?"

Kate stops at the top of the first hill and stares out toward the forest ahead. "That's just the problem. Everyone keeps using those words. It's not so straightforward." She pauses. "Sometimes I hardly think of him, and sometimes it's as though all three of them are sitting on me, pinning me down."

Kate sees a modicum of understanding momentarily tease the corners of Rachel's eyes, and then disappear.

"But it can't be healthy to just lock yourself away. You're young,—you have a life.

"What makes you think I'm not living?"

"I don't know. It just doesn't seem right. It's hard to see you like this."

"Doesn't seem right to *you*, hard for *you* to see this. It's not that hard for me."

Rachel stuffs her hands deeper into her pockets. "I don't get it."

"Membership in this club has a very high price tag. I hope you don't get it for a long time."

They reach the end of the short trail. Up ahead stands a long row of colourful shacks. Ed had told the girls that they were Japanese fisherman's cabins, there since before the Second World War, but Rachel has always thought that they were haunted. There are several of them lining the shore, giving it the not-so-original moniker, *Shack Island*.

"Let's go," Kate says, and she starts to cross the small finger of sand leading to the island.

"Idiot. The tide's coming in."

"We have time. I've always wanted to do this."

Rachel follows, cursing. While it's a simple walk toward the cabins, she keeps looking behind to see if the tide has stolen any of their return passage. Kate strides forward until she reaches the first cabin.

"It's so old. Imagine how remote these must have felt during the war."

They both gaze back across the lagoon, at the hills stuffed with houses. Kate rattles a doorknob.

"Come on. We're trespassing," Rachel starts.

"You're such a teacher."

"It's creepy here. Let's go back. This is an island, you know. And there isn't exactly a ferry back to the other side."

"I can't see in the window."

"They're all boarded up. You're not going to see anything."

"I hope you're better than this at encouraging your students' curiosities."

"Fuck, Kate."

She rattles the next doorknob. This one opens. Kate's eyes widen and she raises an eyebrow to Rachel. "Come on."

"No.

Kate shrugs and enters the dark and dust. When her eyes adjust, she sees a table with an assortment of objects on it. She moves closer.

Rachel sticks her head in the door. "What are you doing?"

Kate picks up a small notebook and puts it in her pocket.

Rachel, still outside, shouts to Kate, "The tide! Kate! We have to go *now.*"

Kate turns to see that the tiny spit is indeed narrowing.

"Fine," she admits.

Rachel leads the way back, Kate following reluctantly, wondering about the person who had entered her own cabin, what their reasons for snooping around might have been. She is certain it wasn't idle curiosity.

They run through icy, stinging ocean and undulating pods of bull kelp, now reaching up to their calves. Kate laughs; Rachel invokes every religious being she knows. On the other side, they take off their shoes and socks, squeeze the water out of their jeans. "I'm freezing," Rachel stutters.

"Move quickly."

Rachel stands rigidly, shivering. "You know what? You're so bossy, but you never know what you're doing."

"What's that supposed to mean?"

"Nothing about you is ever practical. You don't live in the real world. You never have."

Kate stops to consider this. "Maybe the problem is more with the 'real world,' as you call it, and not so much with me."

Rachel shakes her head and stomps back toward the trail.

Back in their mother's Taurus, Rachel turns over the engine and moves the heater to its highest temperature. She flips on the fan and cold air blasts their faces.

"Easy. Let it warm up first."

Rachel shoots her a glare and pulls out of the parking lot, rolling the car over crackling gravel. Kate looks back behind them and watches the tiny bay recede. The distant line of red, blue, and green shacks stands unchanged, tethered to memory. She feels a sudden urge to protect them, to preserve their unaltered vigil.

NORA

CHRISTMAS MORNING. Nora is delighted to have kept her girls home for a whole week. After the quiche incident, she resigned herself to simple meals. Even as children her girls had preferred one piece of meat, one heap of rice or potatoes, and one, maybe two vegetables, none of them touching. *Why put in extra effort to make things fancy? Nothing ever changes and maybe that's okay.* Besides, she's got other things to think about. This would be a Christmas that wasn't just about her kids. Or Ed. She shudders with a nervous spasm. How will they react to her plan?

She stokes a small fire in their wood-burning hearth. Last year Ed had tried to convince her to convert it to a gas fireplace but Nora would have none of it, all because of Christmas. Her own childhood memories of Christmas mornings centered around waiting for her father to get the fireplace going. They weren't allowed to open any gifts until the living room had begun to be warmed by the heat of Dad's own creation. She remembered the anticipation bubbling in her as she watched her father scrunch newspaper and light it, offering its flames to ignite the kindling. The moment when Dad would utter, "Okay," and they'd bombard the tree.

Like most kids, Nora's girls used to go into the living room at the ungodliest of hours on Christmas morning. They'd verify that Santa had visited, and race back into her and Ed's room, pulling them from slumber. Ed would pretend to get up, then flop back into bed. He'd tease the girls this way until they squealed with unbearable impatience. It was always about the kids, as it should be. But now things have to change. *We give ourselves over to them, but it can't be forever,* Nora reminds herself. *We have to make sense of ourselves when the kids leave home.*

Back then it all seemed overwhelming. So much shopping and wrapping, so much crap. At the end of the unwrapping Nora's mom used to proclaim, "Another Christmas has come and gone." This would send Kate into paroxysms of protest. "It's not over yet, Grandma!"

Now it's so small, everything reduced to fit their adult lives. Nora looks at the little pile of presents under the tree and tries to remember exactly when it had started to shrink. Even still, she continues to make her sugar cookies and insists that the girls decorate them with her. She still produces more Hello Dolly Squares and Sex in a Pan than can ever be consumed by their family. She usually ends up giving most of it away to neighbours and freezing the rest for council meetings at the Moose Hall.

"Did Santa come?" Rachel shuffles in, stretching and yawning, startling her.

"Of course he did," she answers, nodding at the tree.

Rachel hugs Nora, wishes her Merry Christmas, and heads to the kitchen to make coffee. Nora settles in to enjoy the service of her youngest child. Not all growing up is bad.

Soon after, Kate yawns her way into the living room, then Ed, both already with coffee in hand. Nora pauses a moment to look at the similarities between her husband and daughter. Both tall and stringy, both night owls, both so goddamned moody. Ed, fortunately, loves Christmas and still lets them glimpse a bit of his happier self on these rare mornings.

"Let's do this," he says, clapping and rubbing his hands together.

"Go for it," Nora chimes.

Rachel unwraps a pair of silver hoop earrings, two scented candles, and a gift set of expensive hair products. Kate gets mainly books, including a book of prepaid tickets for B.C. Ferries. Ed gets a book of football statistics, a subscription to a beer-of-the-month club, and a shovel, which he stares at, puzzled.

"And what have we here?" Nora holds a red gift bag.

Ed looks up, "Not from me."

"Me neither," says Kate. "What is it?"

Nora pulls out a layer of tissue, and then an accordion of folded papers. She feigns surprise.

"Well, isn't this something?"

The other three lean over to have a look at the travel documents.

"Looks like I'm heading to Costa Rica," Nora says.

IVY

IVY REMEMBERS some things and not others when it comes to Isla de Piños, but for the rest of her life this particular day slows down to reveal its every detail. She and Eve stand in Oma's kitchen looking out the window, the winds already so strong that objects like tools, hats, and pieces of wood—things normally tethered to earth, building, or person—are flying through the air. Small angular black disks go whirling past the window, resembling miniature, low-flying aircraft. Since that morning everyone has been talking about a cyclone.

"Mama," Eve says, pointing at the disks. "I can't figure out what those things are."

Their mother races to the window and squints. "Oh god. The roofing tiles are coming off. Get under your bed. Ivy, Eve. Go now."

"Is it really a cyclone?" Eve asks.

"Not yet, but it's not safe next to the window. Laurence, I told you to board them!" Her mother screeches at her father, who shoots her an icy look, then heads for the door. Ivy's not sure if it's him or the wind who slams it shut.

"Papa!" Eve shouts.

"Girls, I told you to get under your bed. Now." Their mother's voice hits the low tone that always commands action.

They grab pillows and blankets and slide beneath the bed Ivy had experimented in with Emilio only weeks before. How a room can change so abruptly.

"Ivy, is Papa going to be okay?" Eve asks, suddenly appearing younger than her sixteen years.

"Of course. Papa's strong. The real cyclone isn't even here yet." Ivy feels the need to speak authoritatively, although in truth she doesn't know anything.

"What about the animals? Is Bonita alright?"

"Animals are smart, especially horses. I'm sure she's already found a safe place to wait out the storm. She knows this island better than we do."

"What about the chickens?"

Ivy sighs. "They're fine, Eve. All of the animals are safer than we are, okay?"

"I've never seen winds like that."

"Me neither," Ivy tells her. "I want to watch." She starts to squirm out from under the bed, but Eve grabs her arm, digs her fingernails into Ivy's skin.

"Ouch! What are you doing?"

"Stay here with me."

"I'll be right back. I'm just going to take a quick look."

"Please. Don't leave me here alone."

Ivy scrambles out from under the bed and walks over to the window. Outside, their father strides through tall grass, wearing the expression of a man in search of a place to relieve himself. His dark hair whips around his face as he leans into a wall of wind, squinting and holding one hand to his forehead. A sudden, forceful gust slams into his chest. Ivy gasps at the shock of his vulnerability. She doesn't think she's ever seen him in a state of weakness.

"What? Ivy, what?"

"It's okay," she tells her sister. Papa struggles to walk back to the house, the wind now tearing at his clothing. It looks as though he is trying to wade through thick ocean current as the unseen thing peels his half-opened shirt from his body and sends it flying. Ivy hurries back under the bed. He will never know she saw this.

They hear voices arguing in the kitchen from their place under the guest room bed. Their father has come back inside, their mother chastising him for not having boarded up the windows yet. "Look, your dad's doing it. I have to help next door. Everything's a mess."

Ivy scoots around and sticks her upper torso out from under the bed. Her sister tells her again to come back, but she's stopped listening.

"Is he on his way?" their mother asks.

Ivy hears Oma's voice. "Don't worry. We've been through this before. Your father knows what he's doing."

"What about the windows?"

"He's getting more boards from the Freisens. He'll likely bring back a few of them, too."

"Windows?"

"Neighbours."

There is a sound of barn doors slamming and an increasing roar of wind. The weather is angry at everyone and everything. Ivy is enthralled by how well air can mimic the sound of ocean.

"Why, Mother? Do we have enough resources for everyone here?"

"We can't think like that at these times."

"Ivy, what's going on?" Eve calls.

"They're arguing about Opa. He might bring some people here."

"Who?"

"Shhhh."

The voices drop away then. Ivy's not sure where they've gone. The living room? Under their own beds? She hates that nobody is telling them anything. Eve's blue eyes are enormous, full of alarm. "How long do you think it will last?"

"I'm not sure."

"Do you think the roof will come off?"

"Not here. I've heard Opa bragging that his house is one of the strongest in Santa Barbara."

"What about the other people? The ones we passed on the way out of the port? Some of them were living in shacks."

It occurs to Ivy how sheltered Eve is, how sheltered she was too, before coming here. "Let's hope that they find their way somewhere else."

"But how could they? There was hardly any warning."

At that moment Oma comes into the room. She puts a lantern on the floor next to their bed.

"Oma, will you stay here?" Eve's voice is plaintive and sing-songy. Ivy detests this.

"I can't. Opa will be back soon and I need to help him. We all have to stay in the safest places. You stay here until I come and get you. Don't go near the window."

A pause. "Ivy? Are you still there?"

"Of course."

"Don't do anything foolish."

Ivy sighs. Do they think she's that stupid? They are not so off-track in a sense, though. All she can think about is Emilio. Where is he? She's never even seen his home. Will he be okay? What about his family? She wishes he would come here, just to show he's alright, although her father would kill him.

"Ivy, what's she talking about?"

"Tell you later."

"I've pretty much put it together myself. Who is he?"

Ivy ignores her, as much as is possible while stuck under a bed together. Her back begins to ache, despite the pillows they've brought. Outside, something big moans and creaks, then crashes against the ground. The house shakes violently and everything loose inside it rattles. Thirty Hümmel figurines dance in the storm, some leaping off the shelves to their demise. Eve, startled, bangs her head against the bottom of the bed.

"Ouch! What was that?"

"I think it was the big tree over by the barn."

"Oh my god."

KATE

CHRISTMAS ENDS in an almost cruelly abrupt way and January trudges on in a grey, bleak fug, the crisp buzz of December having given way to something more sober, ideally suited for hibernation. Kate is back on Brittania and Rachel is at work in the city while their mother and Barbara cavort in Costa Rica, much to Ed's resonating disbelief and confusion. Kate receives a postcard: *Off to the Arenal volcano today ... monkeys everywhere. We might rent horses.*

She hasn't seen Luke yet. He's gone back to Colorado Springs to see his mother. Kate plays games with herself, chiding. They are clumsy together. He is too tall; They're awkward in bed, don't know each others' rhythms. Still, she gets a funny buzz when she conjures his face and the silly, melting effect it seems to have on her. She tells herself that it's common to run to someone else, that she's filling a void, rebounding. But that void has been with her for a very long time, since long before Jeff died. Still though, it is too soon. Everyone would say so.

Nicole's wedding is a week away. It was guilt that made her return the tiny card with a box checked "attending." Kate didn't respond to the letter and didn't see Nicole over the holidays. Everyone was so busy then that it was easy to avoid her. And under no circumstance would she enter the mall.

Rachel calls to complain about their mother's "post mid-life crisis."

"What do you mean?" Kate asks.

"I mean, now *she's* running away? Why's she been so agitated?"

"You have met our mother, haven't you? When has she not been agitated?"

"Seems like more than usual."

"You're just not used to her doing anything out of character. I think it's great. Better than hanging around town."

"It feels wrong."

"Good. I'm glad for her. Hey, are you going to Nicole's wedding?"

"Why would I be invited?"

"I don't know. I was just hoping."

"Sorry."

Kate sits down and writes Nicole a letter. Surely it's not too late to cancel.

Hi Nic,

I got your letter. I want you to know that I'm thinking of you and wishing you well. I'm sorry I won't be there for the wedding after all, and I hope you'll understand. Being here has been good for me. I love the island, the quiet, the chance to think about things. I'm just not ready to come back to North Wailaish or to spend time with anyone yet. Please know that I'm sending big hugs and my very best to both you and Steve.

xo, Kate

She looks at the letter, frowns, crumples it up and tosses it. She's going home again, and this time she has to face what everyone thinks of her.

NORA

"I'M GOING TO SEE that quetzal if it kills me," Nora tells Barb, leaning forward over the platform, binoculars adhered to her eyes, as though a few more inches might make a difference.

"We don't see this bird so often," the guide interjects. "It's very special. Now it's time to put on your equipment."

"Ooh," Barb yelps as a young man drapes straps through her legs. "Now that's more excitement than I've had in awhile." The guide laughs, well-trained in the art of tourist-humouring.

"What the hell have you gotten me into now, Barb?" Nora swats her guide's hand playfully as he tightens her straps.

"It's exhilarating. I did this at Whistler once. It's like flying."

The first zip line is a short one. Like crossing an overgrown ditch, albeit a big one. The woman ahead of Nora can't seem to shut up. She screams her head off as she jumps from the platform. In the middle of the line she loses momentum and stops, dangling helplessly from her climbing harness. The guide has to glide up behind her and heave her over to the other side. Nora fusses with her equipment, examining it for cracks and tears. "You go first," she tells Barb.

"Nope."

She shoots Barb a dirty look, but can't come up with any words. Truth is, she's terrified, so much so that her words are gone. This is extremely rare. Suddenly everything looks like a threat. She knows about the vipers. They might be hanging from branches, waiting to strike. And if she dares look down, how far would she fall? Everything is out of her control and she does not like this, not one bit.

"Breathe," Barb advises.

"Shut up."

Nora inhales in spite of herself, and with a push from the guide, flies out into the trees. The still air gives way to wind and something bubbles up from a deep place inside of her. Laughter. She lets it spill out and into the trees. She laughs so hard she almost lets go of her grip on the harness. She feels like air, like a giant child in a harness-diaper. Barb crosses quickly behind her and Nora collapses, laughing, into her arms.

"You love this," Barb says. "I knew you would."

Nora collects herself. "Wouldn't say love," she mumbles unconvincingly.

The lines get longer and longer, and each one takes them higher, until they are no longer sheltered by trees but hovering high above them instead. Each time they approach a new one Nora feels a gurgle of fear in her stomach and then, as she takes off, its release into something she can only call joy, as she flies, ever higher, over all of the rainforest's hidden things.

During the hiking portion of the zip trek she gets distracted, full of thoughts about Ed, the girls, their troubles—the monotony of a life given over to a kitchen. Nora hasn't travelled much. She's been to Ottawa to visit her aunt, to the interior of British Columbia, to Banff. She and Ed had taken the girls to Disneyland when they were six and eight, but that was it. This is the farthest she'd gone, and the first time without Ed. Everything here evokes delight. No one to cook for, no one to worry about, nothing to fix. Ed, strangely, had become chatty in his emails to her. After his initial tantrum, once she'd been gone a week, she'd started emailing him, just to let him know out of courtesy that she wasn't dead. He had no interest in Costa Rica; he only wanted to tell her about the headlines and to let her know that the snowdrops were starting to come up. *Since when did Ed ever care about snowdrops?* She could sense in his musings, if she allowed herself to, that he might actually miss her.

Lost in this, she almost trips over Barb, who'd stopped with the group at the foot of a giant, metal tower. They all stare up.

"This last one is seven hundred and fifty metres long, and to get to it we climb this tower, three hundred and twenty-eight feet high," the guide informs.

"No. No I won't." The woman who had to be fished from the middle of the first zip line shakes her head.

"If you don't, we can hike back. We'll add about twenty-five minutes to the trip, though," the guide says.

The woman looks furious. Nora turns to her. "If I can do this, anyone can." She starts to climb, shouts to those beneath her, "Better to fly than walk."

At the top, strong gusts of wind threaten. She looks out and then down, clinging to a pole, no longer caring how embarrassing her fear might look. The guide attaches her carabiner and asks if she's ready. She nods, though she never will be, and with a push, enters air so high above the trees they look like stubby broccoli beneath her. Glancing left, she can see the coastline. She'd brought the part of herself that was so afraid, so shut off for so long, to play in the jungle, and this time, instead of constricting, instead of pulling her heart shut, she lets go. "Fuck!" she shrieks, and the laughter comes again. And she is no longer mother, no longer wife, no longer the keeper of kitchens. And what is she then? She thinks she might be the wind.

Later in the Cloud Forest Lodge, Nora won't shut up. "After the volcano let's take one of those canoe thingies down the river. I want to see one of those Jesus Christ lizards. God that was fun. Barb, you've been keeping all this to yourself!"

Barb giggles over her beer. "If you'll recall I've tried to get you to do stuff like this for years."

"Sure as hell didn't try hard enough."

They both howl.

On the hotel balcony she peels layers of clothing from her sticky skin, allows her bare shoulders to breathe in the sultry air, and offers her nose to the fragrance of a thousand flowers. She melts into a lounge chair and glances out at the rainforest tripping down toward the swirling sea, somewhere below. All around are animals. Lazing now on a branch not ten feet away is a disdainful monster of an iguana. Barely moving, it just stares, nonplussed, at a world so familiar to it but completely incomprehensible to her.

She wonders why she's never considered doing anything like this before. From this perspective, she can see how the deep grey of her reality has enveloped her so tightly that most days she can hardly see her way out the door. She knows she's shocked her family by coming here, but why should they not see that like them, she too is changing? She's ready for this, ready to be rid of them, well, at least them as they were, together. As an afternoon rain begins to fill the air with a charge of electricity and the humidity suddenly rises palpably, Nora, under the protection of her balcony's overhang, drifts off into deepest sleep.

KATE

BLUE SKY. Kate hears the two-toned song of a bird. It's the kind that Nora calls the "hee-haw bird," a moniker that has stuck with Kate. A high note, then a low, like a yawn translated into birdsong. She knows that the song is a portent of spring. She sniffs the scent of melting earth like an animal, but reminds herself not to get too attached; it is still only early March. She's seen sudden temperature drops and even snowfall as late as April. Luke calls.

"I rented a speedboat from David. Come."

"I'm glad you were sensible enough not to get out the sailboat."

"I'm dying to get on the water. Please."

Simply talking to him on the phone lifts her spirits. But what does she really want? She thinks for a moment. She wants his honesty, his humility. The way he talks about his mom. "Utterly independent. Eternal admiration. What she did. Alone." A current of heat also rises in her. She wants him, everywhere.

She jogs most of the way into town. Time to get some exercise. She hates the gym, and on the island there is only a small, crowded one at the community centre. She'd rather layer up and brave the bracing cold. It isn't bad after the first ten minutes or so, but she admits that those ten minutes can be brutal; the air is so penetratingly cold, with a moisture that soaks through your skin and into your organs, gripping you to trembling. Puffing breathy snorts of steam, she takes trails so enveloped in silence it feels rude and invasive to place her feet upon them.

She'd been thinking about inviting Luke to Nicole's wedding, but that would be stupid. After Jeff died, instead of hanging around and hashing over what happened again and again with all the people she'd known her whole life, she'd taken off to Brittania. But these people will still expect to have the conversations, to deal with things through their own grieving processes, in which she'll have no choice but to play a part. Her face alone will be a reminder. A trigger. Going home will be like turning the clock back to more than a year ago and living it all over again—as though nothing between then and now has happened. Luke could be a buffer, she supposes, but she also knows that this is hers to face alone.

How inscrutable time can be. She knows that at the wedding, time will collapse around people like Edgar, Nicole, and her parents. She'll be five, ten, fifteen years old even as she stands before them in a grown body. And she will play this role, all the while hating herself for her complicity. But her family is right in a sense, she can't stay motionless or control what part of the world touches her forever. How do you release yourself from caring so much about the opinions of others?

She starts to near the clearing, which looks sodden and forlorn without the cheerful white sails of the Saturday market tents. Five kilometres evaporate as her mind and body work themselves into a different sort of space, where rhythm and repetition take over, and the pain of moving muscles becomes irrelevant. Luke is already at the Wellspring. The plan is to pick up coffee and sandwiches for lunch and then head to the marina. He sits at the counter talking to Kris as Kate pushes through the door. The place is bursting. It's been weeks since she's been here and she is immediately nervous about the crowd.

She defaults to weather. "Amazing out there today."

Kris wipes a blob of cappuccino froth off the bar. "The one day I'm stuck in here with almost no help."

Luke has his booming sailor's voice on, and Kate wonders for a moment if this isn't overcompensation, if he isn't more shy than he lets on. "There's hardly anyone here. Come with us."

"Cruel. Very cruel."

Kate walks over to Luke and kisses him hello. He looks so satisfied, so completely happy just to be sitting there doing nothing.

"You're beautiful when you sweat," he says to her.

"Gross." She pulls at the neck of her running vest. "I need to lose a few layers."

"I remembered the jacket for you."

"Thank you. I hope it's the orange one."

"I wanted to make sure you were visible if we capsize."

"Oh god."

"Don't worry. I've improved."

She watches Luke as he drives the boat over unseasonably smooth waters. His eyes squint toward distance, as though looking for something. He turns to search her face from time to time, always wearing a sort of playful expression.

"You're a natural," she calls over the buzz of the engine.

"What?" A piece of driftwood clunks against the hull.

"Never mind."

He points toward a small, grassy point and begins to steer the boat in that direction. When they dock and tie up, a scrawny teenaged boy comes out to collect the fee, looking irked. He pulls the last remaining drags out of his cigarette and tosses it into the ocean. Luke tethers the boat to the dock laboriously, staring, befuddled, at the thick rope.

They walk up the dock and into the park. A forlorn set of swings sits above full puddles of mud, and the windows of the concession are boarded.

"I love places like this in the off-season," Luke says, pulling the pack off his back and placing it on a picnic table. He sits on the table top and looks out at the bay. There are a few boats moored. Laundry lines hang from some of the sails.

These aren't tourists —these people live on their boats year-round. The skinny boy has disappeared and they stand alone with the crows.

"I know this about you now, Mr. Off- Season," says Kate. "But I'm confused. You seem to also love being around people."

"I do. But it gets to a point when I've had enough and I need to find some open space."

"The older I get the more space I want."

"Were you like this before the accident?"

She considers the question. "I guess so, but I always forced myself to socialize. Thought there was something wrong with me because I'd get so tired."

"Nothing wrong with you." He is standing now, reaching an arm toward her.

"Tell me more about your mom. What's the one word you'd say describes her most."

"Kind. Everyone loves her."

She takes his hand. "Kindness seems so rare, even unfashionable these days."

"One of the things I love about you."

Her breath catches as the word echoes in her head. She's heard it before, a long time ago. But at the time it came attached to something: a promise that she would change, grow into something other than she was. It was predicated on the idea that she was a lump of clay. Mouldable Kate. This time she knows that even though Luke is speaking the word for the first time, he's said it to her before, in the way that he was with her, in their calm and quiet comfort. It is already there, unarticulated, the word itself actually unnecessary. She's waited for what might be attached to it, what expectations, but hasn't yet found anything. Perhaps he is satisfied with the notion that this might already be enough. *Is that even possible?* she wonders.

IVY

SHORTLY AFTER the tree falls, Eve and Ivy hear the front door grunt open and the house rush with air. There is shouting and shoving and a giant slam, then more voices. One of them is screaming.

"Are you crazy?"

Thumping, more shouting, things falling.

And another voice Ivy recognizes as Mrs. Freisen's "Sonia! Stop. We can't do anything." She can now understand this much German.

So much crying and screaming and wailing. Eve and Ivy hold each other tight under the bed. Something's happened to Sonia. Her screams inject ice into Ivy's bloodstream. The house shakes and rattles, transforms into liquid. Framed pictures fall from the wall and books fly off their shelves. Everything is moving, both inside and out. Eve even stops her questions. Something terrible has happened, is happening, but they don't want to know. The voices sink into low murmurs, punctuated by Sonia's animal wails, long and hollow, like the loss of the world. Eve begins to sob.

"Ivy, I wish you'd never come here."

Ivy wants to wish the same. "Just try to sleep, Evey. Everything will be better in the morning."

NORA

NORA CARESSES the coarse fur of the baby sloth. "Sweet boy," she murmurs. "You get better now." The rehabilitation centre is busy. An aid hands her a bottle and demonstrates how to place it inside the small animal's mouth.

What might remain in her of this place? Will she forget it all the second she hops off the plane back home? What is the distance between here and there? And she doesn't mean physical distance. Nora is beginning to feel larger—and not just around the waistband. The animals she's found here are so different from how she'd imagined them—full of colour and personality, even the sick ones. She's embarrassed to admit that previously she'd envisioned them in a cartoonish way, irrelevant and distant. She begins to understand a little about how she can nurture. It's been so long since her capable hands have applied themselves to something more meaningful than the repetitive tasks at the Moose Hall. But will the hopeful sensation of warmth and sunshine, of the immersion into nature, soon abandon her in the grey drizzle that keeps everyone locked inside, in more ways than one? Apart from the T-shirts she's bought for the girls and a pocketed seashell, what can she bring back?

A vacation is a vacation. She's allowed herself that much. No sense clinging to fantasies.

Back at the hotel Barbara is ready to go. She'd packed the night before and now she's fretting about the flight.

"I hate flying."

"That's because you have the privilege of saying so."

"That's what I love about you. You call a spade a spade, don't you?"

"I say what I see. My filter's broken." Nora wanders the room, picking musty clothes up off the backs of chairs, wondering what to put in her suitcase first and whether any of it will be dry in time.

"It's been an amazing trip," Barbara says.

Nora clutches a tank top, looks directly at Barb. "I'd no idea."

"You should do this more often."

"I wish. I can't stand the thought of this being a once-in-a lifetime."

"Well, they say travel changes you."

"That they do, but they should say more about the how and why."

"You know there's more to life than the Moose Hall."

Nora stares at her friend, watching her fold a golf shirt in a manner so meticulous it ends up an almost flawless rectangle. "I think you might be right about that."

"But you have to get past a few things first."

"Such as?"

Barbara inhales, "Rumours. And being so sure about everything—and everyone else."

Nora looks toward the open sliding glass door that leads to their balcony. A tidy line of bulbous ants meanders in, filing straight up the leg of a desk and into Barbara's handbag.

"Would you look at that?" Nora points.

"What? Oh god."

"Did you put food in there?"

"No, of course not. Oh, wait. My mints!" Barbara runs to the bag, which, when she picks it up, is teeming with ants.

THE FLIGHT IS LONG, and Nora spends it bracing herself for Ed's silent treatment. She's not sure how long it will last this time, but a normal one usually lasts around three days. Given the circumstances however, she could be in for a week or more, which might not necessarily be a bad thing. She wills herself enough strength to last well beyond his inevitable outburst, but when she arrives the man who greets her at the door wears a wide smile and pulls her heartily into his arms.

Over the next week he continues his affections, much to Nora's suspicion. She simply isn't sure what to do with them. If she'd only known that this would be the result of leaving, she'd have done so a long time ago. Where in recent years he'd morphed into little more than a disembodied voice behind an unfolded newspaper, now he brushes her arm when she leaves a room, and in the morning leans over and kisses her cheek before climbing out of bed. She wants to shout at him, *What the hell?* But she's no fool. Gift horse...

While part of Nora's mind has remained in Costa Rica, in the warmth of the tropics and the taste of a cold beer in the hot afternoon sun, she soon learns that Ed has taken up the task of learning to cook. He spends Saturdays watching cooking shows and buying ingredients their kitchen cupboards have never seen before. Nora's tongue bleeds from the biting. She's dying to ask him what's happened, but instead she scrutinizes—afraid to break the spell—as he hums along in the kitchen, wearing an unfamiliar mask of calm.

Nora calls Kate, whispering, "Someone's taken your father and replaced him with a pod."

"What are you talking about?"

"He cooks! And he keeps trying to touch me."

"Then let him. What are you complaining about?"
"I'm not complaining. It's just ...I don't know where I am anymore."

"It can be a good thing, Mom. We're not meant to stay the same forever."

"I'm glad you think so. Just like you're not meant to stay in that dark little cabin all by yourself forever."

Kate slams the phone down.

Shit. Too far, Nora.

She remains a dark cloud, Kate. Nora didn't want to come down on her, but she is so stubborn. Why does it feel like everything's a battle? Except with Ed, of all people.

Nora never knows what to say to her oldest daughter. She senses a darkness in the air around them, but is usually careful not to pry, not to chase Kate away again. Nora expected her to snap out of the moping by now, to start living at least a little. She feels helpless and frustrated, but it's so easy to scare her away. Just the slightest verbal misstep and Nora sees her daughter never wanting to talk to her again. And now she's done it.

Nora knows more about the rumours now, but what's the point in telling Kate about them? The failings of the dead should be buried along with them. Releasing secrets would only mean more pain for Kate, and she's had enough of that. Nora worries about how long things are taking, how stuck her daughter seems. Over the next few weeks she reads articles about grief and mails them to her daughter until she tells her to stop, *for fuck's sake.*

And so Nora continues to teeter on the edge of a decision: to be sensitive or to break out the strategies of the tough love book she'd bought when the girls were teenagers. The problem was she was never quite able to agree with all that crap. Kids are all different, and it didn't help that back then the girls had found the book and read parts of it before she'd grabbed it back and shouted at them for rummaging through her drawers.

In the meantime, she'll enjoy the gourmet meals and the long-awaited, albeit mystifying affections of her husband.

KATE

"I'M LOSING MY MIND," Kate tells Luke over the phone. "You're sure there's no sign of a break-in?"

"No. I'm telling you, I just keep finding things in places I didn't put them. But maybe I'm forgetting I put them there. It's early Alzheimer's. They say it happens practically overnight."

"I don't think so."

"There's no explanation."

"Unless someone has a key."

"The locks have been changed."

"Come stay with me."

"I can't."

"Why not?"

Kate hears the exasperation in his voice. All week she's been restless, back-and-forth with him, consumed by thoughts of Nicole and her wedding. Part of her needs to rally, to move her mind away from him, even if only temporarily. To a certain extent, she is already back at her parents' place, preparing, fortifying against the onslaught of her mother's concern and the presence of more people in one room than she's seen in many months. She needs to focus, needs to peel away from Luke, just for awhile. In doing this though, she can feel herself beginning to sabotage her own happiness, but she doesn't know another way to prepare for being back home. She can't be there in her mind and here with Luke simultaneously. If she admits it, there is something almost gratifying, or at the very least familiar in this. There has to be something wrong with how comfortable she's become.

"When do you leave for the wedding?"

"Two days."

She doesn't see Luke before she leaves. Somehow the world of her home and the artificial one she's made here with Luke don't match. She is a coward, playing house with someone who deserves better. She doesn't even call him.

THE ROOM LOOKS SMALLER than she remembers it. Over the span of her life Kate has come to think of this as the room of funerals. Here she's been to girl guide meetings, wedding receptions, baby showers, anniversary celebrations, and award ceremonies for the local fishing derby, but more than anything, it is the room of funerals.

The room is set up with a long, rectangular head table and a spattering of circular ones. It's empty of humans, except for her, and she is sure that no one will have noticed that she'd left the claustrophobia of the wedding early. "Beautiful ceremony," she'll say when the others file in to the hall, and then she'll let them do the rest of the talking.

She walks to the display cabinet in the corner, where her mother's bowling trophies rest, unpolished, which is very unusual. Traces of her mother are in fact everywhere in this place. From the placard listing the Moose Hall executives in the entryway, to the trophies, to the very reception decor, over which Nora always presides.

For a moment Kate dissolves into the last time she was here. Jeff's grandparents had sat at the front of the room, near the photographs. She'd taken a seat on the other side, somewhere near her parents, although it felt more like she was hovering above the scene—if she sank into it, she might never crawl out. Sometimes it was easier to leave your body. What was it Bruce Lee had said? "Be like water." After Jeff died, Kate had learned how to do this, how to be in a place and be liquefied, how to flow around the furniture and bodies in a room, how to spill under and out the door, how to evaporate. The funeral was like the opposite of a wedding ceremony. That day, she'd been returned to her own family just as easily as she'd been given over, she was no longer *theirs*. It was a disunion, an unbelonging.

People murmur and mill outside the door, greeting each other. Kate realizes that she isn't supposed to be inside yet, that there will of course be a receiving line. She slips along the wall and into the ladies' room.

What kind of a person hides in bathrooms? It feels absurd, but at the same time it's impossible to think of looking into so many eyes. It was a mistake to come. People are not what she needs. Not yet. She hears her heart hammer throughout her whole body as the sound of voices begins to enter the hall. Mentally she calls up the quiet little cabin, wishing she could in this moment, walk out the front door and jump straight into the blue-black depths, into an ocean that would muffle sound, render her blind and deaf.

At that moment a group of women giggles its way through the bathroom door. Two bridesmaids back in, trying to squash the bride's crinolined skirt into a shape that might conform to the dimensions of the door frame. They wash and dry their hands, releasing wads of paper towel onto the floor.

"There you are!" Nicole shouts, seeing Kate.

Kate affixes a smile. "Congratulations, Nicole. You look beautiful."

Nicole stands in the pile of paper towels. The round toes of her bright satin pumps nest within the folds of brown paper, like otherworldly eggs.

"I really have to pee. That was crazy."

The three women disappear into the larger stall, bumping the walls and laughing in a manner normally reserved for women younger than themselves. Kate thinks she detects an air of recognizable derision in their laughter, and they seem well on their way to drunkenness. Nicole's soccer friend Shannon calls back to her with a grin, "Hi Kate." More laughing.

The funny thing is that Kate is beginning to lose her ability to care. Perhaps there is some kind of ingredient mixed up within all the grief that allows for this. She isn't sure, but as she watches the women she sees her shadow self go into the bathroom stall along with them. There would be a place for her there if Jeff hadn't died, if she hadn't left town. But she doesn't want that place now. And if he hadn't died, would she have known otherwise? In some ways, witnessing death is like waking from a dream—a nightmare maybe.

She takes a deep breath, opens the bathroom door, and steps out into the cocktail crowd. She needs something for her hands to do. A country song she can't name plays as she approaches the bar. Questions float up in her mind one by one, as though standing in line to have their say. *What kind of people mark every important occasion in the same place? Why does this room have to contain all of their sorrow, all of their imagined joy?* The questions, once asked, settle themselves unanswered in the lower part of her solar plexus. The music grows louder.

The bartender is an old friend. In high school biology class, they'd been paired up as lab partners for the dissection of a fetal pig. He'd broken his arm that week and left Kate to do all the cutting. She remembers the tiny snout.

"Hi Grant," she calls to him. A tentative smile curls her lips, but doesn't quite reach the eyes.

"Kate!" He brightens. "How's my old pig partner?"

She sighs with momentary relief. He seems genuinely glad to see her, but she's not yet sure if everyone will feel that way. "I need a drink."

"I know what you mean. What's your pleasure?"

"Gin and tonic."

She takes her drink and smiles gratefully at him. Apart from Nicole, he is the first to talk to her. They catch up a little, and she begins to lower her shoulders—which have crept up somewhere next to her ears—and makes her way toward the seating chart, which is in fact not a chart, just a sign that reads, *Come as you are, stay as long as you can, we're all family, so no seating plan.*

Kate freezes. She looks around the room. A few people are still standing and talking, but most have begun to find seats. She can't see her mother, but she knows Nora will be impossible to locate anyway—she'll be flitting about, running the show. The Moose Hall would have no one else at the helm. Her dad never bothers to come to weddings anymore, and Rachel is writing report cards in Vancouver. *Fuck. Where am I going to sit?*

Nicole and her bevy make their way toward the head table. Kate knows she'll have to move quickly, before her options grow even slimmer. She slides as silently as she can into the seat next to Edgar Watkins, whose tiny eyes seem to bulge slightly when he sees her.

"Oh, Kate." He shifts in his seat. "You came."

She tries to smile. "Of course. Nicole's an old friend."

"Yes, yes. We all are more or less, aren't we? I just haven't seen you in a long time."

"I'm staying on Brittania right now."

"Oh. At the cabin?"

"Yes."

"I remember that place well. Mike and Ann used to have the best Labour Day parties..." He trails off.

Kate tries to catch Edgar's wife Marjorie's eye to say hello, but she is remarkably elusive. She shifts awkwardly, wondering if she ought to keep trying or if it would be better to fade into obscurity. If she were honest with herself, she would say she has no real desire to talk to either Edgar or Marjorie, so why try?

The question remains: is there anyone here that she does want to talk to? What does she want from them?

The mercifully loud intervention of "Cotton-eyed Joe" engulfs the room as spots of light dance against the walls. The disco ball has been set into motion even before the speeches, even before dinner. Nicole and her bridesmaids let out a whoop as they shimmy their satin skirts toward the dance floor. Once there, they settle into a sort of formation and begin to line dance. Kate stares, transfixed as the women lift their skirts and shake them side to side, then twirl around each other's elbows. When the musical number finishes the crowd cheers, as everyone stomps their feet and begins to clink their glasses. Nicole runs over to her new husband Steve, dips him, and plants a wide-mouthed kiss.

Also at Kate's table are Brian and Suzanne Peters, owners of the local marina. Edgar starts a conversation about outboard motors with Brian, and Marjorie jumps in eagerly, her chunky plastic bracelets clicking against one another. Kate knows Marjorie has no interest in outboard motors. She takes a long gulp of her gin and tonic. When she and Rachel were children Brian and Suzanne and their twin daughters went camping in the Gulf and San Juan Islands with Kate's family and a few others. Everyone had a boat back then. Kate remembers bumping over the whitecaps while she and Rachel sat on the bow, legs wrapped around the bars. There was something like the sensation of flight when the bow lifted up, and a soothing spray would cool their bodies when they thumped down. It was exhilarating and sometimes frightening. The closest she's come to this sensation in her adult life is during plane turbulence on a family trip back east.

Nicole's family has splurged on a sit-down meal rather than a buffet, so Kate is relieved not to have to get up again. She sits and picks at her steak, finding a numb but comfortable place in her solitude. The conversation segues into what everyone's adult children are up to. The tone of the table is set and Kate is invisible. She'd expected worse.

But as the others engage themselves in the comparison of their children's accomplishments, Edgar turns toward her, draws in a long breath and says, "I know your mom is still angry with me, Kate."

Kate sits confused for a moment. *Doesn't he want to ask me about the night of the accident? what happened to his friends? What my role in all of it was?* Kate has mostly forgotten about the funeral, hadn't even thought that this might be a cause for discomfort at their table.

"I don't know, Edgar. She's probably over it by now."

He shakes his head. "It's a funny town, but people like your mother just don't want anything to change."

"I know. What happened, anyway?

"It was in his will, Kate. It was Charlie's way of letting everyone finally see who he was."

"It wasn't the friends' idea?"

"No, he came to see me years ago. He loved this town and everyone in it, but he knew he couldn't really live here. Not in the important ways."

"And everyone was so sad about losing him…"

"Which didn't change, even when they found out."

Kate stares at the single lily, floating in water in a low, wide vase in the centre of the table. "Too bad he had to live his whole life that way."

"I tried to talk to him about it, many times. But he'd gotten used to a double life. We all get comfortable, I guess."

"Funny how death can shake things up."

"I've done so many eulogies now, Kate. You've no idea."

The first to get up and speak is the best man, Roger. Back in high school Roger was a temporary obsession for Kate. Over her senior year she'd spent her lunch hours taking furtive peeks at him, sharing her fantasies with Nicole. He always sat with the wealthy kids, the ones who came from junior high schools on the north side of town. Although she'd never dare approach him, she filled her head with silly mirages where he would read her sonnets, walk with her along the rocky beaches at the bay, and cook her experimental foreign meals. These fantasies must have generated some sort of materializing energy, for at their graduation dance Kate's date disappeared and suddenly there was Roger, holding her in his lumpy, overly muscled arms and slow-dancing to "Cry me a river."

Before this night Kate had already created a voice for Roger: soft, deep, and tentative, one that housed a thoughtful curiosity, one that softened his football player-like demeanor. A beautiful irony. But the actual voice that emerged to her expectant ears was high-pitched and squeaky, and unfortunately wanted to sing along with Justin Timberlake. This was disappointing. Still more disappointing was the cavernous mouth that landed sloppily on hers partway through the song, a muscled tongue emerging from its depths, clinically probing. Still, she was prepared to dissolve herself into the din of music and inhabit her well-developed delusions. Perhaps she could tease out some sort of sensuality, provided he didn't talk.

But her night was marred by Roger's drunken stupor and attempts to do anything but relate, as two people who'd just met each other might be expectected to do. Instead, she spent the evening preventing his advances from going any further than making out, even when as a group they relocated to watch the sun rise out over the ocean at the lagoon. Kate remembers hoping that none of this was symbolic.

Now, Roger stands at the head table talking about the times that he and the groom got drunk together at bush parties. He periodically truncates his stories with the words, "Okay, buddy, I won't go there," and a slap on the groom's back. Nicole stares at him, unblinking.

IVY

EVE AND IVY both manage to fall asleep in an unexpected hour of silence, until Oma comes into the room and taps the floor.

"What happened to Sonia?" Ivy immediately asks.

"Her little boy."

There aren't words. Her body contorts to reject the news. She doesn't want to know how it happened.

Eve snorts and sputters her way into confused wakefulness. "Is it over?"

"Not for awhile yet," Oma answers.

"I don't hear anything."

"It's the eye, it's right above us now. Do you want to come to the living room?"

Ivy is already out and on her way, every muscle aching to be off the rigid floor, her nausea pulsating. In the living room, her father, Mr. Freisen and Opa are drinking. Sonia is doubled over on the sofa, her face in a pillow, her body convulsing. Mrs. Freisen rubs her back.

Oma breaks the silence, turning to Opa. "Frederick, the well will be contaminated. Please tell me you brought more water."

"On the front porch. Two barrels."

"Good. We'll have to be prudent. First we'll get through the rest of the storm. There will be nine of us for a while."

Ivy can see her mother's contempt. "We'll have to assess things after the storm, though."

Oma whispers to her daughter, "There is nothing left to assess."

Mother whispers back sharply, "Where will they all sleep?"

"It's the last of my worries right now."

Eve and Ivy each take a glass of water and some bread from a tray in the middle of the room. Sonia refuses all but the water. Her eyes, when she turns their way, are terrifyingly unoccupied.

KATE

THE WEDDING hasn't gone too badly. Of course, no one accuses her outright of murdering her husband and in-laws, and as people drink more and the evening moves on, things slip into the familiar. Kate stays for dessert and then quietly gets up from the table during the couple's first dance. It feels like a good time to leave. Everyone at the table has relaxed and become drunk and reminiscent. The shock of her re-emergence is over, if it even existed. This is much better than any of her imagined confrontations.

As she reaches the door she feels a hand on her shoulder.

"I was wondering if you'd be here," Shannon, the bridesmaid who called to her in the bathroom, eyes her from beneath a confusing web of bedazzled eyelashes.

"I'm here," Kate shrugs, not knowing what else to say. She wonders why Shannon is so interested in her tonight. They'd known each other a little in high school, but apart from having a few friends in common, they hadn't ever spoken about anything important. "Why?"

"I don't know. Too many reminders of Jeff, maybe."

She looks into Shannon's blue-lidded eyes, takes in the meticulously curled, bright blonde hair, her petite frame. She hasn't heard another person speak Jeff's name in such a long time, and it doesn't feel nice, more like an invasion. And not only that, but the way she says it carries a confusing sense of familiarity. But she doesn't remember Jeff ever talking about Shannon.

"I'm going to head home now." Kate moves again toward the door, her heart racing.

"We should get together and talk sometime. I work at Hilldale." Shannon calls to Kate's back as she speed-walks toward her mother's car.

In that moment, the same feeling she had after the cabin was broken into washes over her, stealing breath. She stops and turns to look at Shannon, standing in the doorway.

"No."

She says it aloud to herself, gets in the car and drives home.

IVY

THEY DON'T GO back to sleep, nor do they go back under their beds. Eve wants to be close to her mother, and Ivy is nauseous and sore everywhere. The women take turns bringing things to Sonia: mostly food, water, and compresses. From time to time she slips back into hysterics and runs toward the door, so the men take up a constant rotating vigil there, while Ivy and Eve's mother continues to supply her with palm-slipped pharmaceuticals that her daughters had never before noticed in her possession.

"If that door opens, the roof will come off," Ivy's father booms, suddenly knowledgeable in the ways of hurricanes. Fortunately Opa's prediction about the strength of his house is accurate so far. It's holding its own against the storm, even though they've lost a few windows in other rooms. Ivy hates to think about what it must look like in those rooms now, behind the doors they had hastily pulled shut.

It is morning when the storm finally passes, at least when they feel safe enough to move around. They'd all slipped in and out of random bouts of sleep, never more than two of them at the same time. Ivy is sleeping when Opa nudges her shoulder.

"Rubia, come and see what a cyclone does."

Eve, incessantly curious, is not far behind Opa and Ivy.

It's astonishing, the power, the devastation, everything unrecognizable. Ivy trips on a fallen branch and lands on her knees.

"Be careful," calls Opa, "Nothing will be where we left it."

"Oh my god. The chickens!" Eve shouts.

Opa looks sadly at the ground. "Guinea hens."

Six of them lie flattened on the ground. Oma will be so upset to lose the eggs she uses in her baking.

"Look!" Eve points.

One of the hens lifts its head and peers around cautiously, the rest of its body still adhered to the ground.

"Unbelievable!"

Opa chuckles as the hen cranes its neck and peels its chubby body from the earth. It fluffs its feathers and begins to peck and scratch. Slowly, the other five hens do the same. Ivy, Eve, and Opa stand and stare as each hen takes up the usual business of clucking and scratching at the earth, as though nothing has happened.

"Do you think they stayed like that the whole time?" Eve asks.

"I don't know. I can't say I've ever seen anything like this," Opa tells her, holding out some grain.

"It's as though they decided to be part of the earth—the only things that weren't flying around," Ivy says.

Opa shakes his head. "They missed their opportunity, as flightless birds. Good thing your papa wasn't around with his fishing rod." He laughs.

Ivy can't resist nudging Eve. "I told you the animals would be fine."

"Yes, many of the animals are. So far," says Opa. "Not so much the people, though."

Later, while they eat breakfast, the men go over to the Freisen's property. Sonia is installed in the guest room, in a drugged sleep, and the task of removing Hannes's body from under the tree that had fallen on him has to be done before she wakes up. Ivy's mother, Oma, and Mrs. Freisen discuss funeral plans.

As the day moves on and the nausea comes and goes, Ivy notices her parents' distraction. She wonders if there might be a moment for her to slip away, but she feels physically terrible and never really knows when she'll need to run to the outhouse. She comes to terms with the notion that there will be no opportunity to find Emilio today.

Oma chuffs about the Guinea hens. "I can't believe such a stupid animal still lives." Bonita the horse—Ivy's horse—as she now thinks of her, has returned with no clue as to where she's been, other than a filthy coat. Over the next few hours other people come and go with reports. Oma gives bread to everyone who shows up. There are stories of huge ships awash in the harbour and bizarre anecdotes like that of the two Americans who couldn't find shelter quickly enough and had to climb into large oak barrels. They'd spent a good portion of the storm rolling around and miraculously survived with only bruises and broken bones.

"But they survived," Ivy says perhaps too optimistically. Mrs. Freisen gets up from the table and leaves the room.

"Ivy, how could you be so insensitive?" her mother chastises.

"I didn't mean anything!" Ivy is learning to shout back at her.

"Since when do you speak to me like this?"

They are locked in a place they aren't used to navigating. But Oma breaks their standoff.

"We will have to learn patience with each other. Especially now with so many under one roof. And soon one more, right Ivy?"

The room falls into silence. Deeper than that within the eye of the hurricane.

NORA

NORA IS BEGINNING to mistrust her memory. Costa Rica could only have been a dream. It's been more than three weeks, but Ed continues to fuss and create delicious messes of enormous proportions in what used to be Nora's kitchen. Nora prides herself on her non-confrontation. She's trying to take her daughter's advice—to let go—but well, she's still Nora.

She's trying not to let on how pleased she is that Kate has been lingering at home since Nicole's wedding. Nora watches her and her father, side by side, wearing aprons, not talking about anything important, only the latest cooking showdown on TV. The two of them do nothing but chop, dice, and sauté. Nora fidgets; she's been the family cook for so long she's no longer sure what to do with herself. She sidles up to her daughter.

"Did you manage to get together with Nicole?"

Kate flips a cookbook page. "We had lunch yesterday."

"How was it?"

"Fine. She's trying to get on at the paper now."

Nora starts to perspire. "What about you? Still thinking about going back?"

"I don't know."

Nora tries to hit a light, jovial tone, but knows her intentions are transparent.

"You might want get back in there before Nicole takes your job."

Kate sighs. "I don't really care, Mom."

What Kate doesn't know is that Rachel is coming for the weekend. Nora had called her about Kate, and they'd secretly planned an intervention of sorts—to keep her talking, or more realistically, *start* her talking. Nora knows that if Kate will open up to anyone, it will be Rachel. At least she hopes so.

KATE

IT'S STRANGE, Rachel's sudden appearance at their parents' house in the middle of a busy school term. Kate is immediately suspicious that her mother has staged some sort of intervention. Not only has Nora been leaving clipped articles on her bed, but she's also been eyeballing Kate in a not-so-inconspicuous way when she thinks Kate isn't looking. Even though she knows Nora means well, it's annoying.

Luke calls a few times to ask about the wedding, but she doesn't spend long on the phone. Finally she tells him she wants to be alone for a while. It's too difficult to imagine Luke when she's here. She's never found it easy to be in two places at once, especially when they are separated by a span of water.

She and Rachel sit at Serious Coffee downtown, drinking cappuccinos and tangling with the sticky mess that is their signature cinnamon bun. Kate notices that Rachel is looking increasingly urban these days, with her trench coat and gamine hairstyle. With less hair though, she looks more vulnerable, the normally averted expressions in her brown eyes no longer easy to hide. Kate has yet to cut her hair since Jeff and his family died. Not out of any articulated intention—she just doesn't want to hang out in a salon. Now it falls dark, long, wavy, and salt-coarsened around her shoulders.

"How was the wedding?" Rachel asks.

"They're all kind of the same, aren't they?" Kate answers,

clipped and critical, feeling detached, and particularly unin-
terested in weddings.

"Did you spend any time with Nicole?"

"No, not really. Her bridesmaid was interested in talking
to me, though."

"Who?"

"Do you remember Shannon?"

"Can't place her."

"Shannon Murray from my school year. Blonde hair, small.
Really into soccer."

"Doesn't ring a bell. Why did she want to talk to you?"

"She was talking about Jeff. She said something about it
being hard to see so many reminders of him. It was weird.
I've hardly ever said two words to her. Even back in school."

"Did she know Jeff?"

"Apparently."

"Have you talked to Mom? She'll know."

Kate puts down her mug, agitated. "No, and I don't want
to talk to her. Not everything needs to be hashed out. I hate
small-town gossip."

"Okay, okay. How long are you staying home?"

"I don't know."

They turn to more benign topics as they finish their drinks
and abandon the remainder of the messy cinnamon goo.

"How about we go and find Shannon," Kate suggests.

"Are you sure that's a good idea?"

"I think it might be."

Rachel reluctantly follows Kate to the Hilldale Recreation
Centre. It isn't a long walk, and as the building comes into
view, so too do Kate's memories of elementary school swimming lessons.

She recalls the frigid water, how huge the pool looked back
then, and the sign that read *Welcome to our ool; Notice there's
no p in it? Please keep it that way.* She wonders if the sign is still
there. Part of her wishes Luke was at her side, the other part is

embarrassed at what he might think of her hokey hometown.

Shannon isn't at the front desk, but her co-worker is happy to call for her. In a few short minutes she comes out of the change room—loopy blonde hair in a ponytail, the edge of a clipboard pressed against her hip, in shorts and a t-shirt.

"Hi Kate." She drops the clipboard on the front desk.

"This is Rachel, my sister."

"I think I remember you." She shakes Rachel's hand.

"I'm glad you came," Shannon says, her expression attempting something like concern.

"You said you wanted to talk," Kate says.

"Yes. Do you mind if we're alone, though? There's a room upstairs."

Rachel shrugs. "I've got a book."

Shannon quickly leads Kate up the narrow staircase and into a large rec. room. Kate immediately recognizes it as the room in which she used to take karate lessons. The instructor used to comment on her popping knees and her inability to hold a straight face during *kata*. She was often sentenced to push-ups due to her lack of coordination or composure. Karate didn't last long.

Shannon sits in a plastic chair and motions to Kate, who shakes her head.

"I won't be here long. What did you want to say?"

Shannon stares at her for a long moment, brushes aside an escaped chunk of bang, and looks down at the floor. "I don't think you understand how it's been for me."

Kate feels a surge of something hot. "For you?"

"It was more than what you're thinking. It actually meant something. He meant something."

A cold shard pierces Kate's body. She didn't expect the admission to be so abrupt. "Why do you need to tell me this?"

Shannon looks straight at her. "I need to tell you how angry I was with you."

"Me?"

"Who else?"

"What the hell are you talking about?"

"You got behind the wheel."

Kate feels a full push of rage. She imagines pulling Shannon's head back by that stupid ponytail and giving it a firm yank. "Exactly what are you assuming?"

"I don't need to assume anything. You made a poor judgement call."

Kate is shaking now. "The only one making judgement calls here is you. And you have no idea. Were you there?"

"I should have been," Shannon says, under her breath.

The two women lock into silence. While Kate is no longer surprised about Jeff and Shannon, she's also sick of guilt, sick of how easy it's always been for people to manipulate her because she cares so fucking much about them. But she's no longer willing to take the blame. While she has no idea when the turning point was, it was decisive. No one else would ever voluntarily shoulder as much blame as she's allowed herself. Now it can rest with the dead. She knows that the affair isn't all, though.

Kate speaks quietly. "It was you in the cabin, wasn't it?"

"What are you talking about?"

"What are you looking for?"

It looks for a moment as though Shannon will continue to deny, but she instead gazes at something invisible on the floor.

"So you have a key?"

She nods. Kate thinks for a moment. "But I changed the locks."

"I'm from North Wailaish. We can get past those sorts of things. You should know that."

Kate asks again, "What are you looking for?"

"Nothing in particular, just a reminder."

"But you were there more than once."

"It started to feel like being with him again." Shannon's eyes pool.

"Did you think about how I might feel about all of this?"

"*You.* Ever since it happened it's been about you. Everyone cares about how you're doing, but I can't even grieve in front of anyone. I have to keep it secret, even now."

Kate grimaces. "I'm sure you haven't kept it completely a secret. Do you really feel you have the right to break into my home?"

Shannon's lip takes on a nasty curl. She stands and faces Kate. "It is not your home."

"It ends now. Do you hear me?" Kate flushes, her pale skin anger-blotched.

"Not until you tell people," Shannon returns.

"Tell them what?"

"That you weren't his wife anymore."

"Go to hell."

"I know a lot more than you think."

Kate leaves the room. Shannon calls after her, "Stop thinking about yourself."

At the bottom of the stairs Kate turns and looks back at Shannon, halfway down. "Actually it's about time I started thinking about myself. You can have your grief, but don't you dare assume anything about mine. And whatever you say, I don't give a shit. You know *nothing*. Guilt not accepted."

Both Shannon and Rachel stare.

Kate pushes authoritatively through the exit doors. Rachel scurries to catch up to her as she runs past the trophies she's never won; past the photos of swim teams aging in reverse, from colour to black and white; past the parts of a life unclaimed in this town.

IVY

A MONTH PASSES. Ivy paces the floor at five in the morning, furious with Oma, plotting escape. While fully aware that things can't be kept secret forever, she'd wanted a bit of time to make her own plans, or at least to come to terms with things on her own. She'd wanted to tell her parents when she was ready, not in someone else's timeframe. *How long has Oma known?* It still doesn't feel real, at least mentally; physically is another story.

Fatigued, she slumps into the sofa. Could she really leave and be back in time, before they noticed? The farm scents of humus, shit, and the steam from Oma's relentlessly boiling sausages have been sending her body into revulsion. This body, an oven in the muggy heat, already feels much larger and given over to its own pursuits. Last night she threw up dinner, and she could hardly bear the despondence on Opa's face, that is, when he looked at her at all.

She' s not sure who Oma has told, but when she went to the bakery with Eve yesterday, she sensed eyes boring into her, felt the kind of shame that burns from the outside in, the loss of Hannes doubling that shame when she's at her grandparents' house. She's stayed as far from Sonia as possible, despite the fact that the Freisens have taken over the guest room and Eve and Ivy now sleep in the living room with their parents. They are on top of one another, and almost every day someone new comes to the door asking for help of some sort. Even though her grandparents are busy restoring the back of the bakery, which was crushed by a falling tree during the hurricane, they never say no. Before now Ivy had no idea of the extent of their generosity, and how much of it she's abused. Oma talks about how lucky they are to escape the storm with minor damage, but none of this looks like luck to Ivy. Much of La Isla is in shambles.

The only good thing is that they've stopped watching her so closely. Now that her parents and sister are locked in to staying on the island for a few more months, and Ivy's gotten into as much trouble as she possibly can in their eyes, they've relaxed their concerns regarding her whereabouts. Or maybe they've come to believe she wouldn't attempt anything more. Maybe they're just exhausted. Along with the baby, another seed germinates in her—a need to find out if Emilio is okay, and to let him know what's happened to her...to them. They are connected now, and while she can't even imagine how he'll respond, she needs him to know. And after that? Who knows? She doesn't want to take her thoughts any farther. She doesn't need him to take ownership, nor does she want a baby to tie their lives together in ways that they never could be otherwise. She just needs him to know.

But how to find him? He knew they had come—he must have been watching the farm—and has stayed away ever since. Surely though, he would have stopped doing that a long time ago.

The other problem is Eve. She's angry with Ivy, and she hates the heat and the bugs that seem bizarrely attracted to mostly her. "What do these insects do when I'm not here?!" she'd shouted once in frustration. A teenager in the throes of peer attachment, separated against her will from her friends, she places all blame on Ivy, who remembers how dramatically important her social life used to be. She understands, but can't count on Eve to keep secrets or to help her in the least. She will have to leave the house without waking her.

Night insects still claim the soundscape, but apart from that the morning is still. Ivy slides quietly from the sofa, very gently out of her sleeping clothes, and into a dress Oma had let out a couple days ago to accommodate her increasing waistline. She moves slowly, her breath heavier, inefficient, and keeps a steady eye on her sleeping sister as she crosses the room, pulls the door gently back, and creeps out into the waning darkness.

She thinks of her father, his face a perpetual rictus of sneering derision. He hates the tropics, but not as much as he hates the reason that brought him here. She's watched her mother disappear regularly into Oma's bedroom, where the Freisens are staying, and returning splotchy-faced. She has always found it easy to cry.

Ivy's not supposed to take the horse out in her condition, but she doesn't see how it can be a problem if they go very slowly. As she walks out toward the stable she can hear Bonita's awakening movements. She seems happy to see her after so long. She nuzzles the oats from Ivy's palm with the velour touch of her flaccid lips, and Ivy saddles her as quietly as possible, whispering gentle endearments in her ear.

"You made your own bed," were her father's words, and he's left her with little apart from that, only talking to her about practical things, if at all. He still wants her to go to college, despite the need to postpone. The plan is to have the baby and adopt it out to a family in Havana. No one back home will ever know, and Ivy is to move forward as though this never happened. To her, despite her nausea and steadily growing girth, none of it is real. Since the hurricane Opa is the only one who spends time with Ivy. He doesn't talk much, though. She doesn't feel well enough to resume their hikes. Ivy helps him tend to the animals, but even when they are in the same room she can't meet his eyes, can't connect to the notion that she is giving his family away.

She walks toward the edge of her grandparents' property, holding Bonita's reins and leading her into the grasses. She glances back at the house as night begins to lose strength against the coming light and mounts the horse carefully, the excess weight creating an unfamiliar balance that she has to compensate for in order to raise herself up. The insects have gone back into hiding as the first deep calls of tropical birds establish their shifts. Still no sign of movement in the house. As she and Bonita slip off slowly toward the trailhead, she isn't exactly sure where she is going, but the leaving part feels good enough.

NORA

THEY SIT IN THE CAR at the ferry terminal. "Do you have to go now?" Nora locks her weepy eyes on Kate. She is trying to find the place of connection that's come and gone so capriciously in recent days, although she's less worried about her after the few somewhat real talks they'd managed to have, the ones in which Kate had momentarily relaxed her suspicion of Nora. Surprisingly, Nora is starting to get tired of the need to control the situation. The yoga class Barbara had dragged her to in Costa Rica helped her a little with that. Still, she hopes to convince Kate to stay home now, to rebuild. It's time, Nora knows. Even if she'd been wrong before.

Kate moves her eyes away and looks down at the backpack between her knees. "I need to get home and take care of some things."

Nora winces at the word "home." "You know you can stay with us as long as you want. I won't make you do too many chores." She tries to make her voice sound light and welcoming instead of suffocating. It's a fine balance with Kate. She's quick to retreat, and it's a lot of work getting her back.

"I know, but I need to see Ivy. I have a commitment."

Nora bites her tongue. A volunteer commitment, not a real job.

"Okay, just remember your home is here and you don't have to worry about anything when you do decide to come back."

Kate hugs her mother and walks over to the ticket booth. She turns and waves as she sets off down the long parking lot toward the ferry. Nora feels a sharp, sudden pang that Kate won't be coming back home, at least not to stay. She sighs and tries to push away the thought. It stings like a premonition, but it's likely no more than her usual frustration at not having control. She laughs a little to herself. Wasn't so long ago she'd never have admitted to that.

Truth is, Nora can feel the fight in her starting to dissipate. For days now she's felt less inclined to care about people doing what she wants them to do. Now a sort of resignation, not entirely unpleasant, starts to take its place. *What if I just sit back and watch?* she asks herself, wondering if she's ever really been in control of anything. She's even started to think about what she might do next, right after Ada discovers her letter of resignation from the council on her desk. More travel is the first idea, whether or not she can peel Ed's arse out of the kitchen or his favourite chair long enough to have an adventure. If not, she's fine with going alone.

"Couldn't change her mind?" Ed meets her at the door—he's been doing this ever since she came home from her trip—takes her coat and hangs it.

"No, unfortunately." While she's still unsure about Ed's behaviour, she's smart enough to keep her mouth shut, no matter how hard it is, and stifle any sort of joke that might break the motivation, or the spell. Whatever it is. She kisses her husband and marvels over how he's come back, wondering where he went in the first place.

SHE SQUINTS AT NEVILLE FROM OUTSIDE the big picture window fronting the Mud Puddle. He isn't here in the usual way. Fidgety. He rubs his forehead, and looks at his watch repeatedly. Something about his manner makes her feel hesitant about going in.

He forces a smile. Still, Nora can see that something's not right.

"You okay?" Might as well get to the point. Unlike Ed, Neville is usually amused by Nora's impatience.

Again, only the smallest of smiles. Still, he tries to push it up toward the crinkles surrounding his noncompliant eyes.

"How was your trip?"

"Great. What's wrong?"

He sips his fancy coffee. His beverage of choice changes depending on the weather and his mood, but it always takes over a minute to order. Nora watches his eyes dart uncomfortably. She'd like to put him at ease, but she'd never take the liberty of showing up first and ordering for him. *Whatever happened to just plain coffee?* Despite how nice he is, Neville is a complicated man, whereas Nora prides herself on her simplicity. He isn't a snob; he just has the uncanny ability to taste things most regular people can't, maybe even see or feel things too. Things Nora isn't entirely sure exist outside of his imagination. And what's bugging him now? She wishes she could read him. Helplessness embarrasses her.

"I'm done." He puts the mug down, still half full. "Can we walk?"

They follow the harbour path, heading past the marina and over to the mall. The fountain in front spills soap suds. For years, teenagers have upheld the tradition of adding dish detergent during graduation prom week.

"I need to pick something up if you don't mind." Neville heaves open the door to London Drugs with one shoulder. He never touches public door handles. So fussy, always worried about germs. Nora, irritated, shoves the door with both hands as she pushes past him.

"Will you tell me what's up with you?"

Neville doesn't answer. They walk the aisles. He picks up coffee mugs, bowls, salt and pepper shakers, and puts them down again. By the time they hit cosmetics, Nora is incapable of dragging this out any farther.

"For god's sake, Neville. Are you going to talk to me?"

He looks so pale and tired. He stares at Nora. "This is harder than I anticipated."

She waits, right eye twitching.

"I'm afraid I haven't been completely honest with you."

He twists a lipstick, puts it back into its plastic holder. "Let's sit over there." He points to a bench inside the mall. Nora follows.

"You look beat," she tells him. And he does. His face still wears the creases of his bedsheets, as though they hadn't wanted to let go of him.

"I am. I was dreaming all night long. Weird dreams."

Nora is familiar with this. Her own dreams often leave her exhausted come morning. "About what?"

"About the dead."

"Sounds morbid."

"Not so much, my friend. I'm always happy to see him again."

"Who?"

Neville fills himself with breath and releases it, looking down. He sits silently for what feels like a very long time, then presses his words out in a whisper.

"My Charlie."

For a second Nora spins. *What is he talking about?* But in the turn of that moment she knows suddenly how she'd recognized Neville the first time they'd met. Before then she'd only seen him from behind. Recognized, but not placed him into the order of elements that fit neatly within her world. She looks back to that day and sees him on a folding chair inside the Moose Hall, shoulders shaking.

"We were married for twenty-five years."

Nora doesn't speak. Neville goes on about the endless ferries and float planes in their early days. Every Saturday night Charlie would come to the city. They had an apartment. The grocery was closed on Sundays and holidays. Their days.

Nora doesn't move, sits staring.

"He couldn't leave the island permanently, though. I needed to know why. I wanted to come closer to the people here. It was always a bone of contention between us. I wanted him to sell the store and move to Vancouver. Sure would've made our lives a hell of a lot less complicated."

Nora is plastered to the bench. She tries to erase what she's come to know about Neville, her fondness for him, and tries to replace it with the stranger who now sits next to her. She is the last to know. Again.

"I came here too, but we stayed private. We went out a lot in the city, but never here. I kept my legal practice small so I could be flexible. It was a sort of a life. I didn't like it, but Charlie ... he needed it that way."

"You didn't tell me." Nora can't look at him. She imagines lurid things.

"You'd never have given me the time of day." He's right about that.

"He's gone. I have questions. He loved it here and I never understood why. The people and the place. But I think I get it now. You helped me find my way back to him, Nora. I really needed this."

She scowls.

"Your stories, the way you live here—there's a culture I'll never be part of, but it was him, *is* him, everywhere. You've really been a friend." He reaches for her hands. "You've helped me, Nora." He says again. "Can you see that?"

Nora retracts from his grasp, sits still as a stone. "I don't..." She can't finish. There isn't a place for him in her framework. Her cheeks are hot.

"I'm going to let you digest this. Please come and meet me again, day after tomorrow."

He smiles at her a little sadly, then gets up and walks out the door.

ED IS NEVER SURE WHAT TO SAY when Nora rants. While he himself has always been fond of ranting, his speeches are always of a different nature than his wife's: lost things, overspending, politics. Nora, when she goes off, chooses almost always to bite into people more local than the government.

"Why does every single person I know have to treat me like some child who can't handle the truth?" she shouts to her mug of tea, slamming it down on the scarred table, unconcerned about spillage. "Years and years of lies. Charlie, Jeff, Neville. Why the hell can't people tell the truth?"

Ed knows better than to tell her why. She knows why. And he can tell it hurts like hell.

"What's next? Is Rachel going to tell me she's a hermaph-rodite?"

"Jesus, I hope not. Even I couldn't take that."

Nora shoots eye fire at him.

"The worst thing is that everybody else knows," she withers, a little more sadly. "I've pushed everyone into corners. It's my fault."

The only offering he has is his arms, into which he brings his wife of nearly thirty-seven years. This time she doesn't stiffen. This time she lets the tears flow, hot and insistent. There's so much to purge.

KATE

THE FERRY IS RUNNING LATE, as usual. Kate realizes she'll be getting in after dark and will have to find her way back to the cabin without much light. Maybe she can stop at the Wellspring and borrow a flashlight from Kris. She sits on the green vinyl seat, eating soggy fries and gravy, watching the larger island disappear under the strata of a few purpling clouds and a wide, foaming wake. She still reels from what she's learned about Jeff and Shannon. Despite the shock though, it makes so much sense. It explains Jeff's behaviour that last Christmas, more than a year ago now. How he'd been even more distant than before, how quickly his anger came, how he found more things wrong with Kate's every move, every word. He was looking for something to validate what he'd been getting up to, some infraction of hers that would morally elevate him. At the time Kate had felt the shifts in his behaviour, the amping up of things, but they hadn't yet made sense, had never reached fruition. And for that Shannon must be carrying enough anger for both her and Jeff. It occurs to Kate, bizarrely, that Shannon's grief might actually be even deeper than her own—or at least composed of different things.

She knows she's never going back to her hometown. Not to stay. The life that was relevant to her there has sealed itself off and now hangs suspended behind some sort of impenetrable membrane, not because of any intention on her part, but, Kate suspects, because of the way sections of life seem to naturally cleave themselves from one another. She certainly sees the span of her life so far as occurring in neat little sections, each one distinct from the other and unrelated to or disconnected from the next. She still feels an interminable ache, but she knows now that it started long before the accident, at the precise, indefinable moment when she'd decided to lose herself for the benefit of others. Her low regard for herself, she realizes, was convenient for Jeff. It kept her small, gave him reasons to belittle her further, made what he'd done with Shannon seem right to his mind and perhaps others'. It isn't the accident that keeps her from fulfilling Nora's wish for her to move back to North Wailaish. Rather it's the fact that no part of her can live there anymore. She needs to go farther, to go away. It's good to see this now.

She isn't sure that she lives at the cabin either, but she likes the simplicity of easy routines for now. She likes the earth and trees that surround her, protecting the soft parts of her that she'd long ago locked away. She likes the way in which she feels a part of it all from the low sink of a kayak. She likes Luke. She is excited about him in fact, in spite of herself. The recent trips back and forth between one island and another, and perhaps acknowledging that Jeff's heart had long left the company of hers, have shaken something loose. She cries often these days, and although it exhausts her, she can discern a slowly increasing ability to not apologize, an inner assurance that she will be still be here, in spite of it all.

The ferry slips into dock with unusual soundlessness as the last of the day's light falls away. Kate heaves her backpack up the slope and onto the open field, where the flashing lights of the Wellspring illuminate a clear path in front of her. She's forgotten what day it is. In order to drum up business, Kris came up with the idea of an eighties disco night every Saturday. She can hear a drunken group whooping rhythmically inside the place and a predictable beat pounding the earth as she walks closer. She has no idea how she'll be able to get anyone's attention

IVY

S HE KNOWS THE NAME of his village and that it isn't far from the new prison, but she she's never been there. Her hips are spread wide around the girth of the horse, whose white flanks quiver under the graze of her heels as they tread slowly along the path, through her grandfather's citrus grove, past Nalda's house, into dense, leafy trees and finally open space. The prison construction continues at a rapid pace despite the setback of the hurricane, its circular buildings now flanked by a few rectangular ones. *Bunkhouses for the workers?* The thought of this beautiful island becoming a sort of penal colony sends horrible shivers through her upper body. *How will this change things?* It is a morose thought. Even though this was never meant to be a permanent home for her, she wants to hold herself here much longer. Why can it not be her choice to do so?

She and the horse tromp back into the forest and circle behind the mountain at the top of which she and Emilio had spent the afternoon together not long ago. A nervous flutter blooms in her chest as the sun moves above the pines. She knows that when she comes out of the trees, it will be intense, exposing. Suddenly she's not so sure about what she's doing. *Why can't I just leave things alone?* In several months the baby will be born and then gone from both her life and Emilio's as though it had never existed. It will ask nothing of her, but what will it take? She'll forget most of her time here. Other things, other people will happen to both of them. Still, something presses her on. Something in a deeper place wants her to find him, determines that it's important for him to know.

The trail ends at a small creek, and she follows it down toward a clearing. She sees a few people walking and the corrugated roofs of what must be Emilio's village. Much has been devastated in the hurricane, and rudimentary construction is everywhere. She stops at a point where there is a clear view of peoples' movements. The cinematic part of herself wills Emilio to walk by, stop, and look up at her.

Of course this doesn't happen. Nobody sees her, in fact. At least not at first. The scene in front of her, despite being so close, feels far away, encapsulated in something that someone like her could never penetrate. She wonders if it might not be safe to enter it, even to have come this far. The part of her that is already a mother, the part that wants to protect, tells her to turn the horse around and go back to her grandparents. She dismounts, takes Bonita's reins, and leads the horse onto the red dirt road running through the village.

An old man with a cigar stands up, his head turning to follow her as she passes by his front porch. She nods, acknowledging him, and he says something she can't understand. She shivers. Continues. As she walks, people stop what they're doing all around her to stare. Their dark glares tell her how bad an idea this was.

A woman walks toward her, eyes intent.

"*Busco Emilio…?*" She trails off, realizing that she doesn't even know his last name.

"*Eres tu.*" Shit. She is known.

The woman stands in front of her, pokes herself repeatedly in the chest. "*Soy es la esposa.*" I am his wife.

And then Ivy sees him, running toward them. For a moment she forgets the woman in front of her, despite her clear despair and anger. He is beautiful, as always, his curled hair hanging farther into his face than it was the last time they'd seen one another. He stops a few feet away from Ivy, her condition registering on his face, and not in a good way.

His wife is staring too. In lightning fast recognition, she speaks to Emilio. At first her tone is eerily quiet, but soon they are shouting. The Spanish is too fast for Ivy to understand. Emilio's wife sobs and pounds at him. She spits at Ivy's feet. Bonita dances nervously.

Emilio says nothing.

Her tears are hot. She jumps on the horse, shouts "*Estoy teniendo su bebé!*" and digs her heels hard into Bonita's flanks. They fly out of the village and into the bush. She keeps the horse at a canter until she can see that no one has followed. Her heart is a metronome—fierce, disbelieving beats batter her insides as though trying to escape.

ON THE WAY HOME she rehearses her speech to her parents. I was just out for a ride, needed to think. None of it is untrue. She saw nobody, spoke to nobody. They will be worried, but no one can prove she did anything.

She isn't prepared for the scene, however. As she rides up to the farmhouse, her mother and sister run out, spewing frantic questions. She can't discern anything from the cacophony of their voices. Confused, all she can do is repeat, "What? What?"

"Your father is out looking for him," her mother says, gasping for breath. "How could you be so stupid?"

"Nothing happened! I was just riding."

"We thought you ran away. He was planning to leave him alone, but now your friend is not going to be so lucky."

"I told you, I was just out riding, Mother. Why all this?"

"Because we're sick to death with worry about you. And angry. Your father is very, very angry."

"What does he think he's going to do?"

Ivy's mother throws up both her hands, then turns and walks back to the house.

KATE

"I AM AN IDIOT. Kate faces the popping fire where she's sat silently for what seems like all night long. Ivy had answered the door, seen the look on her face and let her in wordlessly. Kate had made tea, and the two of them had been sitting silently for a long time.

"My husband was cheating on me," she tells Ivy, finally.

Ivy nods slowly. "It's not as bad as the other things he did to you."

"He did nothing."

Ivy looks at Kate sorrowfully. "Honey, I know that's not true. I've known that since I met you."

Kate is startled. "What do you mean?"

"Suffering is a conversation. We've been having this one for a long time."

Kate moves a chair next to Ivy, leans over her wheelchair and falls into her thin arms. She weeps loud tears into Ivy's chest. Ivy embraces her, absorbs the long-withdrawn grief.

"That's it. Give it to me. I have enough room for all of it."

She tells Ivy about the wedding, what she'd learned about Shannon and Jeff, how that detail had begun to pry apart the layers of her guilt, to lighten her. She tells her how these past few days she'd started to entertain the idea that maybe she wasn't so culpable. She wasn't the one who'd suggested the extra drinks for her in-laws, in fact she was the one who'd resisted the idea of driving, even though she'd had nothing to drink. Jeff was high, claiming fatigue, and those roads were notoriously dangerous, especially in winter. She isn't making excuses now.

There's been a shift. Maybe it has nothing to do with Shannon's news; maybe it is just time to stop sabotaging her own happiness, to believe that she can live and thrive and that none of it needs to contain any sense or meaning. Maybe it isn't between her and the world anyway, but rather between her and herself. A life isn't something to be summed up or neatly defined. And it can change in an instant. At the very least, she might take her place at the table.

"It's the search for meaning, the endless storytelling that keeps everyone unhappy," she tells Ivy. "Everyone creates their own story when something happens to them, but inside they know it's inaccurate, and the discrepancy makes them bitter."

Ivy's eyes are sharp. "You're lucky to learn this so young."

"I don't need Luke to understand any of it, though. I just always felt so good around him. He could see who I was, and that was enough. It was easy."

"I'm sure all of this is still true."

"He used the word 'love,' Ivy. I think I might have felt it, too. Am I losing my mind?"

"This can only sound like a cliché, but love is never simple."

"I'm the kind of girl men cheat on."

"There's another story behind what you saw. Remember your own advice."

"It's a good thing I saw them. Now I can focus on important things, like getting a job. Putting my life back together. My mother will be thrilled."

"You don't have to show me any bravado."

"I should go."

"You're welcome to stay here. You seem angry."

"No, I should get home."

"Take Nancy's car. She's asleep. You can bring it back in the morning."

THE CABIN FEELS COLD WITH NEGLECT. She's stayed away too long. Kate busies herself building a fire and unloading her backpack. Slowly, she warms the small sanctuary, feeling its peace wash over her. She isn't afraid of intruders anymore. Instinctively, she knows that Shannon's visits will end. The baton of grief has successfully been passed. All that remains here is what she brings herself.

She spends the next few days at Ivy's, helping out with the endless chores required of an old farmhouse, even though Nancy is there. There's always something in need of repair. It's warm enough to be outside, so she paints the fence in long strokes that her mind follows in contemplation. Ivy comes out for occasional breaths of fresh air. Nancy pushes her, tiny and bundled in her wheelchair, and gently probes Kate for news about Luke until she shuts down, becoming agitated.

Kate sends out a silent "fuck you" to Luke. She wants to focus on the future, build strength to go forward, to "move on," as everyone is constantly intoning. Her phone rings constantly. Although she sees his name on the display, she doesn't answer. But in spite of herself she is desperate to talk to him, to feel his warm eyes lifting her heart from where it has slept for so long, but she forces herself to remember how she'd seen him hold Kris that night, how happy she looked. There is a small bit of tearing inside, but she talks herself out of any right to be involved.

Until he shows up at the cabin.

She shouldn't have opened the door. His arms go immediately around her, the warmth of him.

"I missed you," he keeps saying.

But she stiffens. The image of that night, assaulting.

"What's wrong?"

"I need to be alone."

He pulls back, keeping his hands on her shoulders. "Why?" he almost whispers.

She shakes her head. Fixes her jaw.

"You didn't call me. You don't answer your phone. I didn't know you were back," he says.

"No."

"What's going on?"

She feels herself beginning to weaken, but holds on to the image of him and Kris. It gives her a weird, almost subversive sort of strength.

"I need to be alone."

"Jesus Christ. I don't get you. You feel this too, I know you do."

"I lost my husband and his whole family. I can't do this. Too soon."

He stops and stares at her. She sees his confusion, that he knows she's lying.

She turns and walks out of the room. There is a brief moment of silence as she senses him, standing there befuddled at the front door. A minute later she hears it close.

She spends the rest of the night weeping, more so than she's done in a year.

IVY

HER FATHER REFUSES to tell her if he found Emilio that day, but he does find his fists, letting them fly into the side of the house. Eve sobs. Rarely do they see him lose composure, and it is formidable. He comes into the house with a small group of nervous-looking men, including Nalda's husband, close behind. When he sees Ivy standing in the living room he slaps her hard in the face.

"I did not raise you to be a whore."

Her mother shouts at him to stop. He only hits Ivy once, but he says terrible things to her, while she stands and absorbs it. Why does he need to control them all? Why do they all put up with this? Everything happens in his shadow. The problem is, she's come out from beneath it and there is no way back. She searches for the most despicable words to hand him, her most potent offering. "I have never, and will never love you."

She has tried to see her father as a product of his own strict upbringing, how his fear of losing all that he'd successfully earned drove his almost every move. But even now compassion is difficult to find. To side with him would mean the destruction of her own heart.

OVER THE NEXT COUPLE MONTHS, as Ivy grows heavy with heat and discomfort, she finds ways to avoid her father, even if he is in the same room. Despite his presence she feels as though she's eradicating him as best she can. If he is inside, she goes outside. She is forgetting the colour of his eyes, the sound of his voice. She can't allow a moment's wondering whether he'd done anything to Emilio.

A heavy, tense air thickens the house and its surroundings. Opa and Ivy's father spend every waking hour rebuilding the Freisens's home, until finally enough of it has been completed for them to move back home while they finish the work. Ivy's sure they are happy to leave them all—they have enough family trouble. Her mother is relieved, as she's been worried about how Sonia will do in the presence of a baby, even though it will remain with them only for the time it takes for it to utter its first cry. Eve asks their father why they can't adopt Ivy's child, but he shouts at her, "This child will have a life far away from any of us, with its own people."

IT STARTS TO HAPPEN IN THE MORNING. Ivy stares at her swollen feet, ruminating. They look as though they belong to someone else, to an obese woman. She can't even wear shoes anymore. She heaves her body around not unlike the oxen on Opa's farm.

Her mother had given her a book that she'd found at the local library, but she was afraid to read it past the first few chapters, even if she could make out a lot of the Spanish. Most of the descriptions of childbirth were terrifying. There were pictures of women in labour wearing unfathomable expressions of agony. She could hardly look at their undignified faces, and their exposure to the world seemed humiliating. But suddenly she wishes she had. As she walks out of the kitchen, a surprising gush of wet warmth releases from her, soaking her dress and saturating the wood of her grandparents' front steps. She calls her mother.

"Are you sure?" she asks.

Ivy stands and shows her mother the wet shadows on the wooden steps. She storms inside, calling Ivy's father. "Take the horse. Get the doctor," she commands.

Her father leaves without saying anything. Ivy, her mother, and Oma go to the now vacant guest room. Ivy is annoyed that her father is taking Bonita out, more annoyed with that than anything else for a brief moment. But then, the pain.

Oma brings ice and water. Her insides seize and harden momentarily, then release. The beginning. The contractions are far apart, but their intensity is surprising. Ivy's body becomes a thing of its own, completely separate from her mind. It seems like forever before her father returns with the doctor. By now she lays sweating, her mother mopping her brow softly with a cool rag. Eve holds her hand.

"You can all leave now. The doctor is here." Her father still won't look in Ivy's eyes.

"I want Eve and Mama to stay," she tells him.

"You made this decision on your own. You will face the consequences alone."

He hustles everyone out of the room. Ivy's mother whispers something to him, tries to turn back, but he grasps her elbow firmly and guides her stiff body straight out the door.

She is alone with a stranger. Having a baby.

Ivy didn't think it was possible to hate her father any more than she already did, but she is suddenly overflowing with it. It empowers her. She begins to scream, knowing that he can hear her hate-fuelled pain. "I hate you. I want you to die," she cries, until the pain is so sharp she can do nothing but submit to the task at hand.

The doctor is curt and professional. The pains soon become more frequent. Terrified, Ivy cries out, asks him if its all normal, imagining twisted limbs, strangling cords, gushes of blood.

"It looks as it should," he responds without a glance at her face.

She doesn't know where everyone is during these many hours. More than once she is sure she might die from agony. It's taking too long. She is ripping open. At one point she thinks she hears a familiar voice:

"Ivy. I'm here." Eve. Outside the window.

In that moment, she loves her sister more than anyone. Eve would never risk her father's anger for anything, and yet here she is, telling Ivy in her own way that she is not alone. She will never forget this, the only offering of strength to do what she needs to in that moment.

The doctor pretends not to notice. And as Ivy weeps, her son enters the sodden heat of this godforsaken world.

KATE

K ATE WAKES UP in darkness and her thoughts go immediately to Ivy. She conjures the young woman astride a
white horse, hair trailing cinematically behind her as she gal-
lops the beaches of the Isle of Pines. Ivy with her huge ocean
eyes, surveying. Ivy in her wheelchair, her sharp mind always
endeavouring to release itself from her withering body. Ivy
shaking her awake. Tendrils of Ivy wind themselves about the
delicate parts of Kate's imagination, growing lush and fertile.

During their conversations Kate had always marvelled at
how small her own life seemed in comparison to Ivy's. How
simple, how free from struggle. Until now she's hardly spent
any time on her own, outside of a relationship, let alone as
a single woman who never knew what had happened to her
child. She wonders if Ivy's strength came naturally or by necessity ... or both. She rolls over and pulls the duvet up close
to her chin, willing her head to drop into her pillow, to return
to softness, to dark. But thoughts of Ivy are insistent. The last
time they talked she'd been pushy about Luke.

"So that's it. You're just going to let it go?"

"I don't have a choice. He's obviously made a decision."

"Bullshit. He's obviously confused."

"I'm in no position to talk."

"You're in the position to start. Do something—" At this
she'd thrown up her thin arms. "Don't just let things happen
to you—or not."

Kate groans. Such an aggravating woman. She tries to decide between coffee or a further attempt at sleep.

Ivy has had a big life, but with Kate she mostly liked to talk about La Isla. Kate pictures a small tropical island, the idyll of heat, and a young woman kidding herself into the pretence of freedom in 1926, thinking she could be with someone who wasn't from her culture or class, believing she could penetrate those reinforced walls, not even seeing them. It would be simple to say that Ivy was born at the wrong time—Kate knows no elderly person like her. In some ways the young Ivy that Kate imagines is a different person altogether, but at times there are intersections—when she talks about the hurricane, when they debate over books. Ivy is always forceful, full of opinions, and yet she listens to Kate, gets inside the very kernel of what she means to say even if she's articulated it clumsily. *Why do points in our lives seem so segmented?* she wonders again. *When does one person disappear into something else? What is it that follows us, connects us from one point to the next? If anything.*

She is the same person. The same Ivy insisting herself into Kate's room. The same Ivy, full of advice. The same woman who whispers, laughs often.

The phone.

"Kate, it's Nancy. You need to come."

She doesn't remember getting dressed or picking up the phone to call Luke. A bizarre spring snow had arrived last night and fat, downy flakes have settled in on the ground. It would take her too long to run to Ivy's. She found a pair of yoga pants somewhere on the floor in a tangled embrace with her sweatshirt. Her coat is slung over the sofa. All parts of her body begin to point themselves in a single direction as she pushes away thoughts of what Nancy's words imply.

Hurry up, Luke.

She's leaving.

No. Not possible.

Kate wonders who to bargain with. God had left long ago. Her heart is awake and pounding, despite the lack of caffeine. She paces the small hallway of her cabin, fearing that if her body does not move consistently forward she might be engulfed ... by what? The idea of being alone again, being left in that cold, final way?

In the small hallway is the one photo of Jeff's family she hasn't yet removed. She hardly notices it anymore. She pauses to look closely at Jeff's face. His half-smile already so distant, like a newspaper photo reporting someone's demise. Would it look the same to someone who didn't know he'd been dead for over a year? Would someone be able to look at that photo and intuit that the life it depicted was gone?

The muffled crunch of tires in snow breaks the insistent silence and Kate shoots out the door. In the cab of the not-yet-warm pickup Luke sits unshaven, looking across at her from his own distance. His eyes crease, taking in only part of her.

"Thank you," she says, silently begging him to not look at her that way. Hardness. Defence.

"What did Nancy say?"

"Nothing. She just said to come."

"So you don't know?"

"I don't know anything."

"Are you sure this is a good idea?" His words soften around the question.

"I need to see her."

It surprises Kate how well Luke knows how to be with her after such a short time. He knows not to talk. She can't help thinking again about how Jeff would have been, how she would have needed to think about his feelings rather than her own, would have had to worry about his reactions. She could never lose herself in something like this with Jeff around. Would he even have taken her to Ivy's? Despite what's happened, she feels uncommonly knit to this strange man sitting next to her.

As he drives he places a large, gloved hand on Kate's thigh.

Through the layers of material something surges into her veins, warming, travelling to the place in her chest that has begun to swell with a familiar pain. It's only a moment though, before he seems to remember and removes it.

And Ivy's voice: *He is gentle.* At the same time Kate's mind continues to pull back to thoughts of what they might find when they arrive at Ivy's house. Kate envisions her own body flying off in the opposite direction each time the truck winds around the switchbacks of the gravel road leading to the other side of the island. There is only stillness in the frigid, spare breaths of early morning. She feels herself splitting in two.

Luke drives quickly, but with an ease that comes from knowing the roads. When they reach the beginning of Ivy's driveway Kate's eyes travel immediately downhill, beyond the house and over the ocean where the sun, having risen high enough now, lights the sea. She pauses first at the beauty of unfamiliar rays of light breaking the grey, then looks toward Ivy's house.

There is an ambulance. It isn't going anywhere.

Kate jumps out of the truck and runs ahead.

Nancy is already at the door. Her eyes are red. She doesn't need to say it.

Kate stands for a moment, impenetrable. Then a sound from another place tears through her. Any living thing would stop if they heard it, would both recognize, know, and fear its source instinctively. Luke comes up behind and put his arms around her. She grabs onto them and squeezes, pushes the agony into her body, where it washes down and through her.

She needs to keep moving—there isn't anything else to do. She runs into the snow, finding branches from low-slung trees and snapping them off. Four deaths shriek their way through her thin body as she runs and runs until finally she sits down, panting, unable to feel the cold of the inexplicable snow beneath her.

Luke runs behind her. When he catches up he reaches down, grabs her hands, and pulls her up. "Come inside."

He walks her to the house and pulls out a chair from the kitchen table, sitting down silently next to her, his hand on her arm. The two of them remain still while Nancy moves back and forth between the kitchen and Ivy's bedroom, where one of the paramedics remains. There are hushed, indistinguishable mutters. The other paramedic is outside in the ambulance, head down in her paperwork.

Kate looks around the familiar room. Someone should be making tea, someone should be reading. *What the hell am I supposed to do right now?* she wonders. She stares at the still functioning cuckoo clock, the uneven dangle of its pine-cone-shaped pulleys. On another wall facing the table is a photo of Ivy and her group of friends in front of their swimming hole in Cuba. The women in bathing caps, the men looking stern. Heat shimmers, even through the muted black-and-white. Emilio is not in this picture.

Nancy is full of the same kind of confused movement, pacing in and out of Ivy's bedroom, babbling. "Everything was the same this morning. She wanted her glass of lemon water, the CBC. It was all quiet, and then she started having trouble breathing. Started making the most horrible sounds." Nancy stutters over this last word, shoulders trembling.

"I had to open her eyelid to see if she was really gone."

Kate looks down at Ivy's glasses, attached to their silver chain on top of her copy of *Twentieth Century Poets*. They look oddly still. She doesn't dare move them. They seem as though they are still imbued with Ivy, as though her touch might be felt through the cover of the book, through the things she'd engaged with, not just touched, but sent through her system, interpreted, lived. In the last few weeks she'd wanted to read only poetry. At the time Kate didn't think of it as noteworthy, but now it seems important.

"Do you want to see her?" Nancy breaks her thoughts.

The question curdles her insides. "No."

"It's okay, Kate. She looks really peaceful."

She feels a sudden flush of rage at these words. Why does everyone say this about dead people? How can it have been peaceful for Ivy? *Massive heart attack* were the words translated to her by the paramedics. How could that have been anything but excruciating? Has anything in Ivy's life ever been peaceful? This isn't about peace, it's about struggle. How it ends, or doesn't. Even the skin covering Ivy's face carried this, despite her attempts to dismiss it—she was in a wheelchair, she'd been unable to feel wind touch her face without wincing, she had already said goodbye to a sister and a child she'd never had the pleasure of knowing. She'd had enough pain to propel her into life more abruptly and authentically than anyone Kate knew. Surely there are more accurate words to make meaning of this.

Kate isn't finished with Ivy yet. Between Ivy and Virginia Woolf, the space between the living and the dead had been bridged, Only Ivy had penetrated the numbness that Kate had existed in since the accident. Somehow, she had seemed comfortable lingering there. Ivy could see through the subtle layer that separated Kate from everyone else. She was a reminder that Kate still lives and that there is more to come. Kate doesn't want to see a body—she wants to remember Ivy alive. She wants to remember her sarcasm, her immediate, comforting certainty about things, her solidity, her trustworthiness. She wants to remember the mischievous, raspy laugh and her sharp, cutting wit. She wants to remember how she'd come to feel okay about herself in this place, in the presence of a woman whose shrunken body held a huge, magnificent life. If she sees Ivy in death, will all this be erased? As Kate searches for the answer, she realizes that there is a part of her that that doesn't believe Ivy can be gone, doesn't believe it's possible for her to just evaporate into nothing. She was ninety-three years old, but Kate just needed her to stay a little bit longer. She lifts herself out of the chair and follows Nancy to the bedroom.

The form on the bed holds the same stillness as the snow-covered earth outside. She looks even tinier than she had a couple days ago, when Kate last saw her. And yes, Kate would use a word other than peaceful to describe Ivy's expression. Her face already has the unmistakable pallor of death—a grey-blue sort of cast that proves itself to Kate's remaining doubts. She sinks to Ivy's side, shaking with sobs, twisting her soaked and mangled tissue.

Ivy isn't there anymore. Whatever accompanied this body through life is elsewhere now, or has completely vanished. Kate no longer knows what she believes, but she knows with certainty that Ivy is not in this room.

THE SUN RISES GARISHLY THE NEXT DAY. Audaciously even, after such a long absence. *Fuck you*, Kate thinks. Weather should never be so incongruous. For a moment she thinks she's fallen asleep on Ivy's sofa again, but as her eyes adjust to the light she sees that she is in her own bed, fully clothed. Somewhere outside her room she hears pots rattling, the rush of steam and bubbling water being poured into a carafe. Luke had stayed the night.

It doesn't take long for yesterday to return. Her body is heavy with loss, with the hollowed emptying of tears, with angry, dark thoughts. *I destroy everything.*

She remembers how invasive her thoughts of Ivy had been yesterday morning. It must have been just shortly after she'd died. Luke had told her that Buddhists believe the soul wanders around confused, visiting familiar people shortly after death. Today though, there is less of her; she is already distant. Kate feels the tug of that empty void, the one she will eventually enter at some point.

Luke comes into the room, also wearing the same clothes. "I made coffee," he says, offering the mug with an outstretched arm.

She feels the sorrow leap out of her body, through her eyes

and into Luke. It is palpable. She watches him receive it.

"I know how hard this is."

She has no words for him. The familiar sensation of tears builds once again to the spilling point. She never wept for Jeff like this. She grabs a tissue and motions for Luke to put the coffee on her nightstand.

She touches his arm. "I'm glad you're still here." Even as she says this and sees his darkening eyes she doesn't care that he is now just on loan from someone else. Something in this loss has stripped away deference and restraint.

He touches her hand, looks down. "Nancy's here too. I hope you don't mind. She's a mess."

"Of course not."

DAYS PASS IN A STATE UTTERLY REMOVED from the normal constraints of time. Morning disappears into afternoon, afternoon into night. The three of them remain in the cabin together, floating in and out of each other's presence. Sometimes they look at pictures, make dark jokes. At other times they just curl around the woodstove drinking wine. Kate keeps waiting for Luke to leave, but he maintains a sort of vigil, letting his phone ring and ring.

As yet another darkness begins to make its hasty return and Kate comes close to embracing sleep, she hears a shuffling at her door. She sees Nancy, peering tentatively into the bedroom.

"You look like crap," she tells her, taking in the wrinkled clothes and a face that looks aged and weary.

"You look pretty shitty yourself." At this Kate smiles. She wonders if she'll remain friends with Nancy. They have almost nothing in common apart from Ivy.

Nancy places something on the bed awkwardly, followed by a second item. Kate puts on her glasses and looks once again at the poetry anthology she and Ivy had been reading, along with Ivy's glasses case.

"I think she'd want you to have these."

Kate is silent. She turns to the bookmarked page and runs her finger over the lines of Sylvia Plath that had lain quietly in the anthology, waiting for their next reading session together:

This dream budded bright with leaves around the edges,
Its clear air winnowed by angels; she was come
Back to her early sea-town home
Scathed, stained after tedious pilgrimages.

She stops there, aware that Ivy is with her, no matter how improbable. She doesn't believe in God, but she does believe in the endurance of a soul and, as Ivy did, in the power of words. She spends the rest of the day finishing the book. As she reads she cradles herself in Ivy's presence, asks her to sit, to listen as she always had. So attentively as to feel the words breathe something fresh into the stifled air, and back to settle in her body. When Kate finally closes the book, she picks up her pen and writes.

Thank you, Ivy, for finding me in this place, and for being unafraid of the ugly things that surrounded me. You helped me to see that I continue.
I know you felt ready and I I didn't want to hear that. It was selfish, I suppose. I guess I always saw how strong your mind was, and ignored the frustrations of your body. I've spent too many months thinking mostly of myself. Now that I think about it, I've never heard you complain.
I hope that something of you stays with me. I want to remember you swearing, drinking wine, and finding things in books that speak so clearly to what we feel right now, the things in life that aren't so easy.
I'm sorry that you didn't die with a room full of people who admire you as much as I do. You deserved to. I hope you know I love you.

I don't know what happens next and don't want to pretend I'll see you again, but I wish you flight, and better things than you had in this life.
    With love, Kate

Luke calls to her. "Kate, it's your mom on the phone."

"I'll call her back."

That night she dreams of Ivy. She waits down the path near the mouth of Kate's driveway wearing a sequined bathing suit. None of this appears odd. Kate sprints toward her.

"How did you get here?"

Ivy is casual, as though nothing's happened. "I wanted to stop by and say hello. I just finished my show."

"What show?"

She looks at Kate as though she is an idiot. "Synchronized swimming, of course."

"Luke is here. And Nancy."

"That's excellent." Ivy's eyes glint lasciviously.

"Stop."

"Yes of course."

Kate leans over and kisses Ivy on the cheek. "I guess I should go back."

Ivy sits back in her chair, wheels herself backward and disappears. This is the only dream.

On the fourth day Nancy goes home. Luke convinces Kate to come with him for groceries. In the store she watches a group of three young women from the city, overdressed for the island with spidery, made-up eyes and dark, edgy clothes. Their sleek hair has been given more attentiveness than Kate can imagine ever having the energy for. Their efforts are confusing, absurd, pointless.

Time has become something different to her. Like a wave, it is rhythmic, cyclic, rolling itself into spirals of imagined experience. She has no trust in memory. Why weren't she and Ivy contemporaries? She worries that Ivy left not knowing how highly she thought of her. She hasn't yet looked at the idea of her own death. When she thinks about it now, she sees it is only a hair's breadth away.

We stand so far from the other side, she observes. *And why? It's not so far from us.*

IVY

SHE BRIEFLY SEES his face, and then he is gone. His skin, olive. So much hair. These things remain with her. After three weeks of sitting in the darkness of her grandparents' living room, healing physically but breaking apart inside, Ivy feels a keen pull to the north. The child that was taken away took her ties to her own family with him. She doesn't know if this is permanent or not. All she knows is that there isn't a place for her back home, and university at this point seems an unanswerable question. She asks Luisa, whose uncle runs the ferry to Havana, to do her a favour. It's all quick to arrange.

She has to leave before the bakery opens. It's dark, moonless. Luisa comes partway down the path with a lantern to meet her. They don't have much to say to each other. Islands are small; she knows everything. Ivy has packed a little clothing and enough food to carry. Her father's money has always been easy to find.

IT WAS IN THIS WAY THAT SHE LEFT Isla de Piños. So much happened there after that departure. That same year another baby was born. One day he would spend time in that huge prison, along with other revolutionaries. Many of the expats Ivy knew would eventually leave. What she found along her own roads eventually returned her to a colder, more hidden island. She knew that one day her parents would want to see her again, but they had to first see the suns of their anger rise and fall, many times, over years. When that day came they would only talk about fishing for birds. This doesn't end. They still walk the shores of this island.

NORA

"MOM, IS EVERYTHING OKAY?" Rachel sits in Ed's recliner while he's at a cooking class at the high school. Nora had been talking on the phone, but now stands with her eyes locked on a small, red spider climbing up the wall.

"What happened?"

"The old lady died."

"Oh no. Poor Kate."

"She seems more upset about this than she was about Jeff." Nora claps a hand over her mouth. "Shouldn't have said that."

"It's just a reminder," says Rachel. "Was she close to her?"

"I guess so. She sounds terrible. I could hardly hear her."

"Is she alone?"

"You know, just the usual hippies. Go help her, Rachel. I don't care if she gets mad. Just show up."

"I can't right now, Mom. There's too much going on at work. It'll have to be you."

SHE'D DELIBERATELY MISSED MEETING HIM in the cafe, as he'd requested. Nora has to go all the way to Vancouver to see him. He doesn't want to come to the island anymore. On the phone he asks if this is okay, if she can understand. She tries.

The mountains are more abrupt on the mainland, thrusting up with narcissistic drama to poke at the dotted clouds. Nora stares at the glassy faces of modern-style homes perched precariously up their slopes. She thinks about earthquakes, and the bridge her bus will have to traverse; she hopes for timing to favour her.

Neville waits in Delaney's. He smiles immediately when he sees her, and gets up to give her a giant hug.

Nora is so glad to see him.

That night he takes her to one of their haunts, his and Charlie's, where the floor undulates with dance. Nora and Neville drink scotch until, finally, the drag show begins. Biting, caustic jokes, music, dancing, and enormous hats. Nora laughs and forgets, tears tumbling.

KATE

"I'M STAYING WITH RACHEL for a while, she tells Luke. "Then there's one more island I need to see."

"Can I come and see you?" He reaches for her. She notices how big his hands are, a contrast from the rest of him. He's shaved off the beard and she can see the vulnerability in the face he's been attempting to cover. She looks down the hill and surveys what the water is doing. No chop. High clouds today—enough space for her to travel beneath without too much doubt or claustrophobia.

"Sure, in awhile." She's lost the anger.

On the third day of her grief-induced house arrest he'd deemed her able to converse. "You know I had no idea what had gotten into you." He was sitting on the edge of her bed. Her back was turned to him, and she didn't roll over, not caring to meet his eyes. "Nancy finally told me what you saw, that night at the Wellspring."

Kate cringed.

He went on. "It might be hard to believe, but it was all her. I admit, I was pissed at you. I felt rejected by you, and I was confused, but nothing went beyond that. I was out the door not long after."

She lay there and breathed the air around his words. They felt like honesty. She had every right not to believe him, but, undeniably, she did.

After a moment she sat up and leaned forward, into him.

Allowed. She put her arms around his neck and he kissed her, held her silently.

She's been looking at flight maps, allured by so many paths, the dandelion seeds of possibility leading out of one city hub and into so many others. After *La Isla,* which lines will she follow?

She feels expansive. An aperture lures her gaze toward land that stretches on, to places both surrounded by water, and not. Whether she returns to this island or another will depend on calculations made in the distance between now and then, both temporal and physical. Not all islands are tear-shaped. Luke doesn't talk about lost time or expectations like Ivy's parents did. Kate doesn't think these things exist for him; he seems open to possibilities beyond his own contrivances. The test will be of the endurable things, she believes. She still has money in the bank and is willing to go, see other things and perhaps photograph them, to be alone in ways she's never been before, and to find company so different from what she knows. If they eventually move in the same direction...

NORA STANDS BESIDE KATE at the farmer's market, her head encircled by a garland of vine and flowers. "It itches," Nora says, attempting to remove it.

Around them, vendors scramble to pack up their wares. The Thai food has sold out, most of the favoured scents of soap have been picked over, and the unsold art is being placed gingerly into boxes layered with foam. Only the crêpe guy continues to produce, attempting to fill final orders scrawled haphazardly on post-it notes.

"Leave it," Kate tells her mother, "It looks fetching."

A ruddy-faced man with a portly midsection stands onstage at the bandstand. "Attention ladies and gentlemen, we shall henceforth commence with our May Day celebrations. Would all men of strength and virility please approach the pole."

A pod of varying generations stumble-walks toward a supine

post, all wearing ridiculous hats. One man sports a pair of furry pants, a half-shirt with vest, and goat ears. Kate almost falls over when she spots Luke, resplendent in a costume of felted leaves. A woman Kate recognizes from the library bumps her while taking a photo.

"Sorry! I'm just so excited. It's Ryan's first time to hold the pole."

They watch the Morris dancers in shredded black-and-white, clack poles and sashay back and forth around each other, the trills of the recorder a pale accompaniment to the drums. When they finish, the portly man announces the winners of the raffle. Kate blows a kiss to the members of of Ivy's book club as they offer their usual stack of books to the lucky recipient. She knows that they would have spent months arguing over the titles.

"We shall now make our procession down to the fields," shouts the master of ceremonies. Nora raises an eyebrow at Kate, who nudges her arm and sends her following.

They march down the road, led by the Morris dancers and a sea of locals clad in gauze and florals. A huge, papier-mâché May Queen is held aloft by procession leaders and drums mark the beat of their footsteps. Many dance. Finally, they arrive at a field and walk over to the labyrinth. In the centre is Luke, covered in felted leaves and sweat. The crowd silences and he speaks.

"It is my honour to choose my May Queen. A woman of ripe fertility within whom I shall spread my seed."

"Who's that idiot?" Nora says, "Does he really think that the kids don't get what he's saying?"

But Kate isn't listening. She trembles with repressed laughter as Luke looks straight at her. Holding his hand forward in a courtly manner he walks through the labyrinth, bows before Kate, and lifts her up into his leafy arms. "I. Will. Kill. You," she manages to say to him as the crowd bursts into hoots and cheers and the MC bellows, "Let the pole be erected!"

Later, after the community spiral dance and a make-out session behind the cedar hedge fronting the library, Kate and Luke find Nora puzzling her way through a piece of cake that had been served to her on a leaf. "Where there's a will…" she says, thrusting the gooey mess into her mouth.

"Mom, this is Luke.

Nora licks her fingers and extends her hand. "I'd like to tell you you're the oddest thing Kate's ever brought home, but I'm not really sure."

"I'm honoured," he says.

IVY HADN'T WANTED ANYTHING ostentatious to mark her place, nothing resembling *a godawful, morbid headstone.* Instead, her book club friends planted a spindly maple in the Japanese gardens and installed a small plaque at its base, engraved with her name and below it the words "Mother Fucker." Kate kneels and places four gladiola stems beside it, strokes the crisp, furling bark of a nearby Arbutus, then turns and walks toward the docking ferry.

ACKNOWLEDGEMENTS

It is a joy and privilege to thank Luciana Ricciutelli, Editor-in-Chief, Renée Knapp, Publicist and Marketing Manager, and everyone at Inanna Publications, for giving *Fishing for Birds* a warm and loving home. It is a pleasure to occupy space where the female voice is recognized and celebrated.

So many thank-yous to Sarah Sheard, for her support and keen editing eyes.

Thank you to Betsy Warland, and her incredible creation in the Writer's Studio.

To my dear friend, Stella Harvey: It has been so wonderful to grow in friendship and writing over these fifteen years. Thank you is not enough for all the support you've given, even when your plate is ever-full.

Much gratitude to Caroline Adderson, an extraordinary writer and endlessly supportive mentor. Also one of the funniest women I know.

My immense gratitude to Lidia Yuknavitch and Jen Pastiloff. You are walking love. Thank you for the bravery of your voices, and for opening the doors to so many others who need to speak.

Thank you to Erik Anderson, for so much encouragement and support.

Thank you to Susan Chapman, for such wise teaching and inspiration.

To my dearest friends, Deborah MacNamara and Anita Lau. You are so deep in my heart. Thank you for walking in this world in the enthusiastic ways in which you do, for making me laugh, championing my crazy ideas, and always believing.

To Kelly Thompson: meeting you changed my life. Thank you for all that you share.

To writer friends who get it: Claire Sicherman, Abby Wener Herlin, Jennifer Honeybourn, Stella Harvey, Eric Brown, James Leslie, Eljean Dodge Wilson, Stacey Shelby, and the beautiful souls of the Ojai Ovary.

Thank you to my brilliant cohort and professors at Pacifica Graduate Institute, for opening my mind and heart, and for showing me how to dance on the beach.

Gratitude to Noel Bennett, Jen Parris, and Lou Bennett, for sharing your beautiful and inspiring sanctuary.

Huge thanks to Choli and Ramberto, for outstanding hospitality and making us feel part of the family on Isla de la Juventud.

To my sister, Jennifer Oaten, who makes me laugh like no other, and provides endless enticing tales of island life.

To my beautiful Mom, Carol White: thank you for travelling with me, listening to me, and loving me. Thailand and Isla de Piños are highlights of my life.

To my dad, Thomas Vernon White: you left too soon, but I will forever cherish your guitar strumming, your paintings, and your pride in me. Thank you for teaching me the importance of art, and for showing me how to make space for it in my life.

To my biggest loves, Al, Madeleine, and Noelle: I cannot thank you enough for your love, patience, and encouragement, even when it means many hours behind a computer screen. You are my everything. I love you with all of my heart.

Thank you to the islands, for the home I find there.

I would also like to acknowledge the source of the poems cited in this book:

The poem by José Marti was excerpted from "I Have a White Rose to Tend," published in *José Martí, Major Poems: A Bilingual Edition*, by Martí y Pérez José Julián et al., Holmes & Meier Publishers, 1982.

Sylvia Plath's poem was excerpted from "Dream with Clam-Diggers," published in *The Collected Poems*, by Sylvia Plath, with an introduction and edited by Ted Hughes, HarperPerennial Modern Classics, 2018.

Photo: Yasmeen Strang

Linda Quennec is a writer, traveller, and Ph.D. student in Depth Psychology. An island-dweller at heart, she took inspiration for her novel *Fishing for Birds* from the natural beauty of Coastal British Columbia and the fascinating Isla de la Juventud (formerly Isla de Piños) where her German grandmother was raised. She holds an MFA in creative writing from Naropa University, and is a graduate of The Writers' Studio at Simon Fraser University and The Humber School of Writing. Her work has appeared in *Quills Canadian Poetry, 3Elements Review, Cirque, Emerge,* and *DoveTales* literary journals. She lives with her husband and twin daughters just outside Vancouver, British Columbia.